A NICE PLACE TO DIE

Fiction Titles from Jane McLoughlin

COINCIDENCE
A TURN IN THE ROAD
THE FURIES
THE HIDE AND SEEK CORPSE
DEATH BY PREJUDICE
STRANGER IN THE HOUSE
CHEATED HEARTS
THE UNFORGIVEN
SHADOW OF A DOUBT *

available from Severn House

A NICE PLACE TO DIE

Jane McLoughlin

This first world edition published 2011
in Great Britain and in the USA by
SEVERN HOUSE PUBLISHERS LTD of
9–15 High Street, Sutton, Surrey, England, SM1 1DF.

British Library Cataloguing in Publication Data

McLoughlin, Jane.
  A nice place to die.
  1. Police – England – Fiction. 2. Vicars, Parochial –
  Crimes against – Fiction. 3. Detective and mystery stories.
  I. Title
  823.9'2-dc22

ISBN-13: 978-0-7278-8060-4 (cased)

All Severn House titles are printed on acid-free paper.

Severn House Publishers support The Forest Stewardship Council [FSC],
the leading international forest certification organisation. All our titles that
are printed on Greenpeace-approved FSC-certified paper carry the FSC logo.

MIX
Paper from
responsible sources
FSC
www.fsc.org   FSC® C018575

Typeset by Palimpsest Book Production Ltd.,
Falkirk, Stirlingshire, Scotland.
Printed and bound in Great Britain by
MPG Books Ltd., Bodmin, Cornwall.

PROLOGUE

The old woman did not hear them coming. They burst through the door of her cottage and they set upon her. Some of the older men scattered the blazing logs from the open fire, kicking them across the room so that they set light to the straw pallet where the old woman slept. Tongues of flame began to climb up the wattle and daub walls towards the thatched roof. Whatever the logs touched began to burn.

They dragged Hester Warren to a site on the edge of the village, where the local women had built a great pyre of wood and straw round a strong stake on an open field.

Hester wasn't really conscious when they threw her down on the parched ground. The women who had lost children in the recent sickness vented their grief as she lay on the ground where the men had flung her. They beat her and kicked her, screaming abuse full of hatred and misery. Then some of the men hauled her upright against the stake and bound her there, while the women heaped kindling around the base of the pyre.

Then they set it alight.

The whole village heard the witch scream. They couldn't see her frantic face behind the flames, but long after she should have been safely in Hell they could hear her curse them, and all future inhabitants of Catcombe down the generations, for what they had done that day.

Then the screaming stopped and there was only the sound of the fire, crackling and hissing. Some wag had called out, 'See you in Hell, then, Hester Warren,' but no one took up his jeering. It was as though they were awed that they had witnessed divine justice done. The mothers of the children who'd died at the witch's hands began to weep. Most of the people there looked shocked, as though the burning of the old woman had come as a surprise to them.

The parson stepped forward then and lifted his arms and spoke some solemn words before he turned his back on the fire.

'The evil among us is destroyed,' he told the people, 'let us give thanks unto the Lord.'

Some of the villagers fell to their knees.

Parson Pearson began to recite the Lord's Prayer. He paused and raised his voice when he got to 'Deliver us from evil.'

'Amen,' the squire muttered, echoed by the doctor, who had played such an important part in unmasking Hester Warren as a witch and the source of the calamity that had come upon the village. The squire and Parson Pearson had too, once the doctor had pointed out that none of the squire's family or the parson's, nor the offspring of anyone else who could afford his knowledge of medical science, had died of the sickness which had broken out amongst the poor village children.

It was Hester Warren who had harmed these children. The mothers' grief and guilt at their own failure to help their suffering welled up inside them and spilled over in a great mass hunger for revenge against the woman who had claimed to be able to cure the children with her ancient spells and herbal potions and had instead killed them.

For Hester Warren was not one of them, not born and bred. No one knew where she had come from, because no one was old enough to remember her coming. No one was sure how old she was. The tight-knit village community thought she must be as old as the huge old oaks in the woods and could not have lasted to such an age by natural means. Anyway, Hester seemed always to have been there on the fringes of Catcombe, in a tumbledown cottage beside the stewpond in the woods on the outskirts of the village. She was a familiar sight to the fishermen in the early evenings flitting like a giant bat in the dusk as she searched the hedgerows for the plants she gathered to take back to the cottage. There, muttering to herself, she brewed the leaves and roots and twigs in a pot over a smoky wood fire to make her potions.

People were afraid of Hester because she was not like the rest of them, but when they had something real to fear in their own lives, they invariably turned to her for help. It didn't matter to them then that she was not right in the head, or that some claimed to have seen her on the night of Samhain, the ancient festival of All Hallows Eve when the spirits of the dead return to visit their old homes, consorting with a black, bear-like animal in the depths of the forest. At times like these, many a young girl who had dallied too long in the dusk with a young man came to Hester for a potion to bring on menstruation; then ageing men who could not satisfy their wives visited the cottage at night for powders made of dried roots which would restore their virility. And more than once Hester had worked with her magic twigs on married women in despair at being with child once too often.

But those who came to Hester Warren came in secret. Those she helped were conscious almost always that they were suffering the consequences of sin. Decent folk would condemn them and cast them out if their troubles became known. So even as they went to Hester for her help, they knew that the old woman did the devil's work.

When it was over and Hester Warren was finally dead, the smell of wet ash hung in the air over the village for hours. In such a drought as they were suffering that summer, it would have been too dangerous to let the fierce blaze of the execution pyre burn itself out. The wind had got up, and sparks set alight first one rick and then another round the village. The farm men who put the fires out worked silently, carefully avoiding looking at each other. There was no moon, no stars to be seen, but in spite of the cloud there was no sign of rain. The heat was oppressive. The men were not sure why they felt under threat, but they did, every one of them.

That night the villagers in their beds pulled the covers over their heads and thought of the sound of Hester's screams and the curses she had brought down upon them, and upon Catcombe, and they were afraid.

The year was 1568.

ONE

Tim Baker was only recently qualified as a vicar. He was young and optimistic and he wanted to help his parishioners be happy rather than good. He believed passionately in the principles of love and family and compassion. He thought that if he could talk to people, he could make them understand these principles and be glad. But Tim was shy and inarticulate, and, in practice, he did not know how best to turn theory into action.

When he was first appointed to the parish of Catcombe in Somerset, Tim saw it as his mission to heal the deep and bitter divisions between the traditional rural community in the old village and their new neighbours in the vast modern housing estate called Catcombe Mead. The estate was built in the late 1990s to house the overspill from a distant city. The villagers saw these urban incomers as a hostile invading force. The incomers looked on the villagers as another kind of farm animal.

Old Catcombe, like many other ancient grey-stone rural small towns buried deep in the West Country, was dying on its feet. Within living memory there had been a cattle market, a thriving woollen mill, and a small brewery to provide work for the locals who were not employed on the farms. But these were gone now, as were most of the farms. Now many of the cottages that lined the single main street, or clustered around the squat church with its imposing square tower, were holiday lets unoccupied out of the summer season. Year by year one shopkeeper after another had gone out of business and moved away, until there remained only a single Co-op store, a post office already threatened with closure, and a small junk shop called *The Antiques Emporium* which was open only in summer.

There was also an untidy garage which no longer sold fuel from the three grimy pumps marked in pints and gallons – two for petrol and one for diesel – under its battered canopy. The butcher's shop selling local beef and lamb had closed the year before when the butcher died and his son sold out; and two years ago the branch of one of the big banks which occupied an impressive double-fronted house opposite the church had closed. The building was now converted to a private house. The only bank business left was a cash machine in the Co-op, and they were lucky to have that.

In contrast, the modern shopping centre of Catcombe Mead flourished. The housing estate was a large development of jerry-built red-brick family homes served by a shiny new glass-fronted secondary school, a supermarket, and the usual DIY and furniture stores.

These houses were intended for executive workers who would commute every day to the city thirty miles away. Shops, the new school, a health centre, were all within walking distance – a community purpose-built for the new millennium.

The developers congratulated themselves on how many homes they had managed to fit into the site where once upon a time fat Red Devon cows grazed on the water meadows in the summer. They claimed they had built the houses without losing what they called 'rural amenity value' because there were still a few fallow weed-filled fields beside the road between Catcombe and Catcombe Mead to remind the incomers that they were enjoying the benefits of country life.

But a slump in the national economy affected jobs in the city. The cold east wind of economic blight made itself felt in Catcombe Mead. The housing estate began to reflect a rundown air of depression and neglect.

And, as the incomers themselves made no effort to take responsibility for the eyesore that had been created for them, the resentment of the Old Catcombe villagers towards the incomers began to harden into outright antagonism.

The villagers began to feel that they were under siege by barbarians. During the day the bored young unemployed from Catcombe Mead drove stolen cars at speed through the old village. They raced their motorbikes round the town hall and through the arches of the historic market cross. They terrorized old ladies as they tried to cross the street, and shouted obscenities at mothers walking with prams or small children.

At night these same outlaws stalked the streets, threatening the people and stealing from homes and garages. In the morning, trails of broken glass and discarded beer cans, used condoms, puddles of vomit and urine, remained as evidence of the night's disturbances.

In the Co-op in Old Catcombe, the old ladies asked each other, 'What have we done to deserve this?' And the middle-aged woman behind the counter could only shake her head and say, 'It's like there's a curse on this place.'

Nothing much came of complaints to the police or the council. The police sent a constable round the village houses to offer advice on security; the council provided a man with a mechanical street-cleaner early on Monday mornings to clear up after the weekend. But the intimidation continued and the villagers still felt themselves besieged.

Something had to be done. And, the Reverend Tim Baker told himself, it's my job to do it.

As was his wont, he looked first for solutions in books. Unable to communicate easily with his parishioners, he looked to local historical precedent and tradition for guidance. In the parish records he came across a contemporary account of the burning of the witch Hester Warren in 1568.

The next Sunday, the Reverend Baker delivered an impassioned sermon. He used the terrible fate of Hester Warren to call for an end to the ignorance and intolerance which still existed in the parish. He appealed to his congregation to seek reconciliation between the two Catcombe communities, divided, he said, by a lack of mutual understanding.

His regular churchgoers, ten elderly residents of Old Catcombe, showed no sign of having heard or understood anything he'd said. Some complained among themselves afterwards that they didn't like the way the vicar had shouted at them, it wasn't proper to raise his voice in church.

Tim told himself that if he was to achieve his goal he must get his message across to younger, more active people. That meant that he would have to look for converts to his cause among the residents of Catcombe Mead.

So, one breezy afternoon not long before Christmas, the young vicar, telling his wife that he'd be home for tea, mounted his new blue mountain bike bought for getting around his scattered parish, and made his way down the still pleasant country lane to the housing estate. There he intended to foster the spirit of the season of goodwill to all men among his new parishioners.

If the people of Old Catcombe and Catcombe Mead would only *talk* to each other, he thought, all this ill-will could be sorted out. As he approached Catcombe Mead and the main road, he saw ahead the vast glass school and the supermarket car park. He didn't want to go there. People there would be too busy to listen to him. He intended to make contact with the people living in the residential areas, the ordinary people. He was naive enough to imagine that he could call on them in their homes as he did when he visited the Old Catcombe villagers. The newcomers were people like himself who would surely respond to a friendly approach just as his parishioners in the village did.

The Reverend Tim took the first turn on the right into Forester Close. This was a quiet-looking cul-de-sac of detached three-bedroomed houses. Nowhere looked its best this time of year but the leafless ornamental trees and the muddy grass verges in this street spoke of pretensions to human warmth and communal pride not even hinted at by the soulless blocks of flats and concrete pavements which bounded the main road. He thought the street looked promising.

He thought he saw a light on at the back of one of the houses and this made him happy. Here was a proper full-time mother, probably baking scones for her children's tea when they came home from school. He found the image comforting. This, he decided, was a good place to begin.

It was only after he dismounted from his blue bicycle and propped it against a low garden wall outside the house that he saw the group of teenage boys hanging around outside the front door. They were gathered round a tall sturdy youth with dark greasy hair. He wore studded black leathers and heavy laced boots which seemed to mark him out as some sort of leader. He was playing with the controls of a shining black motorcycle.

Tim Baker suddenly felt nervous. He was a small, thin, pale man who wore spectacles with thick lenses to correct his short sight. He had a nervous dithery way that irritated him as much as he knew it put off other people. Also, he had learned from childhood that there was something about him that triggered ridicule and sometimes outright aggression in the young.

But it was too late to retreat now. He took a deep breath and started to walk towards these new parishioners of his. He was acutely aware that they were watching him, and that they had formed a semicircle and were moving towards him.

'Hallo, lads,' he said brightly, and tried to make his smile convincing. 'Nice bike,' he said to the boy with the motorcycle. He thought that made him seem rather cool. He tried to deepen the high pitch of his voice. 'I'm your new vicar,' he said. 'My name's Tim. I'm hoping to get to know some of my parishioners here, right? If you've got any problems you'd like to talk about . . .'

He knew he sounded ridiculous, and frightened. But he couldn't help himself.

Tim wished they would stop staring at him. It made him even more nervous.

'Quite,' he said, as though someone had said something. He asked himself, what's the matter with me? They're just kids, all they need is to feel someone cares about them.

He laughed. It came out all wrong, very shrill and forced, which it was. He said hastily, hearing his own desperation, 'I think I've come at the wrong time. Everyone seems to be out today. Perhaps you could mention to your parents that my door's always open, right?'

He was sweating. This was absurd. They were harmless kids. But he started to move away, knowing that he must not turn his back on them. It seemed to him that he could smell his own fear. He'd always thought that was just something people said about fear, but now he knew that it was true.

'Got a day off school, have you?' he said. 'That's nice. You must study very hard these days to pass all those exams. I feel sorry for you kids today, there's so much pressure on you all to do well. But one day you'll be glad you worked so hard.'

The teenagers looked at each other and showed their teeth as though they were about to laugh but they didn't laugh.

You fool, Tim told himself, of course it's school holidays.

'That's your advice, is it, Rev?' the boy on the motorcycle said. 'That's what got you to where you are today, is it?'

The boy slowly and deliberately rolled a joint, lit it, then inhaled and passed it to one of his mates.

'You want a drag, Rev?' one of the younger kids asked, pushing against Tim and blowing the aromatic smoke in his face.

'Don't you know that stuff's dangerous,' Tim said, trying to sound like an older brother, not the heavy father. 'You could get addicted,' he said. 'It affects your brain, leads to short-term memory loss . . .'

'What brains are you're talking about?' the first boy said. 'Don't you know we don't have no brains?'

The kid with the joint reached up to touch Tim's dog collar. 'Woof, woof,' he jeered and they all laughed. The boy, encouraged, grabbed the collar and pulled it off.

'Walkies, walkies,' he said, imitating Tim's voice and accent. 'Look, Kevin, I've let him off the lead.'

Tim suddenly felt horribly vulnerable.

'I'd better go,' he said. 'Things to do, places to go.' He very nearly giggled in his embarrassment. It was a nervous habit he had never been able to break.

'Yeah?' Kevin said. He picked up Tim's new blue bicycle and threw it at him. Perhaps he didn't actually intend it to hit him, but the young vicar was moving forward and the bike knocked him down.

'Oh, I say,' Tim said.

He could hear the way he sounded and he knew that they would mock him for it because he was old-fashioned and had nothing in common with them.

His spectacles had fallen off. Without them he was almost blind.

'These what you're looking for?' one of the boys called, and Tim heard the crunch of glass as his tormentor stamped on them.

The boy pushed the spectacles roughly against Tim's face, nicking his skin with the broken glass so that blood began to dribble down the side of his nose.

'Four-eyes, four-eyes, you got a bloody nose,' one kid began to chant.

He was so young his voice hadn't even broken.

'No, it's just a scratch,' Tim said, trying to wipe away the blood with the back of his hand.

'Not good enough for you, Rev?' Kevin said, 'You looking to be some kind of martyr, are you? I'll give you a bloody nose.'

He hit Tim hard in the face. The sudden pain left the young vicar confused, struggling to catch his breath as blood poured out of his nostrils.

Tim tasted the blood at the back of his throat. As more teenagers began to hit him in the face, he put up his hands to try to hold them off, but he couldn't see where the blows were coming from. He couldn't speak, either; he just made a silly little protesting sound that seemed to enrage his tormentors further. He began to pray silently, Please, God, what do I do now?

He started to blubber, trying to get to his feet because he knew from the old days at school how his tears inflamed bullies. He could make out Kevin's voice, deeper than the rest. 'You trying to run out on us, Rev?'

'No, please, we can talk this through,' Tim was trying to say, and as he heard his own words in his head, he was mortified at the absurdity of what he was saying even though he could not make himself heard.

'You're not going anywhere till we've shown you what we think of people like you,' Kevin said. 'You want to talk? Here's what I've got to say.'

He kicked Tim hard in the crotch. Then the others joined in. Someone hit him at the base of the spine with something metal, and then there was a flash of iridescent white as one of the teenagers pulled a knife and sliced through his sleeve and forearm to reveal the bone and a silvery tendon. Then it disappeared under the dark flow of blood.

In Tim's last conscious moment, he remembered something he'd heard recently about a gang of girls seen playing football with a live rat. Somewhere in Yorkshire. Who'd told him about that? Had it been on television? It was no good, he couldn't think. Please, God, what is the world coming to?

He was unconscious by the time a car turned into Forester Close and the teenagers scattered.

In the car Donna Miller had seen her sons Kevin and Nate among the group gathered around something lying on the pavement. She saw them look up and then take flight like a crowd of crows rising from a dead rabbit in the road.

She telephoned for an ambulance.

'Do you know who he is?' one of the paramedics asked her.

Donna shook her head.

The police asked, 'Did you see who did this to him?'

'No,' she said. 'I found him lying in the road like this when I came home.'

A policewoman in plainclothes seemed to be in charge. She gave Donna her card. 'If you think of anything that could help,' she said, 'ring me. In confidence,' she added.

'It could've been a hit and run, couldn't it?' Donna said.

There was something about Donna's face that caught the police-woman's attention. Shock, of course, but more than that an expression where primitive fear struggled with an unexpected defensiveness.

'No, it couldn't,' she said. 'This was a vicious attack and whoever did it will be on a murder charge.'

'I didn't see anything,' Donna said.

TWO

Hidden behind the curtain at the window of her front room Alice Bates watched the murder of the young vicar.

The position of her house at the top of the cul-de-sac facing down the street gave Alice a clear view of what went on in Forester Close. She spent a great deal of her time watching everything that happened there. Nor was she a mere casual observer of her neighbours' doings. She had never even spoken to most of them, but she felt nonetheless intimately connected to them. Watching the secret lives of others from the safety of her front room provided Alice with a kind of virtual life of her own. That, and the television, were the emotional and spiritual touchstones that connected her to other people. They offered her an illusion of being involved in society but at the same time distanced from it. She did not distinguish between the real lives she watched unfold and the fictional 'realities' of television drama. Thus she protected herself from the brutal actuality of life by refusing to believe that it was really happening.

So, for Alice, Number Three Forester Close contained the entire outside world. She was still the same person who would once have written on her prized possessions: Alice Bates, Three Forester Close, Catcombe Mead, Catcombe, near Haverton, Somerset, Wessex, England, United Kingdom, British Isles, Europe, the Western Hemisphere, the World, the Universe, the Mind of God.

She watched the young vicar cycle up the street. She was afraid he was going to come up to her house and knock on the door. Alice didn't like visitors. She had no friends to come and see her, and strangers only called if they wanted something.

So, without losing her vantage point, she moved behind the sideboard so as not to be seen. She saw the young man's pale, anxious, holy face outside her house, looking as though he was searching for something or someone. She saw that his dog collar was too big for his thin throat.

He must be mad, Alice thought, coming on his own to a place like Forester Close dressed like that.

She knew that something bad was about to happen.

Alice had noticed the gang of teenagers hanging about in front of the Millers' house before the vicar turned into the Close. They were there most afternoons when Donna and her partner Alan were out. They spent their time drinking and smoking, and jeering at anyone who passed by. Very few people did pass by because there was something savage about these youngsters; they were intimidating and no one wanted to run the gauntlet of their foul language and abuse.

Alice's heart was in her mouth as she watched the young vicar get off his bright blue bike and approach the teenagers.

The older Miller boy, Kevin, said something to him, and suddenly they were no longer a group of kids, they were a pack on the hunt, predatory and menacing. Alice thought, that poor little man, what's he going to do now?

She herself had often known what it felt like to be afraid of other people. It was what happened to shy, scared spinsters like herself who never learned to assert themselves. For her, fear was a way of life. Alice was aware – and then ashamed as she watched what was happening to another vulnerable human being beaten – that she felt a thrill of primitive excitement that had nothing to do with concern for the young vicar. The man was weak and helpless and he was a born victim. Some instinct of self-preservation compelled Alice, herself habitually a victim, to be glad to see someone else suffer for once. There but for the grace of God, she thought. But, she said, he's one of the Lord's own, how can God let this happen?

The vicar was knocked down and the youths set on him.

It never occurred to Alice that she could or should do something to stop the teenagers kicking the poor man to death.

Because she felt helpless to act, she saw herself somehow exonerated from responsibility for what those thugs were doing. She didn't even go to the telephone to dial 999. If she moved, those kids might see her and know that she was there, watching. They could turn on her.

Then Donna Miller drove up and the teenagers fled. The poor young vicar was taken away in an ambulance, like a prop no longer needed on set. Alice thought, he looks badly hurt; he could be dead.

The policewoman who seemed to be in charge was so smart and well-dressed that Alice thought she could be a television presenter. She looked quite out of place in the Millers' rundown front garden. She doesn't look to me like any kind of a serious detective, Alice said to herself.

This police officer gave Donna Miller her card.

Much good that'll do her, Alice thought. Donna will cover for her boys whatever they do. She's their mother, she won't get them into trouble; mothers never do.

There was no point in hoping that Alan, Donna's present partner, would play the heavy father either. He wouldn't dare. All three of the Miller children were Donna's, but by different fathers.

Nor would anyone else in Forester Close get Donna's boys into trouble. The Millers terrorized all the residents in the street. The entire family recognized no laws or social restraint as applying to them. Donna and Alan, a slob who spent most of his waking hours watching pornographic DVDs from the sitting room couch, had abandoned any effort to control Kevin, who was nineteen, or his younger brother, seventeen-year-old Nate. Or Jess, the youngest.

Alice felt a certain sympathy for the daughter. Fifteen-year-old Jess was a sullen, doughy-looking creature with weighty tattooed arms and shoulders. She was apparently addicted to having parts of her sizeable body pierced, so that she looked like an overstuffed sofa held together by safety pins. When the Millers first moved in, Alice took the girl to be a blowsy thirty year old, perhaps Donna's sister, but then she overheard a shouting match about a forthcoming birthday party and realized that Jess was still a child.

The girl brought a bit of lurid colour to Forester Close. Alice took her to represent what passed as yob glamour. She wore glittery blue eye shadow and thick black mascara, and her hair was dyed a fine dark purple. In the street, where she and her brothers hung around for hours at a time, she was always smoking, and swigged constantly from big brown bottles. In the house, when she wasn't sulking, Alice could see her slumped on the sofa in the living room watching the clash of aliens on DVDs.

Jess also screamed colourful abuse at her mother, at her brothers Kevin and Nate, at the stepfather Alan, and even at her own young baby which the rest of her family combined to try to force her to care for by ignoring it themselves as long as they could stand it crying. Jess's body language made it clear that she resented this pressure of motherhood. Sometimes she shouted at the older of the two boys, Kevin, that the kid was just as much his as hers and he could look after it himself, she had better things to do. Kevin ignored her. Jess tried to ignore the baby.

Alice was bemused by Jess. The girl was plainly unhappy. She appeared bored out of her mind by everything to do with her family and Forester Close. Living on the housing estate seemed to strike her as little better than being abandoned in a wilderness peopled by primitive apes. Alice sympathized with that. The girl was lost in her own life.

Alice believed that as a fellow female, Jess, too, must live in dread of the yobs in her own family.

But then Peter Henson, a retired doctor who lived with his wife opposite the Millers at Number Four, dared to complain when he discovered Jess having loud and violent sex with what the doctor called a Neanderthal against his garage wall. And the Miller family turned on him as one to defend their own.

The Hensons, Peter and his wife Jean, became a target for vandalism. The elderly couple could not leave their car outside their house without the windscreen being shattered or the paint-work scored. Every time the Hensons came out of their home, the Millers jeered and swore at them. And Jess was the worst of the lot.

No, Alice said to herself, all the Millers are the same. No one in the street is going to dare to admit to the police that they saw what happened to the young vicar.

Alice had no doubt of this because, watching the residents in secret, she had a more intimate knowledge of her neighbours than they could possibly guess. Although she kept herself to herself, and they were strangers to her, she knew things about these families that they kept secret from each other.

She knew they had one thing in common. They were all afraid of the lurking undercurrent of mindless violence, like the thudding bass beat of Kevin's music, exuded by the Millers.

They, like Alice herself, would try to put the incident of the young vicar's death out of their minds. Alice, like the rest of them, was petrified by what those Miller boys might do to her if she told the police about them. What had happened to the poor vicar was a tragedy but it was something not to be spoken about. Alice understood that. As long as no one knew what she had seen and she herself kept silent about it, she could persuade herself that she hadn't seen anything. There was nothing to be done, after all.

She went into the kitchen to feed big, beautiful Phoebus, a ginger cat which for several months now had taken to coming round to her back door every afternoon. Alice thought of him as her own. She could hear him miaowing in protest because she was late.

Alice thought, it's nearly Christmas, *The Sound of Music* will be on television, and all those other old films with nice children and happy endings. Best not to dwell on the bad things, there's nothing to be gained by it.

THREE

The morning after Tim Baker's death, Detective Chief Inspector Rachel Moody sat in her car at the bottom of Forester Close trying to gather her thoughts.

This case particularly distressed her. She was finding it hard to maintain her professional cool. In all her previous experience of murder, the killer was usually driven beyond endurance before he did the deed. He lost control and lashed out. She could understand that, however much she disapproved.

But the savagery of this young vicar's death was new to her. What possible motive could anyone have for such an unprovoked attack? It was almost as though some sicko had done it for fun. And, Rachel told herself, something like that happening at Christmas time makes it even worse.

DCI Moody couldn't get out of her mind the sight of Mrs Tim Baker's terrified white face last night when she and Sergeant Reid broke the news of her husband's death, or the way the poor woman had looked down at the Christmas presents piled under the decorated tree in the living room. 'But it's not possible, it can't be true, it's Christmas,' Mrs Baker said. And then, with trembling lip, 'What can I tell the children?'

Now, parked at the bottom of Forester Close before starting to go through the motions of the routine investigation, Rachel Moody looked around her at the bleak street. It was so ordinary; it could be a cul-de-sac on a faceless housing estate almost anywhere at all. Except that Rachel could still see, like a ghost image in a photograph, Tim Baker's broken body lying like litter on the muddy patch of garden outside Number Two.

She asked herself, why am I taking this case so personally? Why can't I see it as just another murder?

She tried to imagine what Forester Close would be like in summer, when the trees lining the pavement were in leaf and the gardens in flower. Quite pleasant, probably, full of dappled shade and the smell of the honeysuckle which covered several of the walls dividing the front gardens of the houses from the street. But in the depth of winter the leafless branches of the trees and the drab colourless gardens gave the street a grim and desolate aspect. The blue and white ribbon of the police cordon outside Number Two was a touch of frivolity in comparison.

There were tears in Inspector Moody's eyes as she thought of the way the young vicar had died. It's no good, she told herself, there is something personal about this case. He was acting on behalf of all of us who want the best for others. He was trying to befriend those bastards who killed him; like a puppy wanting to be loved. And it's Christmas.

She thought, If I can't get someone punished for this, everyone who ever wants to do something positive to make the world a better place might as well give up trying. That's overloading it a bit, but I know what I mean. At least, I think I do.

Her train of thought was suddenly broken as Sergeant Reid opened the passenger door of the car and got in. Thanks to her they had arrived too early to start their house to house interviews. She invariably did arrive too early. Resigned, Jack Reid had volunteered to go to the café near the supermarket to buy takeaway coffee and sandwiches to eat in the car to pass the time. Nothing was to be gained by starting on door-to-door enquiries while people were still in bed.

Flustered, DCI Moody put up a hand to brush away tears that might come. She didn't want to be seen as soft. Not long promoted to Detective Chief Inspector, Rachel Moody had only recently transferred to Avon and Somerset police from Eastbourne, and she was having a hard time of it earning her male colleagues' respect. But Sergeant Reid didn't look at her. He was trying to take the sandwiches out of their plastic containers.

'What time is it?' Rachel Moody asked.

She knew the answer. She had only just checked her watch. It was 7.30 a.m.

'We'd better give it another half hour or so,' Jack Reid said.

The voice of experience, Rachel thought, and felt that she had made herself ridiculous. He thinks I'm neurotic, she said to herself, he's wishing he didn't work for a hysterical woman who was only promoted above him as a gesture to equal opportunities.

But then Reid said, 'Here, I wasn't sure how you like your

coffee so if I guessed wrong and you take sugar, you can have mine.'

He didn't sound as though he was holding a grudge.

'No, no sugar, thanks,' she said. 'God, I'm starving.'

He handed her the sandwich he had released from its packaging.

She wondered if she was wrong about Jack Reid. Perhaps he didn't have the resentments and prejudices she was ascribing to him.

They were silent while they ate bacon sandwiches, both thinking of the young vicar and his bereft family.

'You never get used to it,' Jack Reid said suddenly, 'not something like that.'

So he did see me crying, Rachel thought, and was surprised at his sensitivity.

'I suppose I wouldn't want to get used to it,' Rachel said. 'It would be terrible to get to the stage where you take something like that for granted.'

'It makes me think how my wife and kids would feel if it were me,' Reid said. 'Sandy's given up trying to make me get out of the force and do something else, but at times like this I feel guilty about what I put her through.'

'We don't get many like this,' Rachel said. 'This is different.'

She asked herself, why would anyone suddenly want to kill a man like that young vicar here? He looked so harmless, what could possibly have triggered the violence and rage involved in his killing. The motive wasn't even robbery. There was still thirty pounds in notes in the wallet found in his breast pocket at the morgue.

The crime had seemed even more inexplicable once Sergeant Reid identified the body. Personal papers in the dead man's pockets revealed that the victim was the local vicar, a married man with two young children who had only moved to Old Catcombe, his first parish, six months before.

'What in God's name was a man like that doing in a place like this?' Rachel Moody asked.

'It beggars belief,' Jack Reid said. 'Can you credit that a man can be killed practically in the street in broad daylight and no one saw anything?'

'So you tried talking to the neighbours?'

Reid couldn't disguise his frustration. 'We tried, but no one was in,' he said. 'At least, they weren't answering their doors. So much for Christian principles and good Samaritans and all that guff.'

'Don't let it get to you,' Rachel Moody said. 'We've got to treat this like any other murder. Whoever killed Tim Baker murdered the man, not the vicar.'

'I wonder,' Sergeant Reid said. 'Where was his dog collar? The killer might be a freak who hates Christmas, or someone who has it in for religion.'

Rachel Moody remembered the giant Christmas tree she had seen yesterday evening as Sergeant Reid drove slowly through Old Catcombe looking for the vicarage. Where the bereaved Mrs Baker's decorations had seemed pathetic, the sight of that other radiant symbol of love and joy at the heart of the historic village had given Rachel a warm festive glow. It was the season of goodwill and this tree on the village green, covered in coloured lights, gave a real feeling of community. There was a placard beside the tree announcing that everyone was invited to an open air carol concert on Christmas Eve.

Tim Baker must have organized that, Rachel Moody told herself.

In contrast, there was not even a token sense of community in Forester Close. No one had got around to putting up decorations yet.

'They'll have to cancel the carol concert,' Rachel said suddenly. 'It wouldn't be proper, would it?'

Sergeant Reid didn't know what she was talking about. 'I like a good carol concert myself,' he said. 'The kids love it when they sing a very odd version of *Good King Wenceslas*. And, of course, *Shepherds wash their socks by night*.' He laughed.

The DCI wasn't listening. 'You know,' she said, 'that woman who called the ambulance? There was something odd about her.'

'The blowsy bleached blonde job, you mean?' the Sergeant said.

Moody thought how odd men's perception of women was, so subjective and always sexually coloured. What she had noticed about the woman from Number Two, Forester Close, was the desperate expression of fear in her eyes. Of course Donna Miller had been very shocked by what she'd seen, traumatized, practically. She'd been extremely pale under her make-up, and she couldn't stop shaking, which was natural enough. But to Rachel her eyes had told a different story. It was as though something she had long expected had happened at last and it was that which scared her. She was frightened, and she was defensive.

'That woman's hiding something,' Rachel Moody said. 'We've got to find out what it is she's not telling us.'

FOUR

A mile or so away from Forester Close, on the other side of Old Catcombe, young Mark Pearson was on his way to the village rugby club to celebrate his twenty-first birthday. He drove slowly round the bends in the narrow twisting lane. He'd almost knocked the vicar off his new blue bicycle the day before. He wondered where Mr Baker was off to, cycling away from the village like that as if the devil were after him. That's all we need, Mark thought, vicars on bicycles wobbling all over the road in front of farm vehicles.

Mark had lived in Old Catcombe all his life, as had his father, his grandfather and his great-grandfather. Like them, too, he played prop forward for Catcombe Corinthians rugby team, and batted number three for the village cricket XI. He was big and strong with a mop of curly dark hair, not all that dissimilar from the Aberdeen Angus and Hereford beef bullocks he and his father raised on the family farm. Most of the residents of Catcombe Mead would dismiss him as a simple-minded son of the soil, an obsolete relic of a dead and irrelevant time.

Mark shared his family's attitude, which dismissed the incomers of Catcombe Mead as an unwelcome infestation of parasitical vermin who made no effort to control their sheep-chasing dogs, and habitually left gates open whenever they slipped into a field to trample on a crop.

But even so, for Mark's generation of the Old Catcombe order, there were already changes under way. The future for farming looked bleak. Many of Mark's friends who had been at school with him had tried to find work in the area, but failed and moved away to the city, or to another country.

Bert Pearson, Mark's father, assumed that he and his son would work together on the farm and then Mark would take over and employ a future son of his own in turn. Mark wouldn't say so to his father, but he couldn't see this happening. It was becoming more and more difficult to make a living from the land. And he couldn't help but resent the kind of money his former school friends were earning in the city. They came back on visits driving new cars, wearing sharp clothes. Mark wanted these things. He began to feel that life was leaving him behind. He wanted to have money in his pocket and know the feeling of simply spending it for fun. For him and his family, spending money was a painful process of juggling priorities and doing without. They spent on necessities, not for pleasure; just using money was a source of guilt.

Most of his life Mark hadn't questioned that he would work on the farm with his father and then take it over when his parents retired. Dad and Mum would move out of the farmhouse and live in a cottage nearby when Mark married and started a family of his own. They all took this process as preordained.

But that was then, Mark thought. It was the foot and mouth outbreak in 2001 which started it. Dad and Mum had kept the horrific details from their eleven-year-old son, but they could not hide what was happening on the farm itself.

The precautions were bad enough, the restrictions on where they could go, the stinking black antiseptic dips for their gumboots wherever they went, the anxious night and morning checks on the cattle and sheep for the slightest sign of lameness or sore mouths.

And then the government vets identified a case of the disease on a local farm.

In those days Bert Pearson ran a mixed farm. Mainly cattle and sheep, with a few pigs; arable land to grow wheat for sale and maize as winter feed, and water meadows close to a small river for the stock.

Mark came home from school one day to find Ministry vets in white protective clothing destroying the last of the pigs. All the cows and sheep were already dead. Mechanical excavators had uprooted a field of wheat to dig a vast pit where the carcasses were already piled high. A pall of smoke hung over the pyre, but this did not hide the open-eyed faces of lifeless animals Mark and his father had known as friends.

That night was the first time Mark saw his father in tears.

A few days later, they learned that the rush to destroy all the farm animals within the prescribed exclusion zone had been a false alarm. There had been no local outbreak of disease. The vets had made a mistake. No one even said sorry.

That day, something inside Bert Pearson died. And Mark Pearson started to smoulder with anger against the smug ranks of outsiders who could not be called to account for the damage they did so carelessly.

Bert and Mark restocked the farm; at least, they bought new cattle and a few pigs. The sheep were not replaced. Nor were these new animals any connection with the carefully line-bred stock that had been wiped out by the agents of panicky politicians. It sometimes felt to Mark as though that one incident alone destroyed everything his Dad was: a father, husband, friend, and citizen.

Mark knew that since that time his laughing, lively Dad, rugby player, cricketer, the first to offer to mow the outfield on the pitch or provide a pig for the hog roast after the annual fete, had disappeared forever.

Bert Pearson now haunted the farm like a spare grey ghost. Some days he did not leave his armchair in the kitchen, but sat there all day in silence staring at children's programmes on the television. If he went out it was to walk, stiff and awkward, through the fields and down to the river. There he would stand without moving, staring at the water, taking no notice of the wildlife seething around him.

He took to going to bed early in the evening, about seven o'clock usually, or soon after the children's programmes on the TV gave way to the grown-up stuff. He didn't want to watch that.

Once in bed, he lay sleepless in the dark ignoring his wife and son, everything except the old sheepdog who padded after him to his bedroom and spent the night in there with him.

It was all too much for Joyce. She tried to help him. She had forced him to go to the doctor, who diagnosed severe depression and prescribed pills that seemed to make Bert more zombie-like than ever. She tried to interest him in going out with her to the pub for a meal, or to a film. He shook his head and slumped back in his chair, or turned the sound up on the television to drown her voice. Unable to face going to sleep with him in the bedroom where she was only too conscious of his lack of response to her, she moved into the spare room.

At first she wept a lot. Then she decided that she must make some sort of life for herself. To do that, she told herself, she had to give up on Bert. She didn't want to, but she was frightened that he would take her down with him into the misery he wallowed in. She couldn't stop herself, she did think he wallowed in it. He didn't even try to help himself.

She told Mark, 'He's my husband, I married him for love. I know he's ill, he can't help it, but I'm only forty-eight, I can't go on like this.'

Mark didn't understand. So when his mother started to go out socially in the evenings, he blamed her. She had a group of women friends with whom she enrolled in adult education classes, played bridge, sang in a choir, or went out regularly to play bingo in the community hall of a town not too far away from Old Catcombe. The house was crowded with chairs she upholstered, patchwork quilts she stitched, and stuffed toys she won at bridge.

Mark, too, might have made a fresh start somewhere else. But he would have felt like a traitor to himself. The knowing eyes of the cattle when he came to check them in the afternoons, the jolly grins of the pigs as they scampered towards him when he brought their food, the sight of wheat turning gold before harvest, and the smell of cut grass at silage time; these things were part of him, as much a part as the beating of his heart or the pumping of his lungs. They gave him life. He knew this without sentimentality or poetic fancies. He rather wished he didn't.

One cold bright day after a long spell of dry weather, Mark heard a commotion in the field where the cattle had been let out at last after being shut in the stockyard during a long wet autumn. The farm dogs were barking as though repelling a small army. Mark shouted for his father, but Bert did not respond. Meanwhile the noise of motorbike engines being gunned sounded like several chain saws from the lane.

Mark jumped on the farm quad bike and the dogs leaped up behind him, barking wildly. He sped out of the yard and down the lane towards the field where the cattle were.

He had only gone a few hundred yards when he was met by an eye-catching young girl running up the lane towards him. At first sight she looked to him to have no clothes on, except for a pair of ridiculous high-heeled scarlet boots, but then he saw that she was wearing a skirt like an elastic band and a skimpy top several sizes too small for her rather large breasts. She looked terrified, her eyes wide with fear and her mouth open as she screamed for help. He couldn't hear her screams over the sound of motorbike engines and the bellowing of the herd of bullocks which was stampeding up the road behind her.

Mark's first reaction was furious anger. This ridiculous girl with her stupid clothes and her purple hair was putting his animals in danger. She reached the quad bike and clung to him. Her over-tight clothes had split, and he caught a flash of her breasts. Part of the side-seam of her bright red skirt had burst open and he saw dark pubic hair. It was an extraordinary feast of female flesh for him to encounter so suddenly. But he didn't have any time to enjoy it.

'Get behind the quad bike and keep still,' he shouted at her.

The cattle had slowed down at the sight of him and were milling in the narrow lane, the leaders lowering their heads to challenge the dogs, which had raced forward to confront them.

'Oh, my God,' he heard the girl gasp, 'they're trying to kill me.'

'Shut up,' Mark said. This time he said it quietly, almost hissing at her.

He had got off the quad bike and was walking slowly towards the angry, frightened bullocks. He addressed the girl in a soothing, slow tone but not for her benefit, only to quieten the animals.

'What do you think you're doing?' he said.

The sound of racing motorbikes almost drowned what he said.

'These monsters ran out when Kevin and Nate went into the field to ride their motorbikes,' she said. Her voice shook with shock and fear. 'Nate left the gate open and I couldn't stop them. I thought I was going to die.'

Snorting and stamping, the animals now turned back the way they'd come, calmed by the sight of Mark and the dogs and the familiar quad bike.

'Are those yobs out of their minds, taking motorcycles into a field full of bullocks?' Mark said, still in his quiet voice although he was finding it hard not to shout at her.

He got back on the quad bike and slowly followed the animals, which were now moving restlessly towards the gate to their field. The girl climbed up behind him and held on to him. He

could feel her trembling as she clung to him. The dogs had raced
ahead and were in position in the lane to turn the animals in
through the gate.

Mark could now see two youths on motorbikes racing in a
wide circle on the pasture.

'Who are they?' he asked the girl. 'They're going to pay for
this.'

His threat sounded a little pathetic even to him. There was
nothing he could do. He didn't even have a mobile phone to call
the cops.

But the revving engines and the flashes of colour on the lads'
helmets enraged the bullocks anew. They surged through the
gateway into the field and charged, bellowing furiously, towards
the motorcyclists.

The girl screamed, 'Kevin, look out,' and then he heard her
say under her breath, 'Oh, please God let them be all right.'

'To hell with them, what about my bullocks?' he said.

The two youths seemed suddenly to realize they were in danger
from the approaching animals. The bullocks were almost upon
them. Not sure how to escape, they revved their engines again
and sped away across the field and through the open gate out
into the lane. The sound of their motorbikes was audible long
after they had disappeared.

Mark jumped off the quad bike and closed the gate. For several
minutes he watched the bullocks, deprived of their quarry, come
to a halt. Slowly, one after another, they lowered their heads and
started to graze.

'Bastards,' Mark said, turning back towards the girl.

She was still perched on the back of the quad bike and looked
good to him even with her teeth chattering and streaks of mascara
smeared on her pale cheeks.

'Now how am I going to get home?' she said, and her voice
was shaking. 'I told Kevin this was a stupid thing to do.'

'If you're from the housing estate it's not that far to walk,'
Mark said.

'What makes you think I'm from the estate?' the girl said,
suddenly on the defensive.

'Where else would you be from?' Mark said.

He was shocked at the contempt he heard in his own voice.

He looked at her to see if she had noticed. She bit her lip, and he saw that she was trying not to cry.

'I meant no one who belonged here would do what you and your boyfriend just did.' Mark was trying to show sympathy.

'He's not my boyfriend, he's my brother, my half-brother,' she said. 'They both are.'

Mark looked at her more closely. She tried to smile at him. She had a nice smile. But with the smeared mascara on her cheeks, and her purple hair, she looked like a clown. In the silly high-heeled red boots she was wearing, the thought of her walking to Catcombe Mead struck him as funny. He couldn't imagine how she had managed to run away from the bullocks at all. She must have been really scared.

'What's your name?' he said.

'Jess,' she said. 'Jess Miller. Who are you?'

'Mark,' he said, 'Mark Pearson. I live at the farm there.' He pointed back up the lane.

She was shivering again and he felt sorry for her. 'Your brothers are morons,' he said. 'Tell them that from me. Stupid shits.'

'It wasn't Kevin's fault,' Jess said. 'I made him let me ride behind him. I told him if he didn't let me, I'd tell Mum he stole a bottle of brandy from the supermarket.'

Mark didn't like to tell her that when he called Kevin a shit, it wasn't because he'd abandoned his sister to walk home.

'Come back up to the farm with me and I'll lend you a sweater,' he said.

She looked doubtful.

'It's all right,' he said, thinking she was worried about anyone else seeing the state of her, 'there's no one there to see you except me.'

He hoped his Dad was out in the fields somewhere staring gloomily into the distance.

At the farm, Mark led the way into the kitchen. Thank God, he thought, Dad's not here.

The girl walked around the room touching things in disbelief. 'It's like a museum,' she said, 'where are the real things?'

He was puzzled. 'What do you mean?' he asked.

'Oh, you know, the microwave and the washing up machine?'

She looked around. 'You haven't got a proper kettle or a toaster. How do you boil water for tea?'

Mark pointed at the Rayburn in the inglenook.

'I don't believe this,' she said.

There was a short silence, then he said, 'I'll get you that sweater.'

In his bedroom he knelt down to root through his drawer for his best sweater. He felt suddenly ashamed of his everyday clothes, afraid she would say something about how old they were.

She had followed him upstairs. 'Anything will do,' she said. 'Anything warm.'

She came into the room behind him and leaned across him to take the sweater. He turned to get up and felt her legs brush his cheek. He felt his face going hot, bright red.

She bent over him, sniffing his hair. 'You smell of sweat,' she said, and her voice sounded husky. 'The smell of men's sweat always turns me on.'

Her breasts pressing against his face as he tried to get to his feet were large but very firm, not pendulous at all. He kissed her hard hot nipples and she grabbed his head in both her hands and pressed him against her so that he was almost forced to open his mouth to her breast. He put his hand between her legs and felt how wet she was.

'Quick,' she muttered, 'do it now.' And then she was tearing at his clothes and he was lost.

Afterwards, he seemed to climb back from a deep, soft place to find her head on his stomach. He could feel her warm breath against his skin.

He stroked her hair, seeing through half-closed eyes the purple strands bright against his fingers.

'You're beautiful,' he murmured, 'you're so beautiful.'

She lifted her head and smiled. 'I've got to go,' she said. 'Kevin may come looking for me. I don't want any trouble.'

They both knew what she meant. The hatred between Old Catcombe and Catcombe Mead was like a death threat between them.

She sighed. 'We must find a place,' she said. 'You do want to see me again?'

He could only nod dumbly, not trusting himself to speak.

FIVE

Detective Chief Inspector Rachel Moody and Sergeant Jack Reid chose Number Three, the house at the top of the Close, to start their search for witnesses to the young vicar's murder.

This was the home of Alice Bates.

'Anything known?' Rachel Moody asked.

'Name and address, that's it,' Jack Reid said.

'Whoever she is she must have a panoramic view of everything that goes on in the street,' Rachel Moody said. 'Isn't that a good place to start?'

'Sure it is,' Jack Reid said, 'and apart from that, I'd put money on some old girl living there alone. Best source of information there is, that.'

Rachel stared at him. 'What makes you think that?' she asked. 'It looks like all the other houses to me.'

'Oh, no, the signs are all there. There's something defensive about that house, the way it looks. Net curtains at every window and absolutely nothing in the garden because whoever lives there expects anything she leaves out will be stolen. Sure sign of old age. And no car, a dead giveaway she's on her last legs.'

DCI Moody laughed. 'You're crazy,' she said.

'Oh, you can laugh,' Jack Reid said, and grinned. 'But I'm right, you'll see. I'd put money on it.'

'Well, if your little old lady in Number Three really saw someone being killed, surely she's just the type to be only too pleased to talk to us,' Rachel said.

Jack Reid shrugged. 'Let's hope so,' he said. 'More likely she'll pretend she doesn't know anything about it. This killer's local; she'll be much more scared of the neighbours than she is of us. Want to bet?'

'No fear. You've made a fortune off me already,' Rachel said. 'Here goes.'

She rang the doorbell.

They waited.

When Alice Bates finally answered the door, Rachel was startled at the sight of her. The DCI had to admit that Alice Bates was exactly what Jack Reid had told her to expect.

Miss Bates stood in the doorway shivering in a faded blue candlewick dressing-gown. She was thin, with colourless hair pulled back into a wispy knot. She had prominent pale eyes which she did not raise to look at her visitors. The skin of her face and on the backs of her hands was dry and neglected. She certainly looked like an old woman.

So, like everyone else, Rachel Moody initially identified Alice Bates as a kind of formless structure supporting shapeless clothes of nondescript colour, a woman without any noticeable appearance at all. When Alice reluctantly let them into the house, and turned to shuffle ahead of them down the hall, she moved, even in her own home, like someone who did not want to be noticed.

Sergeant Reid, following the DCI, whispered, 'You owe me a tenner.'

But it seemed to Rachel that Alice was not really old, or at least not ancient as Jack Reid thought her to be. Watching her, Rachel decided that age was a part Alice had got used to playing, a deliberate impersonation of an invisible woman.

She doesn't know she's doing it, Rachel told herself. When did she start acting out this old persona to avoid living a real life?

She was curious to find out more about this nondescript woman.

Alice led them into the kitchen at the back of the house. Through the window they could see a small bare patch of garden and a broken wooden fence which the locals seemed to use as a short cut from Forester Close to God knew where through the backs of the adjoining gardens.

DCI Moody noticed a vast ginger cat sitting on top of the fence, staring at her through the window.

'Nice cat,' Rachel Moody said to Alice, hoping to break the ice. 'Is he yours?'

'Yes,' Alice said. 'Do you like cats? He's beautiful, isn't he? Now, we can be a bit more private here. How can I help you?'

'We're inquiring into an incident that took place in this street yesterday afternoon,' Sergeant Reid said. 'Did you see or hear anything?'

'Oh, no, I'm afraid not,' Alice said. 'Nothing at all.'

Alice could not meet the policeman's eyes.

Why's she so scared, Jack Reid asked himself.

Alice Bates thought, I should have asked what happened, and what sort of incident. I should have made it look as though I don't know what happened.

But Rachel Moody seemed not to have noticed that.

'Perhaps you can fill us in on a bit of background for some of your neighbours,' she said. 'It strikes me that you probably know most things that go on in this street.'

Alice began to look more frightened.

'Just background, you understand,' Jack Reid said quickly. 'A chat off the record, you know, just for our information, nothing else. It could save us hours of research.'

'We'll be talking like this to all the residents,' Rachel said. 'We just want to get a picture of what life's normally like here.'

Alice relaxed. As long as this policewoman didn't actually ask her direct questions about the young vicar's murder, she was not too alarmed.

'Well, people round here don't mix much,' she said. 'We keep ourselves to ourselves, you know. There's a nice couple next door at Number Four, they're very quiet.'

'Oh, yes?' Rachel said. 'What can you tell us about them?'

'They seem nice,' Alice said.

'Well, what are their names? Do they go out to work? That sort of thing, you know.'

Alice tried to think of something to say. She could see from the way this police Chief Inspector was looking at her that she was not going to give up easily. If Alice couldn't say something to divert her she would start asking direct questions about what had happened yesterday.

'He's called Dr Henson and his wife is Jean, I think,' she said. 'He's interested in young children, but he doesn't work now. There was some talk about him being a paedophile, but I don't know about that. It's what people said.'

'Who said?' Rachel Moody asked. Alice had her attention now.

Alice wished she hadn't said anything. Mention of the paedophile rumour brought her straight back to the Millers. It was Donna Miller who had accused Dr Henson after that silly incident back in the autumn. Alice tried to remember. It had been a fine mild morning for the time of year and Jess Miller's baby had been left out in her pram on the driveway of Number Two. The brake on the pram couldn't have been properly applied and something – the child moving, or a sudden freshening of the wind – set it rolling slowly towards the main road. The pram knocked the garden wall and turned over, spilling the baby on to the gravel. The little girl started to wail for her mother, but although her volume increased, her family were apparently shouting at each other inside the house, and no one came out to see what was happening.

It didn't occur to Alice to go out to the baby, because she wouldn't know what to do. But she thought it quite shocking that one of the Millers didn't attend to her. The little girl was making a dreadful noise.

Then Peter Henson emerged from his garage and ran across the road to help the child. He picked her up and comforted her, then smoothed her clothes and used his clean handkerchief to dab at a graze on her arm. She smiled at him and pulled at his neat white beard.

Alice hadn't thought much of it at the time. But the next day the terrifying Donna Miller had barged into her house waving a letter and screaming at her:

'You saw him do it, why didn't you stop him. Why didn't you?'

Alice managed to ask, 'What is this letter?'

'Don't pretend you don't know. It had been put through the door when I came down this morning. It's about little Kylie. It says that evil pervert came out and felt her up and you witnessed everything. How could you let him do it?'

'It wasn't like that,' Alice said. She was so frightened of Donna that she couldn't breathe properly, and when she tried to speak she was so intimidated she had difficulty making sense of what she wanted to say.

Alice tried to explain but everything she said seemed to inflame Donna.

'No,' said Alice, helpless to get Donna to listen, 'he's not a paedophile, of course he's not, he's a paediatrician, a registered doctor.' She struggled to find words, her brain still stunned.

Donna ignored her. 'I can't believe you'd do this,' she yelled. 'What kind of woman are you? You even know he's on the register and you didn't tell me, and now it's too late. My baby's been scarred for life.'

'No,' Alice said, desperate, 'Dr Henson picked her up and comforted her, that's all. He made her stop crying.'

All Alice could think of to say was that none of this would have happened if Donna or Jess had been looking after the child, but she couldn't speak. She was paralysed. She didn't dare say anything. Donna wouldn't hear her anyway, the way she was, she was beyond making sense.

'You're all going to pay for this,' Donna shouted, and slammed the door behind her.

Now, aware that the plainclothes policewoman was watching her curiously, Alice wondered who had written the letter that had so inflamed Donna. She hadn't even thought about that at the time.

She wished she hadn't mentioned anything about Dr Henson to these officers. She certainly wasn't going to allow herself to be drawn into mentioning Donna Miller.

'I'm sure it was nothing,' she said. 'People get the wrong idea, don't they?'

Rachel Moody asked, 'What about your neighbours on the other side, the family who live at Number Two. What can you tell us about them?'

'Nothing. Nothing at all,' Alice said.

Watching her, Sergeant Reid thought, she looks exactly like a tortoise retracting its head into its shell. She's not going to tell us anything useful. She's scared stiff of something.

He and Rachel Moody exchanged glances. They were both convinced that Alice was hiding something.

'What about the people on the other side of the Millers?' Rachel asked. 'Who lives there?'

'Oh, that's Terri and Helen,' Alice said.

The DCI and Jack Reid both noticed that she was relieved to change the subject.

Suddenly and unexpectedly, Alice smiled. 'I call them the Odd

Couple. There's a young girl who looks exactly like Helen, so I suppose they're mother and daughter, and Terri looks after them. She's a sort of father figure.'

'Are you saying she's gay?' Rachel Moody said. She didn't think she was getting anywhere and wanted to stop Alice's pointless speculations. On the other hand, gossiping was giving Alice confidence. Something useful might come of that.

'She's a lesbian,' Alice said bluntly. Then she added, 'She and Helen are like a married couple.'

She wanted to offer them something interesting which might take their minds off the young vicar's death.

'I'm afraid, though,' she went on, 'Helen is cheating on Terri behind her back. With a man.'

Alice had played her trump card. She looked at the police officers with smug satisfaction as though they'd been testing her and she knew she'd managed to exceed their expectations.

'Do you know who this man is?' Sergeant Reid asked. He scented a possible suspect. He was convinced that the Reverend Baker had been killed by a male. It wasn't a woman's crime, he'd put money on that. When Alice mentioned Terri, he'd flirted with the possibility that she might be the sort of female he was no longer allowed to call a bull dyke, a militant who might take revenge on the male sex and the old-fashioned moral attitudes of the church by beating a vicar to death.

He dismissed the idea as absurd. But now the introduction of a red-blooded man with a secret to hide made the Sergeant perk up.

Alice said, primly, 'No. But he's not a gentleman.'

The spinster speaks, Jack Reid thought, she's a virgin, I'd put a stack of money on that.

'What makes you say he's not a gentleman?' he asked Alice.

'He often seems to be drunk,' Alice said. 'He leaves his car outside my house and you should see the way he parks. No consideration.'

Even to her, it sounded feeble. What she'd wanted to say was that when she saw the way he made love to Helen when Terri was out of the room, he behaved like a wild animal, really quite violent with her. Nothing at all like the gentlemen lovers on the television, men like Mr Darcy in *Pride and Prejudice*, or Mr Bingley, even. Not that Helen seemed to object to Dave's ungentlemanly treatment, Alice admitted to herself.

But she wasn't going to tell the police that she watched what her neighbours did in the privacy of their own homes. She said to herself, the less I say to anyone about what I see from behind the living room curtain the better.

Alice took a deep breath and smiled at the police officers.

'I'm sorry I can't help you,' she said. 'I was watching television most of yesterday, there's not much else to do this time of year. I didn't see anything.'

SIX

Next on Detective Chief Inspector Moody's list for interview were Peter Henson, the retired paediatrician, and his wife Jean, a former primary school teacher.

'Pillars of society,' Rachel Moody muttered under her breath as Sergeant Reid knocked on the front door. 'They'll help if they can.'

'Want to bet?' Reid said. 'Once they would have done, but not now they're retired. That changes everything. They had careers, they used to *be* somebodies, and suddenly that's all gone. Now they're nobodies. They won't tell us anything. They'll be afraid of their own shadows.'

'Why would professional people like them end up living in a place like this?' Rachel said.

Sergeant Reid laughed. 'Age is a great social leveller,' he said. 'You're too young to realize. Old people sink to the bottom of the human heap whatever they used to be.'

'You're a cynic,' Rachel said. 'There must be more to it than that.'

'Yes, there is,' Reid said, 'it's a question of confidence. They'll have lost it. You'll see.'

'Don't tell me,' Rachel said, teasing him, 'you'd put money on it.'

She rang the doorbell to reinforce the Sergeant's knock.

Dr Henson was tall and stooped a little. He had white hair and a small neat white beard.

To Rachel Moody, he looked like an actor playing a scientist on television. He was constantly peering over his spectacles as though checking everything against an invisible measuring chart. His wife gave the impression that she was a shy and self-facing woman who had given up the struggle to present herself as something very different, her husband's fantasy of the partner he deserved. She was neat and tidy, and, Rachel noted, dressed in the muted all-purpose costume of someone who attended a lot of charity coffee mornings. She looked habitually puzzled.

She's the sort of person who expects to be blamed for anything that goes wrong, DCI Moody thought.

Sergeant Reid asked the Hensons if they had seen what happened outside the house opposite.

The couple looked at each other and, in chorus, denied knowing anything about it. They'd seen something mentioned on the evening news on television. They couldn't believe someone had been killed across the road. Indeed, they appeared very shocked to know that such a thing could happen in a quiet respectable suburban street like Forester Close. No, really, they hadn't seen or heard a thing.

'You see, we've got better things to do than spy on our neighbours,' Peter Henson said.

Rachel Moody wondered what they'd say if she asked 'what better things?' But she didn't want to antagonize potential witnesses.

'What can you tell us about the Millers?' Rachel Moody asked Dr Henson.

He looked at his wife as though checking that they were going to agree on their answer.

'Nothing at all, I'm afraid,' Dr Henson said. 'We've never actually met them socially.'

'That's right,' Jean Henson said, backing him up.

'You must see them around, surely?' DCI Moody said.

'There are enough of them,' Jack Reid added. 'I'd have thought they were hard to miss.'

'We try to keep ourselves to ourselves,' Dr Henson said.

'People don't mix much round here,' Jean Henson said. 'Least of all the Millers. Why should they? They've got each other. You might say they're a typical twenty-first century family unit.'

'You're more aware of them in the summer, of course,' Dr Henson said, making an effort to help. 'When they've got the windows open, there's a bit of noise. The kids have their friends round. And there's the child. She's a lively little thing.'

'The child?' Rachel asked. 'We didn't know there was a child.'

'Oh, yes,' Jean said. 'She must be nearly a year old now. Jess couldn't have been much more than thirteen when she fell pregnant. Didn't they tell you?'

Rachel said, 'We haven't questioned the Millers yet, except

at the time to take a statement from Mrs Miller about finding the body. We want to try to piece together what really happened before we go any further.'

Sergeant Reid asked, 'You're quite sure you saw nothing suspicious?'

'I expect we were in the garden,' Jean said, and added, 'gardening.'

'There must've been a fair bit of noise when it was going on,' Jack said. 'There were a number of kids involved, according to Donna Miller. You're sure you didn't hear anything at all?'

'No, nothing,' Dr Henson said. 'What a terrible thing, that poor young widow and her children.'

'It makes it worse that it's so close to Christmas, don't you think?' Jean Henson said.

Rachel struggled to get up out of the vast armchair where Mrs Henson had invited her to sit.

'We won't take up any more of your time,' she said. She tried to stifle the irritation in her voice. She was convinced that the Hensons were holding something back. She added, 'If you think of anything . . .'

'Of course,' Dr Henson said.

And Jean said, 'You should talk to Alice Bates. She knows everything that happens in the street.'

'But not yesterday, it seems,' Rachel Moody said. 'She saw nothing.'

Peter and Jean Henson walked with the DCI and the Sergeant to their front door and closed it firmly after them. As soon as they were alone, Peter Henson said, 'They've interviewed Alice, then?'

'And she obviously didn't say anything,' Jean said.

Dr Henson followed his wife through to the kitchen.

'Should I have said something?' he asked. 'I feel bad about keeping quiet.'

Jean put the kettle on. She had no intention of making tea or coffee, it was an automatic action to try and distract herself from the police visit.

'No,' she said, 'no, of course not. I said when you came out to the back garden and told me what you'd seen, we mustn't get involved. You know what the Millers are like.'

'But that young vicar was killed, Jean, he's dead.'

'Yes,' Jean said, 'he is, and if you don't keep quiet, so will you be. You're no match for that Kevin Miller.'

'But if everyone thought like that . . .'

'For God's sake, Peter, there's no point.' Jean was pleading with him. 'If you tell the police what you saw, the Millers will just say you're lying, and they'll back each other up. Who do you think will support your story? Alice Bates? She's too scared. Everyone's far too scared.'

'Alice must have seen what happened. She's always spying on everyone from that front window of hers. I could talk to her. We could back each other up. That would make the police case against that lout.'

'Believe me,' Jean said, 'there's no point in doing the right thing if you're dead.'

'You sound as though you don't care if Kevin Miller gets away with murder,' Peter said. He sounded resigned.

'I don't,' Jean said, 'not if it means he won't murder us.'

'It wouldn't come to that,' Peter Henson said, 'surely it couldn't be that bad? This is England.'

Jean said nothing. She knew that her husband instinctively still wanted to act with the confidence of a man whose life as a high-powered doctor was spent dealing with terrified people who looked on him as some sort of god. He was humiliated that now he did not dare. She also knew that the Millers' retaliation would be more than she could bear.

She was sorry for Peter. It was hard for him to come to terms with being reduced to an ordinary, rather pompous old man whom nobody listened to. We shouldn't have come here to live when the NHS said he was too old to work, she thought. We should have left England and gone to live in Spain or Australia to be nearer Pat and the grandchildren.

'It's nearly time for the lunchtime news,' she said.

She went into the front room and started to draw the curtains to shut out the street.

It had begun to rain; a hopeless, helpless quiet outpouring of fine drizzle which fell silently on the carpet of dead leaves in the road. Jean watched the DCI and the Sergeant leave the scene of the crime across the road and walk to their car.

'They're wasting their time,' she said aloud.

She moved away from the window.

'Time for television, Peter,' she said.

She turned on the set, but as the newsreader's face appeared, she switched channels to a documentary about the Second World War.

Even the War's better than what's happening out there, she thought.

Out there Rachel Moody and Jack Reid stared at each other across the wet roof of the car.

'Don't you dare tell me you told me so,' Rachel said.

'It's just as well you don't put your money where your mouth is,' Jack said, 'you'd owe me a fortune.'

They got into the car out of the rain.

'What's the matter with the people in this street?' Rachel said. 'They're so damned defensive. They're behaving as though some-one's holding them hostages. What are they all afraid of?'

'They've had a shock,' Reid said. 'A man being murdered in their street is a shock.' He paused for a moment and then added, 'But it's interesting that no one seems surprised by what's happened. It's as though they were expecting it.'

SEVEN

Jess Miller, too, watched the police leave the Henson house.

What do they want with old farts like the Hensons, she asked herself. What would they know?

There was no point that she could see to old people, they just got in the way and reminded anyone around that that was how everyone, even Jess herself if she wasn't careful, would end up. A waste of space.

She thought, it's such a con, what they tell you in school, that there's a world of opportunity out there and if you work hard you get the rewards. Old people have done that, haven't they, and look at them. Some reward that is, old age. Jess didn't intend to fall for that. I'll have a ball while I'm young, and to hell with what happens after that, the bloody state can provide. It's like Nicky Byrne says: 'better dead than decrepit'.

Jess was sitting on the wall outside the house texting Mark Pearson on her mobile phone. There was no point trying to talk to him, she wouldn't hear what he was saying because her brother Kevin had turned up the volume on the radio in Alan's car, which was parked on the drive.

Jess glared defiantly at Kevin, who was lying on his back next to the car working on the underside of his motorbike. He'd messed up her life. He was her half-brother, for God's sake, they were family. All he'd ever done for her was make her pregnant with the child she'd never wanted.

He caught her one night about a year and a half ago when she was drunk in a local disco. She'd had far too many vodkas and a few too many pills and she'd been throwing up in a dark corner, but she was ready for love. He'd taken her round the back of the supermarket and pushed her down on a heap of black plastic bags full of refuse and she wouldn't have been able to stop him even if she'd wanted to. Afterwards she thought better of it. He was almost her brother, he was supposed to look out for her.

She was thirteen and a half then. It wasn't the first time she'd done it with a boy, but Kevin was family and it was different with someone nearly eighteen and your own half-brother. Of course, that made it more exciting. She hadn't thought much about it at the time, apart from it being different because they were sort of blood. She never thought she could fall pregnant when it was between family.

Some time later her best friend at school started on about her getting so fat she looked like she was going to have a baby. Jess told her to piss off but she went to a doctor to get some pills to help her lose weight. He told her she was already six months gone. He also told her it was far too late to do anything about it.

'Bastard,' she said aloud, meaning Kevin but not quite daring to say it to his face. If Kevin knew she was texting Mark he'd break her mobile for her. She put the phone in her pocket and scowled at Kevin, or rather at the soles of his trainers where he was lying flat on his back messing about with his motorbike. Maybe he was family but that didn't stop her being scared of him. It was all right if he was in a good mood but when he wasn't he was a right bastard.

He never actually said the kid wasn't his, but that was it. Jess wasn't even sure if he knew the child's name; if he did he never called her by it. Jess's mother was the one who'd called her Kylie. Jess couldn't be bothered deciding on a name. There wasn't much point trying to talk to Kylie anyway, all she did was cry. What pissed Jess off was the way Kevin could get away with having nothing to do with the kid, but she couldn't. That one stupid exciting night had spoiled everything for her forever, and for him it was as though it'd never happened. He'd never touched her after that, either, even though for quite a long time she wouldn't have minded.

At least Mark couldn't get enough of her. That was fine, but for her it wasn't like it had been with Kevin. The most exciting thing about sex with Mark was knowing how angry their two families would be if they knew what was going on. Jess didn't understand or care why the toffee-nosed people from the old village hated the Catcombe Mead incomers so much. But she knew why the people from the new housing estate hated the original villagers. She hated them too, as did Donna and Alan and Kevin and everyone else.

They were almost all old, for one thing. They lived differently, they looked and talked differently. They always had really dirty hands from doing primitive things with them. They didn't know the meaning of having a good time. They were slow and stupid, real hicks compared to the people like her who'd moved in from outside and knew something about real life.

Mark was one of them, but he wasn't like the others. He was really good-looking, for one thing; he was cool.

But Jess was still worried.

She hadn't told Mark about having the child. She had tried once, the first day. She'd thought about telling him, anyway, but it was too risky. He wouldn't want her any more if she did. She showed him a photo of Donna and Alan with Kevin and one of Jess with Kylie and when he asked who the kid was, she lost her nerve and said it was her little sister. Jess was sure that if Mark knew the truth, that would be the end between them. Even if he didn't mind her having a kid, it being Kevin's kid was something else. Mark hadn't actually met Kevin, but he hated him anyway because of that day with his bulls.

Jess was afraid, too, of what Mark would think of her if he knew that she, Kylie's actual mother, wanted nothing to do with her? Jess couldn't explain. She didn't want to be anyone's mother, not now, not for a long time to come, if ever. Maybe she was abnormal but that's the way she was and nothing would change how she felt.

So what if she told Mark the child was hers, and he didn't care? What if he didn't mind taking the kid on if that's what it took to be with Jess? No, she couldn't even think about that. What she didn't dare admit even to herself was that her greatest fear was that Mark might find out that she didn't want her own child and be so repelled by her he'd leave her. She couldn't bear the thought of losing him like that. He was her best chance of escaping to a new life in a different place, somewhere where the two of them could do what they wanted away from Old Catcombe and Forester Close and the state of siege they lived in.

But even losing Mark wouldn't be as bad as having to live at home much longer. It was all very well Donna saying what a nice place Forester Close was to live, with the patch of garden in the front and the pretty trees in the street. But there was nothing there for Jess. Except Mark, of course, and he had to keep away. Even living on a farm like a peasant in the old village as he did, and smelling of animals as he did too, Mark made her life worth living.

Jess took a few swigs from a bottle of cider Kevin had been drinking. She lit another cigarette.

She had to get away from the house without anyone asking where she was going. Mark would be waiting for her, parked a few hundred yards down on the main road. The one really important thing now was to get away from Catcombe Mead and find somewhere they could be alone.

'I'm going down to the shop,' Jess yelled in the direction of the house. And went.

EIGHT

The day the police came to question the residents of Forester Close, Terri Kent and her partner Helen Byrne quarrelled over Helen's daughter Nicky.

Helen swept out of the house at lunchtime to go back to work, leaving Terri miserable and not sure what to do for the best.

How could Helen be so cruel? Terri asked herself, how could she say those things? Did she mean what she said?

She can't have, she thought, we're happy together. Surely we are? She's never said she isn't.

But then Helen never said anything much. She just sort of drifted through life, smiling and distracted, not even seeming to think much about what was happening to her.

Terri's strong hands were shaking and she felt sick. Perhaps Helen never really loved me, she thought, perhaps she only came to live with me because she wanted to leave Dave and she knew I'd look after her.

Terri cast her mind back to the magical early days when she and Helen worked together in the Social Services department at the Council in Torquay. They'd been so close then. Of course it had been awkward because Dave worked for the Council too, except not in the same department. But that had made it more exciting, carrying on under his nose and him never suspecting.

He'd taken it very badly when Helen left him. That was before he knew about the relationship between her and Terri. He took it that the two of them living together meant Helen had moved in with a girlfriend until she found a place of her own. It hadn't occurred to him at first what was involved.

Terri recalled how Helen tried to tell him, but Dave didn't believe her. He thought she was making it up to punish him for something, and that if he could put that right, she'd come back. If Helen had gone off with another man, of course, he'd have believed it. Dave was never the faithful type himself. He'd probably have picked a fight with the other man. He'd certainly have beaten Helen up, but that would've been the end of it.

But when she finally said she was leaving him because she was in love with another woman, he didn't know how to deal with that.

That's why Terri had bought this house in Somerset and they'd moved away from Torquay. Terri had found work as an administrator at the local hospital, while Helen seemed happy to give up her Council job and work part-time at the local supermarket.

But Dave found them. Now he wouldn't leave Helen alone. Terri thought, perhaps he's been causing trouble, unsettling her. We were fine till he appeared on the scene. Is that it?

Terri had insisted that Dave should not see Nicky when he came to visit. She'd argued that seeing her father would unsettle the child, that she should be given time to adjust. Helen wasn't sure.

Perhaps I was wrong, Terri thought. He must miss his daughter. Perhaps he'd leave Helen alone if he could see Nicky sometimes. Terri didn't like to admit that the truth was she was afraid of the competition; she did so want Nicky to accept her as a parent.

Does Helen want to go back to Dave? Terri asked herself. Does that explain the things she said?

All she herself had tried to say was that they shouldn't let Nicky get too friendly with the Millers. Jess Miller wasn't a suitable friend for a child as clever and studious as Nicky. Jess, in Terri's opinion, was a destructive force.

And then Helen had started to abuse her.

'It's nothing to do with you,' Helen had shouted at her. 'Nicky is my daughter, she's nothing to do with you.'

'I'm only trying to help,' Terri said. 'I want the best for her.'

'What makes you think you know what's best for her?' Helen said.

'She lives in my house,' Terri said, sounding desperate.

'If that's how you feel, it's easily remedied,' Helen said. 'I'm not going to stay where Nicky isn't wanted.'

Terri, stung, said, 'You've nowhere else to go.'

'That's what you think,' Helen said, sneering. 'It isn't good for a young girl living here with you. It's not right. She'd be better off with normal people.'

That's when she had swept out of the house, banging the front door.

So that was why, when Rachel Moody and Jack Reid banged on the front door of Number Five, they got no answer. Terri Kent did not want to speak to anyone, she was too upset.

She crouched on the floor of the bedroom where she had taken refuge in an unthinking effort to feel closer to Helen. She had nothing to say to the police. It was their job to find the murderer of the vicar from the village, let them get on with it and leave her alone. It wasn't as if she could help, anyway.

And if, terrible thought, they had come to tell her that Helen had taken her own life because of what Terri had said to her during their quarrel, then Terri definitely didn't want to know. She told herself, as long as they don't tell me then it isn't true.

DCI Moody turned away from the door when she got no reply to her knocking.

'Funny,' she said, 'there's a car in the garage, someone should be in.'

Sergeant Reid tried to peer through the front window into the living-room.

'No sign of anyone,' he said. 'Perhaps they're in bed.'

'In the middle of the afternoon?' Rachel Moody said. 'It's not likely. Anyway, the child must be due home from school.'

'We're wasting our time here,' Jack Reid said. 'It seems to me we're not going to get anything useful out of anyone in this street. It's inhabited by zombies.'

'I'd like to know what they're all so damned scared of, and why?' Rachel Moody said.

'Us, probably,' Jack Reid said. 'They think we're going to find some way of blaming them.'

'That's ridiculous,' the DCI said, 'we're trying to help them.'

'That's not the way they see it,' Sergeant Reid said. 'They'd rather we went away and let them go back to pretending nothing's happened here since the Old Catcombe villagers burned Hester the witch in 1568.'

'That's crazy,' Rachel Moody said. 'They can't be that deluded.'

The Sergeant shrugged and they turned away and walked back down the garden path to the road.

NINE

Nicky Byrne sat on the front wall of Number Five with her back to the road. She was waiting for Jess Miller to pass on her way home from school, but she didn't want anyone to know that. The wall felt very cold and damp on the back of her legs through her school skirt, but she tried to ignore it. Jess's law laid down that doing nothing sitting on a wall making dirty patterns with your heels on the pale blue painted pebble-dash was cool; standing there alone looking bored was pathetic.

Nicky didn't want Jess to think of her as pathetic. She wanted to be as much like Jess as she could make herself, given how different they were.

They were unlikely friends. Big, noisy, uninhibited Jess with her purple hair and her revealing scraps of clothing and her decorative safety pins could never pass unnoticed; Nicky, a colourless little swot with pale sandy hair and red-rimmed milky eyes behind her spectacles, was totally effaced by her.

But friends they were.

Although Nicky was two years younger than Jess, they were in the same class at school. Nicky had jumped a year last term because she was much brighter than the other children her own age. At any rate, she worked a lot harder at her studies. Jess, meanwhile, had failed her end of term tests and been held back to retake the year.

In spite of the age difference, a kind of conspiracy was developing between the two of them. It wasn't obvious at first what drew them together. True, they both seemed freakish to the other children, but at opposite ends of the scale. No one told they were becoming friends would believe it. What, after all, had either to gain from the other?

In fact they provided each other with something both needed. Associating with Nicky graced Jess with a gloss of intelligence, while Jess protected Nicky from the worst of the school bullies, and also gave the younger girl an insight into life on the street in Forester Close. At home Nicky's mother Helen and her friend Terri kept the girl under a form of house arrest. Terri in particular insisted that Nicky was different from ordinary children; she was gifted, she had to be protected from associating with them. But in spite of her, or perhaps because of her, Nicky and Jess had become allies, each protecting the other where she was dangerously ignorant. Jess was the one who'd explained to Nicky that the main reason everyone persecuted her was not only her horrible cheap pink plastic spectacles, but because her parents were lesbians. Jess had had to explain what that meant, too.

Nicky, on her part, persuaded Jess that it didn't pay to be written off as stupid. Stupid people did not get on in the world, and Jess wasn't going to end up like the rest of the nonentities in Forester Close, and in the whole of Catcombe Mead too, for that matter. With superior Nicky for a friend, Jess couldn't be stupid.

The two girls' friendship was a secret, though. It was born out of mutual inadequacy and it flourished in concealment. It wouldn't exist if people knew about it. Then Jess and Nicky would be embarrassed and ashamed and avoid each other because of the preconceptions of others.

In the road, Jess tripped and pretended to take a stone out of her shoe.

'Is the witch watching us now?' she asked, not looking at Nicky.

'Sure she is,' Nicky said, pretending not to notice that Jess was there at all. 'I can't actually see her, but she's always spying on us.'

'I wish we could get rid of her,' Jess said.

Nicky said. 'I'm reading a great book about someone just like her. She gets beaten to death in it. It's called *Crime and Punishment*. It's Russian.'

'Oh, you and your stupid books,' Jess said out of the corner of her mouth.

Jess leaned on the wall and pulled the bright orange hips off a leafless rose bush.

'The old witch will probably complain about what you and your boyfriends get up to round the back of her house at night.' Nicky made a sniggering noise without her face moving.

Jess scowled in the direction of Number Three. 'She'd never dare,' she said. 'I'll set Kevin on her.'

'Where is Kevin?' Anyone more sensitive than Jess would have noted the tone of Nicky's voice when she said Kevin's name.

'Who cares, as long as he's not here,' Jess said.

She expected Nicky to giggle, but she didn't. Jess stared at her. Nicky went bright red and tears filled her eyes.

Jess, forgetting to pretend she and Nicky were strangers, crowed with laughter. 'You're soft on our Kevin. You are, aren't you? Wait till I tell him that. I won't let him live that down. You must be mad.'

Nicky tried to bluster. 'Don't be bloody daft,' she said. 'Who'd fancy your Kevin, for God's sake?'

Stung by any implied criticism of her family from an outsider, Jess said, 'Well, he wouldn't look twice at you, I can tell you that much.'

'Don't you think I don't know that?' Nicky suddenly screeched at her. She swallowed hard and then said more calmly, 'you're more his type, after all, aren't you? Cheap an' easy.'

Nicky thought Jess was going to hit her and cowered away from her. But Jess thought better of it.

'He'd give you a poke if I asked him,' she said.

Nicky looked at her in horror. 'You wouldn't? Oh, Jess, please don't say anything, I couldn't bear it if he knew . . .'

'You done my maths yet?' Jess said.

Nicky nodded. She pulled a folded piece of paper out of her pocket and handed it to Jess.

'I hope you've got some wrong this time,' Jess said under her breath, 'Mr Perkins gave me a funny look last time and said something snide about believing in the miraculous resurrection of the brain-dead, whatever he thinks he means by that.'

'Don't ask,' Nicky said.

Jess jumped off the wall and turned to cross the road to Number Two. 'See you,' she said.

She banged the front door behind her and shouted 'I'm home.'

Donna was listening to music on Jess's iPod and didn't hear her come in and shout. It was only when she reached out for another handful of crisps and found the packet gone that she noticed the girl.

'What d'you think you're doing with my iPod?' Jess said, and pulled the headphones off Donna.

Donna didn't try to stop her. She knew better than to oppose Jess physically. 'Kylie'll need changing,' she said.

Jess turned away from her. 'Bug off,' she said under her breath, and, putting on the headphones, turned up the sound on the iPod.

But that was too much for Donna. She snatched the headphones from Jess's head, pulling her wiry purple hair as she did so.

'Eff off,' Jess screamed. 'That hurt. What d'you think you're doing? Piss off and leave me alone, can't you?'

'So sue me,' Donna said meaninglessly, without thinking.

'I'd have a witness that you assaulted me,' Jess said. 'I know my rights. I could get the law on you.'

'What witness do you think would support you about anything?' Donna sneered.

'The old witch at Number Three,' Jess shouted. 'She watches everything we do.'

Jess was surprised that this silenced Donna. When she looked at her mother, wondering why, she was startled at the expression on Donna's face. 'What's the matter now? Has she put a spell on you?' Jess said.

Donna wished that her relationship with Jess didn't always seem to come down to this sort of sniping. 'Why don't you call the bloody cops, then?' she said. 'I'll make a statement supporting anything you say if it means they take you into care and get you the hell out of my house.'

'Suits me,' Jess said.

'What's stopping you?' Donna said.

Jess said, 'If I get pregnant again I can apply for a council flat even if I haven't been on the waiting list and I'd get handouts for the baby and everything.'

'Yeah? Who's going to get you pregnant now everyone knows you did it with Kevin?'

Jess pretended not to hear. 'What's to eat?' she said.

Donna welcomed a change of subject. 'Since you mention it, where is Kylie?'

'Who said anything about her?' Jess said. 'How should I know? You were looking after her.'

'You're home, you do it,' Donna said.

'I've got homework,' Jess said. 'And I'm off out.'

'Jess, don't you go and do anything you'll be sorry for,' Donna said.

Jess was startled by the sudden seriousness of her tone. She didn't know what to say.

So she fell back on the familiar format of bickering. 'Leave it out,' she snapped, 'as soon as I'm sixteen I can do what I like.'

'Love isn't enough,' Donna said. Suddenly she was fighting to find words to express fears she'd never even thought she had. 'You don't know what you're doing, Jess, I'm afraid for you. I'm scared you'll wake up suddenly when you're eighteen and you'll have two kids and another on the way and no man and that's it. You may as well be dead. It's all so far from what you think you want. You won't even find a lover after that because you'll be dragged down by the kids and you'll get pissed one night and screw some drunken yob you've never seen before and you'll never see again and then there'll be another baby and you won't even remember what its father looked like. Please, Jess, listen to me. I know what it's like.'

Jess turned sulky. 'What do you know? It won't be like that for me.'

She was too used to quarrelling with her mother to take in what she'd said, even when Donna seemed suddenly to have changed tack. Jess dismissed her.

'It may've been like that for you, Mum, but you're not me,' she said. 'Why should I listen to you anyway when you've ballsed up your own life? You're just jealous because you're past it, that's all.'

Donna recognized the familiar pattern of their arguments and refused to resort to the usual personal abuse.

'You're right,' she said, and there were tears in her eyes. 'That's what it was like for me, and I'm afraid of you ending up the same way. No one would ever be jealous of me, would they? I'll tell you one thing, if I could go back to when I was your age, I'd do everything different. I love you, Jess, I'm your mother, I want things to be better for you.'

Donna wiped her eyes with the back of her hand, but she wasn't crying. She meant what she said too passionately for tears.

Jess was staring at her as though she had never met her before. 'What's got into you?' she said. 'If you want things different from the way they were, that means you wish I'd never been born. Is that what you're saying? Screw you, Mum. I'm not you. You go on about how you're unhappy, well, tough tit, there's nothing I can do about it, even if I cared. It's all over for you and it's time you knew it. I'm what counts, I'm young.'

Donna looked at Jess's angry contorted face. She remembered herself at Jess's age, how she too had taken for granted that her mother existed only to do what she could to make her happy. Donna thought, it's no good, she doesn't know, she's too young. She doesn't understand. I can't help her.

Upstairs, the baby started to cry.

'That's all we need,' Jess said. 'Bloody kid.'

Donna forced herself to wait for Jess to do something.

But Jess knew her mother would give in first. She pretended not to hear the baby.

To avert Donna's attention, she changed the subject. 'About that old freak at the top of the road watching us all the time,' she said, 'you know she spies on us, don't you? You'd better watch your step or she'll report you to social services for child cruelty, saying things like that to me.'

Donna stiffened. She gave Jess a hard look, trying to decide if the girl was winding her up or not.

'Do you think she does? Watch us all, I mean?'

Jess said, 'What else is there for her to do? Of course she spies on us. But who cares what someone like her thinks?' The baby was still crying. 'What's that old woman going to do to us?' she added. 'We could get Kevin to give her a warning.'

'Do you think Kevin knows she spies on us?' Donna said.

She remembered how it had felt that day the young vicar was killed, turning into Forester Close and seeing Kevin and Nate and their friends kicking at what looked like a heap of clothes on the ground. For a moment she'd thought they'd got hold of a bag of cast-offs left out for the binmen and she'd been annoyed with the kids for making so much mess. But then she'd realized what they were doing and she remembered how it had flashed through her mind that she was scared of them. And she was their mother.

She'd kept quiet about seeing what they did. She'd even warned Kevin that if any of his friends were involved, to tell them to lie low for a bit. She was careful to pretend she had no idea that he was involved.

'Do you?' she asked Jess again.

Jess was moving to the music on the iPod. 'Do I what?' she shouted.

Donna reached over and turned off the iPod. 'Do you think Kevin knows Alice Bates watches us?'

'Hey!' Jess said, 'so what if he does? What's she going to do to him, for fuck's sake?'

Jess turned the iPod back on and began to sing along to the music to shut out her mother's questions.

'It's what he might do to her if he knew what she might've seen,' Donna said, and as she said it, she was glad that Jess couldn't possibly hear her.

The girl was climbing the stairs, going at last to see to the baby.

TEN

Bert Pearson glowered at the clock on the kitchen wall.
Bert had spent a long time sitting in the kitchen trying
to work out what he was going to say to Mark. The fire
in the range was long dead, and the room was cold. Bert's limbs
were stiff and painful and he couldn't feel his fingers or toes.

He kept telling himself that this was his son and as his father
he'd got a duty to say something, but Bert didn't even convince
himself. He might be Mark's father, but he'd almost forgotten
the days when the relationship had meant anything much to either
of them. That had been when Mark was just a kid helping round
the farm and he'd spent every Sunday morning with the boy
down at the rugby club giving him the benefit of his experience
just like the other dads with their lads. In those days Mark had
been proud to boast that his father was the best player in the first
team the year the Catcombe Corinthians beat Plymouth Albion
in a friendly.

Bert Pearson sighed. It was a long time since he'd left the
farm of a Saturday afternoon to watch Mark play. George Webber
had called in that very day to tell him the boy had scored the
winning try in yesterday's game. George had thought Bert would
like to know, Bert having not been there to see it.

But George hadn't come to tell him about Mark's try; that was
just an excuse. George Webber hadn't come to the farm for years;
there was something serious on his mind to bring him to visit
Bert.

When he came out with it, Bert was shocked.

He hadn't believed George at first. He'd even started to take
a swing at him, but that hadn't come to anything. George said
there were others who would back him up. It was the talk of the
market that week, Mark taking up with a right little tart from
the housing estate, a real tough backstreet low-life whore
from Catcombe Mead who took drugs and had two layabout
brothers who spent their nights molesting the village girls in Old

Catcombe and tearing through the streets on their motorbikes terrorizing old women.

George even told Bert the girl's name: Jess Miller. She came from a bad family, he said; her brother had a motorbike and he was one of the worst of the thugs who caused so much trouble in the village, it would be no surprise to anyone if he'd been in jail. Word had it, too, that he had something to do with the Reverend Baker's murder.

Bert shook his head in disbelief. He protested to George that Mark was a good boy; he wouldn't be interested in going with a cheap girl like that. Why would he? But then, Bert asked himself, where is he now?

'There's not so many young girls in the village to catch his eye,' George said. 'It's not like it was in our day. So many of the young'uns have moved away. Nothing for them round here these days, Bert.'

After George left him, Bert phoned the rugby club. He asked for Mark. The secretary went to look for him but then he came back and said Mark hadn't been with the lads after the match, and he hadn't come in the bar for a drink.

Bert asked himself, what could he possibly be doing out at this time of night when anyone who worked around farming would have to get up early in the morning?

Bert felt depressed and scared. He didn't know what to say to the boy, or even how to start a conversation with him. Mark's mother should be here, this was her business. Joyce should have brought the boy up better, she should be at home looking after him instead of spending her evenings out wasting her time with a gaggle of boring middle-aged women frittering away a few hours on rubbish. This business with Mark was her fault, and now the whole future of the farm, the traditional Pearson way of life, was at risk. Bert thought, I wish she'd come home. I wish she'd come home and tell me what to say to him, she'd know what to say, how to explain to Mark why he must never see this girl of his again. I wish she was here instead of me.

Bert was afraid. He was afraid that when confronted, Mark would walk away from him and go to this girl and never come back. He was afraid that he could lose his son because he hadn't got the words to explain. He couldn't explain to himself, he simply knew by instinct that the incomers were his enemies, people who were out to destroy a rural way of life they could never be part of. Even if they tried to fit in, they couldn't. They used the country like some kind of theme park to enjoy, but they didn't understand that their being there at all destroyed what they claimed a right to share. They didn't even know what they were doing.

Bert knew he was in danger of becoming maudlin. It used to take a few drinks to make him like that, but now it just happened. It seemed to be all he could do these days when he faced something that demanded action.

He was about to give up on tackling Mark and go to bed when he heard the boy come in. Bert could smell him as soon as he opened the back door, reeking of the smell of the girl's cheap scent. He wanted to hit his son. He felt bereft, knowing he was old and it didn't matter what he said. He'd lost the boy already, he was losing his way of life; the farm would be lost. He'd already lost Joyce. There was no point in going through the motions with Mark. He found himself weeping.

'What are you doing up, Dad?' Mark asked. Bert could tell the lad had expected him to be in bed and, seeing his father's self-pitying tears, thought he was having one of his bad turns.

Bert ignored Mark's question. He wanted to say that a son of his should smell of good wholesome beer on a Saturday night, he should be ashamed to come home reeking of a tart. But of course he couldn't say that. He said nothing.

'Dad, what's up?' Mark sounded concerned now.

Bert shook his head. 'Nothing,' he said, 'nothing's up. I hear you had a good game today, son.'

'You should've seen the second try,' Mark said. 'That was really something.'

Bert heaved himself out of the chair. He was afraid that if he didn't get out of the room he might do something stupid like pleading.

'Dad?' Mark was puzzled.

'Mum'll be back soon,' Bert said. He didn't know why he said that.

There was an awkward silence.

Why can't I ask him about the girl? Bert thought. He said, 'I'm off to bed.'

'Goodnight, Dad,' Mark said.

Bert had one more try at talking to the boy.

'Tomorrow we'd better start on the fences along the lane,' he said. 'We've got to do something to stop that scum from the housing estate getting in and scaring the stock.' He could hear his voice shaking with the emotion he couldn't express. He hoped Mark didn't notice.

Mark was surprised. It was years since Bert had talked about the farm like this. He thought, something's happened. What can have happened?

But he was tired; it was too much trouble to question his Dad. 'Sure,' he said. 'Goodnight.'

In bed, Bert lay on his back listening to the sounds of the old house settling in the dark. He heard Mark go to his room. It was a windy night. Then came a sharp shower of rain, driven against the windowpane, drowning all other sounds. Shortly after that had passed, Joyce came in. Her efforts to be quiet were ridiculously noisy.

For some reason, she did not go to the spare room. She came into his bedroom as though she still belonged there.

Bert turned over as though in his sleep.

'Bert,' she whispered. 'Are you awake, Bert?'

He did not speak.

She went away.

He wondered, has she heard something too? Has one of those women told her about this girl of Mark's?

In the morning he was up early as usual, creeping out of bed and dressing as quietly as he could so as not to disturb anyone. Mark wouldn't get up to start the milking for another hour or so. Mark would deal with the stock, too; he was used enough now to his father not leaving the house to help in the mornings.

It would be another two hours or more before it began to get light. Bert listened to the cattle stirring in the barton and the soft sound of their breathing in the dark shed. He could smell their breath, too, sweet with the scent of hay.

He would have liked to linger a while in the darkness close to the peaceful beasts. But there was no time to waste. For once he had a sense of purpose and he was not going to be deflected.

Bert took the pickup and drove down to the village. He couldn't do this from the house. He didn't want anyone to know what he was going to do.

He parked on the edge of the village green, where there was a telephone box outside the post office. He did not get out of the pickup at once, but sat looking at the outline of the familiar stone buildings which had always been part of the fabric of his life. For several minutes he was puzzled that he could see so clearly at that time of the morning. Clearly, but as though looking down into the depths of water and seeing the world reflected there.

Of course, it was the colourless light of the full moon shining on a frosted scene. On the Green, the Christmas tree sparkled in this white light, its dark branches glittering with real ice. He thought, it looks as though it's taken root this year, as though it's part of the scenery.

The dancing coloured lights on the tree were turned off. The season of goodwill, he thought. What kind of goodwill survived in the village now? He remembered the carol concerts his mother had taken him to when he was a kid, how they'd done the rounds of the village houses singing on the doorsteps. The old women had come out to greet them with their plates of hot mince pies and a glass of home-made wine or sloe gin to keep out the cold.

That was a long time ago; probably people stayed at home and watched television these days.

I never took Mark carol-singing, he thought, I should have taken him like my mum took me. I wonder if he ever went with Joyce. Probably not, she was too busy.

He asked himself, is this a good idea? Should I do it? And then he thought of Mark and the girl from Catcombe Mead and he knew that he had to do it, even though he had nothing to go on except fear and the desire to believe that the Millers had to be got rid of.

That lad has caused a lot of grief round here, Bert told himself, and it's time someone put a stop to it. Once the police start looking, they're bound to find something to use against him.

He got out of the pickup and walked slowly across the deserted patch of crisp grass to the telephone box. There were empty beer cans and broken bottles on the plinth of the War Memorial, and he began to hurry, eager to get on with what he was about to do.

It was still early and there was no one about to see him. He had
the telephone number he needed written down on a piece of
paper in his pocket.

He dialled the number of the constabulary headquarters in the
county town, Haverton. The police station in Old Catcombe had
closed more than five years before.

'I've information,' he said.

Bert could imagine the bored young cop reluctant to answer
the phone at all so close to the end of his night shift.

'Name and address?' the policeman asked, plainly wanting to
be rid of the caller.

Bert ignored the question. 'It's about a murder you're looking
into,' he said, 'the vicar from Old Catcombe who was beaten to
death on the new housing estate. I've a name for you, the one
that did it. You get someone out to Catcombe Mead to question
a kid with a motorbike, name of Miller. He's the one you want.'

He put the phone down.

Let those Miller scum prove it wasn't their lad if they can,
Bert told himself, I don't care if he did it or not, that's the type
as would do a thing like that. Mark's a decent boy. I'd like to
see the cheap whore as can keep a hold on my son Mark when
she's next best thing to a murderer.

ELEVEN

Detective Chief Inspector Rachel Moody found the note about an anonymous tip-off fingering the murderer of Tim Baker on her desk when she got to work in the morning. The constable on the night desk had left it there before he went home at the end of his shift. He hadn't dared ignore the anonymous tip-off in case it was important, but he was in a hurry to go home, he didn't want to get involved. He knew that there wouldn't be anyone in CID for an hour or so to follow up the information. Best leave it to them. The vicar's murder was an ongoing case, a few hours wouldn't make any difference.

So he'd written 'Re: Vicar's murder in Forester Close, Catcombe Mead. Man who wouldn't give name says to question youth with motorcycle called Miller. Electoral roll has an Alan Miller at Two Forester Close. Son Kevin on file. Cautions for misdemeanours including theft, drunk and disorderly, and ABH.'

The constable had done the routine checks quickly, not wishing to appear unwilling. There, he thought, at least CID can give me credit for doing the preliminaries for them.

The anonymous tip-off came as no surprise to Rachel Moody. She and Sergeant Reid had made their door-to-door inquiries and questioned anyone who might have seen anything, but no one had anything to add to the bald facts. It was a scenario which often triggered tip-offs like this from members of the public afraid to be identified. Maybe whoever left this message thought they were helping police inquiries, but it didn't really add much to what they already knew or suspected. What Rachel Moody needed was concrete evidence, preferably a witness.

There had only been one suspect, as far as the police investigation was concerned: Kevin Miller. Among others, perhaps, but neither the DCI nor Jack Reid had any doubt that it was Kevin Miller who had actually killed the young vicar.

This anonymous call was proof that the police were not alone in suspecting Kevin. But, Rachel Moody told herself, it's not evidence, it doesn't take us anywhere.

Even so this tip-off was at least an excuse for a new lead to revitalize the investigation. Was it coincidence that it was Donna Miller, mother of Kevin, who had called the ambulance? Had she seen her son attack the vicar? The DCI remembered the woman's face afterwards, a frightened fat woman's face where fear was mixed with a kind of cowed defiance.

When Jack gets in, Rachel thought, it could be worth another try at talking to the Millers, and Donna in particular.

But for the moment Rachel Moody was tempted to push the constable's note under a pile of report forms she should already have filled in. She was frustrated by the lack of progress in her investigation into Tim Baker's murder and it seemed to her that the anonymous tip-off would be another dead end. Already the Chief Super was showing signs of impatience at her failure to make an arrest. The way things are going, Rachel thought, the top priority at present is to keep the Superintendent sweet. Another unproductive interview with Kevin Miller isn't going to help.

She told herself that she would try to get round to the Millers later. First the mound of paperwork on her desk demanded attention. The boss had already mentioned that she was falling behind. And she was not at her best that morning. She had had to change her bedclothes twice because of night sweats, and then a programme on breakfast television about women's sufferings during the meno-pause had made her even more depressed about what she was facing.

Things were hard enough for women climbing the career ladder in the police force, why did Nature have to hit them with this particular handicap just at the moment they could least pretend it wasn't happening?

Then DCI Moody saw her boss walk into his office and slam the door. The Chief Superintendent, too, was plainly in a bad mood.

Moody knew the boss would be looking for her. He must have heard by now that late yesterday the case against a villain they'd been trying to nail for months had been dismissed in court when a witness changed his evidence. Looking for a scapegoat, the Superintendent was bound to blame her as the officer in charge of the case.

The anonymous tip-off about Kevin Miller would at least take her out of the office for a few hours. She'd be best off out of the building.

Rachel Moody took the note with her and escaped to the women's room. There she checked her immaculate make-up. It was time she touched up the colour on her hair, she told herself, even her ash blonde tint didn't cover signs of grey at her temples. Stray strands of damp hair had escaped from her rather severe French pleat and she scraped them back off her face and pinned them firmly in place. Then she went into the corridor where a group of her colleagues was gathered round the coffee machine.

'Come with me, Jack,' she said to the burly Sergeant Reid. 'I may need muscle on this. I've had a tip-off on that vicar killing in Catcombe Mead.'

'You mean you want to get out of the office till the boss has had a chance to cool down,' Jack Reid said. Everyone in the group laughed. They knew what the Super could be like on a bad day.

'Soon would be good,' Rachel Moody said.

She saw the laughter wiped off their faces at her tone. Damn, she thought, I always seem to say the wrong thing.

'Do you want me to drive?' Jack said as they walked down to the car.

'No,' Rachel said, 'you may have to jump out in a hurry and tackle this thug if he sees us coming and makes a run for it. Horses for courses.'

But as she turned the car into Forester Close, DCI Moody had a sudden flashback to that first time she'd been here. The body in the gutter, a fat woman, green with shock, visibly shaking on the grass verge, and an unnatural silence in the Close from which all residents seemed to have fled.

'I don't like this place,' she said, thinking aloud.

'What's wrong with it?' Sergeant Reid said. 'It looks like a nice place to live.'

'There's something about it,' Moody said. 'Spooky, like it's somewhere that's going to be haunted one day.'

Jack Reid laughed. 'You women and your fancies,' he said.

Then he flushed with embarrassment at what he'd said. He had enough experience with women to suspect what was making his boss strangely illogical these days, and he was afraid she'd fly off the handle at his remark.

He added quickly, 'These houses won't last long enough for that. The wife's brother worked on the site when they were building this estate and you should've heard what he said about the way the houses were thrown together.'

'This is us,' Moody said. 'Number Two.'

'Want me to go round the back in case he makes a run for it?' Jack Reid said, flexing his muscles as he locked the car.

'It's probably not really that kind of visit,' Moody said. She wasn't sure why she wanted him to stay close to her, but she did. 'The whole thing could be a bum steer.' She stepped aside to avoid the motorbike propped against the front step.

Donna Miller answered the door. She had just got out of bed and was wearing only a tight T-shirt and a rather tatty pair of pants. She looked startled when she saw DCI Moody. She knew immediately who she was. She'd thought that awful business was over with, and at once she felt at a disadvantage because, compared to herself, the policewoman looked expensively dressed and carefully made-up. Donna resented this. It seemed to her that any woman police officer should look more like a down-trodden servant of the public and not like a successful businesswoman.

'What do you want?' Donna said.

Moody showed her ID. 'And this is Sergeant Reid,' she said, indicating Jack.

'I know what you are,' Donna said. 'You're the cop who came when the vicar was beaten up. I told you then, I didn't see anything.'

'I know,' Rachel said. 'It's not you we want to talk to. Is Kevin Miller in?'

'What do you want with him?' Donna said.

Jack pushed himself forward. 'Just answer the question,' he said.

Donna shrugged. She turned and shouted, 'Kevin, someone to see you.'

Kevin Miller, too, looked as though he had just got out of bed. He was wearing jeans and a dirty vest and he stank of stale beer.

'They're cops,' Donna said. She stood aside as Kevin came to the doorway, then pushed the door shut behind him.

'Hey,' Kevin said, 'it's cold out here.'

He turned to Jack, ignoring Moody. 'What you want?' he said.

'Nice bike,' DCI Moody said.

'What's this about?' Kevin, still blanking her, addressed Jack.

Moody said, 'We want to ask you a few questions about an incident here recently. A man was beaten to death in the street.'

'Oh, yeah, the vicar from the village, wasn't it? I heard about that.'

'It would be easier doing this inside,' Jack said.

'Yeah, I know, but Dad's out and she can be funny about the cops. She won't let us in.'

'You remember the incident, then?' Moody said.

'Sure, Mum found the body. It's her you should be talking to. I wasn't even here.'

'Where were you?' Jack took out his notebook and pen and prepared to write down the details.

'I stayed over with a chick I picked up in a bar in Weston. Didn't get back till after it was all over,' Kevin said, and grinned at them.

'Name?' Jack asked. 'What was the girl's name?'

'Dunno,' Kevin said. 'Didn't ask. We didn't do much talking.'

'Where did you pick her up?' Jack sounded resigned.

'Some bar, mate. Weston's full of bars. I don't remember which one.'

'Why Weston? There's places nearer than that you could pick up a girl.'

Moody was floundering and Kevin knew it.

'Her? I didn't go to Weston for that. The chick just happened.'

Moody and Jack both knew that Weston was somewhere it was easy to get drugs.

'Can your mother confirm all this?' Moody asked. She was trying to retain some dignity.

'Sure she can,' Kevin said, giving the policewoman what he thought passed for a charming smile. He turned and shouted through the letter box, 'Mum, you're wanted.'

Donna opened the door. She had obviously been listening. She avoided their eyes, keeping her gaze fixed on the ground.

'They want to know—' Kevin started, but Moody interrupted him.

'Yes, thank you, Kevin, I'll ask the questions.'

Moody began to go through the motions. Donna confirmed that Kevin hadn't come home till late in the evening of the day the vicar was killed. More like the next morning. She didn't know he'd been in Weston with a girl, but he hadn't been here, she was sure of that.

'Too bloody sure,' Moody said to Jack as they got into the car and drove away.

'Let's face it, Boss,' Jack said, 'we haven't got a snowball's chance in hell of pinning this one on that poisonous bastard and he knows it. They'll be having a good laugh about making fools of us back there.'

But in the kitchen of Number Two Forester Close Kevin Miller was not laughing.

'Why did they come here?' he shouted at Donna. 'Someone must've tipped them off.'

Donna was scared. He thinks it was me, she thought. Who else would he think it was?

'They've gone away, they've nothing on you,' Donna said. She spoke to him in a soothing, caressing tone because she was trying to persuade Kylie to eat. 'It must've been chance. No one knows you were there.'

Donna deliberately said 'You were there.' She couldn't bring herself to say 'You did it.'

'That old bitch Alice Bates next door does,' Kevin said. 'Jess says she spies on us all the time. It must be her.'

Donna said, 'Alice Bates? She wouldn't do a thing like that.' Donna couldn't hide that she felt relieved because Kevin wasn't blaming her. 'She wouldn't dare,' she said.

Kevin sat hunched at the breakfast bar glowering at Kylie, who began to cry.

At last he said, 'It must've been her. That old bitch. I'll make her sorry she didn't keep her mouth shut. I'll kill her for this.'

TWELVE

Parked in a lay-by on the main road between Old Catcombe and Catcombe Mead, Jess Miller sat rigid beside Mark Pearson in the front of his pickup.

She was wearing a new top which had given up trying to contain her breasts. Mark's face, occasionally lighted by the headlamps of a passing car, was smeared with her lipstick.

Now they had nothing to say to one another. Jess had been crying, and her smudged mascara made her look, in the light of her cigarette when she inhaled, like something out of a Dracula movie. Mark gripped the wheel with both hands and scowled at the traffic.

'What are we going to do?' Jess said at last. She knew very well that Mark couldn't answer her question. She got a certain satisfaction from fuelling the fire of their thwarted passion.

Mark said nothing.

Jess found a tissue and wiped away some of the condensation on the windows of the pickup. She opened the window a crack and tossed out the pulpy paper.

'Where can we go?' she said, staring round as though the bleak lay-by or the traffic on the main road could offer a solution. Jess looked at the empty beer cans and discarded cigarette packs scattered across the grass verge and thought, lots of other couples have stopped here like me and Mark with nowhere to go. She said, 'We could get in the back and do it. The traffic's going too fast for anyone to notice.'

Mark sounded angry. 'Someone might recognize the pickup,' he said. 'It'd be just our luck for my Dad to come by.'

'We could go into one of your fields,' Jess said. 'Where there aren't any cows. Please, Mark, just for a little while. I'll keep you warm.'

'Bullocks,' Mark corrected her automatically, 'not cows, bullocks. I'm not doing it in a field like an animal. And if my Dad . . .'

'If your bloody Dad spends so much time out and about, he's not in the house much and I don't see why we can't go to your bedroom,' Jess said.

'Oh, lay off, Jess. We can't go anywhere near the farm.'

'I don't see why not,' Jess said in a sulky tone.

'Oh, Jess,' Mark said.

She could tell that he was getting irritated with her. She knew she was being childish, but like a kid picking a scab, she couldn't let well alone.

'Why don't we tell them?' she said. 'There's nothing they can do to us, really, is there? The worst they can do is throw us out, and then we're together which is what we want. Oh, Mark, why don't we stop hiding and come out with it?'

'We can't do that,' Mark said, and his knuckles were white on the wheel. 'You know we can't do that.'

He was thinking, she always does this, she always starts trying to force the issue. Why doesn't she see that I can't just up and leave and start over somewhere else? What would happen to the farm?

He said, 'I don't see why we can't go to yours. We can tell if there's anyone there . . .'

'No,' Jess said, 'we can't.' She thought, Kevin and Nate might not be there, but Donna and Kylie would be. Mum might not turn us out, but she could easily say something about Kylie. She's always telling people the kid's mine. That's the last thing I want.

'I share a room with my little sister,' Jess lied.

'So?' Mark said. 'We'll be careful not to wake her.'

He knew as he said it that this was no good. Jess could never keep quiet in the act of love.

'Can't we drive somewhere outside the area where no one knows us?'

'Dad would know from the mileage I'd gone outside the village. He checks the diesel.'

'Well, fill the tank so he can't tell,' Jess said. She felt that Mark was trying to make difficulties.

He shouted at her suddenly, 'I haven't got any money, all right? Don't you understand anything? I can't even afford to take you out for the day down to the coast or spend a night together at a bloody bed and breakfast.' Then, more calmly, he said, 'How do you think that makes me feel, Jess? It isn't as if I don't want to fuck you.'

Jess was disarmed. 'I love you too, babe,' she said. 'I'm sorry.'

She lunged towards him, her hand searching his crotch for the zip of his fly. The lights of an oncoming car picked them out.

With an enormous effort, he pushed her back into the passenger seat. 'No,' he said, 'not here.'

A lorry drove into the lay-by ahead of them.

'Quick, I know where we can go,' Jess said, 'we can go round the back of Alice's house. She lives next door to us, but no one ever goes out there at night. There's a sort of covered lean-to where she keeps deckchairs and things. We'll be OK in there.'

Mark hesitated. He didn't want to go anywhere near Jess's family, but she was hot for him and he was hot for her and she seemed to think it was all right so it was worth the risk.

'Who's Alice?' he said. He wanted Jess so much now that his own voice sounded funny to him, hoarse and thick.

'No one,' Jess said. 'Please hurry, Mark, or I'm going to come off all over this seat and your effing Dad's going to see the stain. Drive faster, babe, I'm on fire.'

Jesus, Mark thought, swerving across oncoming traffic into Forester Close, this girl's really something.

He tried to ignore the small voice in his head asking him, this isn't right. It isn't what she thinks, I've got to tell her. One day. Soon.

THIRTEEN

First thing in the morning Alice came downstairs to feed Phoebus.

He wasn't in the kitchen where he usually waited for her, marching up and down on top of the kitchen table with his tail erect and twitching like a water diviner's rod.

She checked the cat flap to be sure it wasn't stuck, but it was working perfectly. She opened the back door and called him. Sometimes if she was earlier than usual he was still outside doing whatever he did when he went out at night.

He probably caught a bird or a rabbit or something and he's not hungry, she told herself. She wasn't worried. Phoebus knew how to look after himself. He'd be back when he was ready.

By evening, she began to wonder if he'd found himself a new home. She felt rebuffed. She thought that she had not made him happy. Even a stray cat didn't want to live with her.

Soon after dark, there was a knock on the front door.

No one called on anyone after dark, no one innocent. Alice went into the hall and listened at the door for the sound of voices.

But the silence was unnatural.

'Who is it?' she called, her voice faint and querulous with anxiety.

'It's Jean Henson.' Jean's voice sounded more frightened than Alice's. 'Please, let me in.'

Alice started to unlock the deadlock and undo the bolts. She had taken off the chain as soon as she recognized Jean's voice. Of course, Phoebus must've gone to Number Four hoping the Hensons would feed him. Cats were so greedy. Jean must be bringing him home.

When she opened the door, Jean was pressed so close against it that she almost fell into the hall. She was carrying something covered with a towel.

She gave a quick look behind her as though to check she wasn't followed.

'Please, quick, shut the door,' she said.

Jean's face was white and pinched, she looked terrified and ill. She had obviously been crying and her eyes were red and swollen.

'What is it? What's happened?' Alice asked.

'Can we go in the kitchen?' Jean said. 'No one can see us there.'

Alice was alarmed now. 'Has something happened?' she asked again. 'Where's your husband?'

'He can't come out,' Jean said, 'he knows they're waiting for him.'

'Waiting for him? Who?'

'Those terrible kids. They'll kill him if they can. If they get him while it's dark, they'll kill him. They've done it before, haven't they?'

'Done what?' Alice asked. Please, don't let her say it, she thought, she mustn't say it, we must try to forget.

Jean was frightened by what she had said already. 'The trouble is, there's no proof,' she said, 'we all know who did it but the police can't prove anything.'

Alice felt oppressed and guilty. She knew that she could have provided that proof but knowing that made her feel all the more terrorized by the feral youths who hung around in the street outside the Millers' at night.

She looked at Jean and saw that her visitor wasn't simply afraid; she was petrified. She was shaking all over, even her lips shook so it was difficult for her to speak. It came as a shock to Alice that Jean and Dr Henson, who, unlike herself, had had real lives in the real world, felt the same terror of the youths as she did. She wished she didn't know that, it made the threat seem much more immediate and real.

Alice hustled Jean into the kitchen.

'Surely they wouldn't go that far?' she said, and her voice quavered like an old woman's.

'Look,' Jean said.

She put whatever she was carrying under the towel on to the kitchen table. 'Look what they've done.'

Jean pulled back the towel the way police pathologists revealed corpses in murder dramas on television.

Alice did not realize at once that what lay on her kitchen table was the carcass of her cat. Phoebus looked like something that had been pulled out of a slurry pit. His orange coat was slimy with drying blood. His beautiful striped tail was stripped of fur. His head had been almost cut off and hung from a thin iridescent sinew. His teeth were bared and the sockets of his eyes were a mass of congealed blood.

Alice could not look. Gently, she folded the towel back over the cat's body.

'No,' she said, 'they couldn't. Surely not on purpose. How could anyone do that?'

Jean said, 'Peter found him. He used to come round to our kitchen windowsill sometimes. We put out milk for him. They must've caught him. They left him on the doorstep. Peter nearly stepped on him when he went out. They must've thought he was ours.'

Alice knew that wasn't true. The Millers knew Phoebus belonged to her. This was a threat meant for her.

Alice thought she was going to be sick. She leaned on the sink and closed her eyes, rocking to and fro in a helpless, pointless, way. Why did Jean have to bring him here, why didn't she just tell me? That would be enough. Or would it? Alice could scarcely believe the cruelty inflicted on Phoebus. Nothing that Jean could have said would have described that.

'They know he's mine,' she said. 'Donna brought him here once when she saw him on the main road. And anyway, why should they hate you or your husband?'

Even as she said this, she remembered the incident involving little Kylie, how Donna had taken Dr Henson to be a pervert who'd targeted Jess's child.

'Do they still think a paediatrician is the same as a paedophile?' Alice whispered. She could not bring herself to speak the word in a normal voice. 'They can't think that.'

'Don't you think so?' Jean said in a queer, faltering voice. 'I do. They think Peter's a pervert. That butch lesbian and the faded creature she lives with probably wind them up. They hate men, women like that. They're always looking for excuses to blame them for everything. And didn't they once work for Social Services? There you are, then.'

Alice didn't know what Jean was talking about. She had no idea how to calm her. All she could think about was the horrible thing that had happened to Phoebus and why anyone should do it to a harmless cat.

It was unspeakable, that act of pointless violence. But she told herself that Jean must also be afraid of what those mindless thugs could do to her husband to punish him for his imagined crime.

'What are we going to do?' she asked Jean at last.

'What can we do?' Jean said. 'You've seen the cat.' Her voice was bleak.

'Not the police? No, of course not.'

'What could they do? We can't prove who did this to Phoebus. He could've been run over. And as for the threats against Peter, they'd say he's a confused old man who's imagining things. The police couldn't do anything. And then those apes would know we'd reported them. It would only make things worse.'

'Apes wouldn't do a thing like this,' Alice said. She didn't know if they would or not, it was something to say, the best she could think of to convey her helpless contempt for the worst of humanity. But she and Jean both understood that it wasn't contempt she felt; it was extreme terror.

Alice took Jean's arm. 'You'd better get back,' she said. 'I don't think they saw you come in.'

'No,' Jean said, 'they'll be watching Peter. They'll expect him to bury . . .' she couldn't say the cat's name, she simply pointed at the heap on the table.

'I'll look after Phoebus,' Alice said. 'He was my cat.'

But when she had seen Jean out through the front door, she went back into the kitchen. What can I do with him, she asked herself.

She fetched a sheet from the airing cupboard and wrapped it around the remains. Then she put the bundle in a plastic bag from the supermarket and tied the handles tightly. She put the whole thing into the rubbish bin outside the back door. She couldn't bring herself to bury the body in the garden, in case someone saw her do it. She felt bad about putting Phoebus into the bin, but consoled herself that he was dead, there was nothing of that glorious creature left in those hideous remains.

They're not going to sneer at me while I bury him, she thought, I'm not going to give them the satisfaction. This is Kevin Miller's way of threatening me, but why should he? Even if he thinks I saw what he did to the vicar, he must know by now I'm not going to say anything.

The best thing to do, she thought, is to ignore what's happened, pretend that I'm still hoping to find Phoebus.

Alice spent the rest of the evening making a notice. She wrote in big letters with a black marker pen on an old piece of cardboard – Missing: Beautiful big ginger cat, last seen in Catcombe Mead area. Reward. Apply Three Forester Close.

I'll put that up outside the supermarket, Alice thought. I'm not going to give Kevin Miller the satisfaction of knowing how he's upset me.

FOURTEEN

The woman behind the counter at the Co-op in Old Catcombe was red in the face with indignation, so strong was her sense of self-justification.

'I've said it before and I'll say it again, there's a curse on this place.'

DCI Rachel Moody abandoned any attempt at the scientific stance of the professional police officer. She asked, 'Why? Why should the place be cursed?'

'Didn't the murder of our young vicar take place on the self-same spot where way back in the old times Hester Warren was burned as a witch?'

The woman peered into Rachel Moody's face in conspiratorial fashion, cutting Sergeant Reid with his sceptical smile out of the secret she was about to tell.

'They do say that as the flames consumed her she put a curse on the village and on the descendants of those who put her to death until the end of time.'

Behind the woman's back, Jack Reid caught the DCI's eye and tapped his temple with his forefinger.

'Ask anyone who lives here,' the woman said, 'they'll tell you the same. That housing estate was sent to blight our lives and that's what's happened. The people who live there came to do the devil's work. And that's what they've done. The Reverend Tim Baker's death is Hester Warren's revenge.'

'But why?' Jack Reid asked. 'Why him?'

'It was the parson called her a witch. They say he was the one encouraged them to burn her.'

Rachel Moody's ears were pounding. She needed to sit down but instead she leaned against the counter and waited for a wave of dizziness to pass.

Jack Reid knew the signs by now. Rachel Moody had a very low boredom threshold, he thought. This wasn't the kind of information the DCI was after and more and more often she'd pretend to come over faint to put a stop to it. Women could get away with that sort of thing.

'Why don't you have a look round outside, Boss,' he said, 'and I'll finish checking if someone in the shop saw anyone using the phone box at the relevant time.'

The DCI nodded. 'I'll leave you to it,' she said. 'I'll be waiting in the car.'

'What's the matter with her?' the woman said. 'Who does she think she is?'

Jack Reid stared at her in amazement. 'I don't know what you're talking about,' he said. 'Can we get back to the point, please?'

'What can I do for you, then?' she said. She did not try to hide her hostility.

'Do many people make calls from that public telephone box on the green?' he asked.

They had traced the tip-off about Kevin Miller to that phone. Reid had little hope that anyone saw someone using the box at six o'clock in the morning, but he had to go through the motions.

'Not many,' the woman from the Co-op said. 'Why should they? More likely a stranger passing through, though they all seem to have their mobiles now, don't they? Could be a delivery driver looking for an address.'

'The call I'm interested in was made at six a.m.'

The woman from the Co-op laughed. 'Only farmers are up at that time of day,' she said, 'and they're far too busy to make phone calls from the village they could perfectly well make at home.'

Sergeant Reid gave her an arch look, asking for her collusion. 'Could be a call he didn't want the wife to hear,' he said.

'Nay, you're clutching at straws, lad. The wives have better things to do than listen to phone calls at that time of day in the middle of winter.'

Jack Reid closed his notebook and put his pen back in his top pocket.

'No, I suppose you're right,' he said. 'But we've got to check everything.'

'Is this to do with vicar's murder on the housing estate?' the woman asked. 'Why you're making such a meal of that God knows. Everyone here knows who did it. Why don't you just arrest that Kevin Miller. He's the one as did Mr Baker in, no doubt about that.'

'We need evidence. We can't arrest him without evidence. And so far there isn't any.' Jack was annoyed with himself. His frustration had made him say more than he'd intended.

'I don't know what's got into your lot,' the woman said. 'What's wrong with the good old-fashioned ways, I'd like to know? Arrest him on suspicion and force the evidence out of him once you've got him in a police cell. That's what you should do. It's the only way to treat scum like that.'

Sergeant Reid smiled at her. He was beginning to have some sympathy with her attitude. 'The old ways are the best, eh?' he said. 'Don't let my boss hear you say that. She wants to dot the i's and cross the t's before she brings a case to court. It's more than her job's worth if she doesn't get it right.'

'But she would get it right,' the woman from the Co-op said. 'Kevin Miller killed the young vicar, we all know that.'

In the car, Rachel Moody was sitting in the passenger seat with the door open. She was staring across the village green with a faraway look in her eyes.

Jack didn't ask her if she was feeling better. He thought it more tactful, and much easier, to ignore the subject of her funny turns.

'Nothing,' Jack said as he got in beside her. 'Less than nothing. We're getting nowhere on this case.'

Rachel looked across the yellowing grass with its patches of dried mud where the kids had been playing football. It was picturesque, in its way; a towering great tree near the centre, and the quaint old cottages surrounding the open ground, each with one downstairs and two upstairs windows looking out on the scene like the pairs of eyes and open mouths of an audience about to watch a drama unfold.

Rachel had heard before about the burning of a witch. It must've looked much the same when they burned Hester Warren, she told herself. I wonder if the people here clammed up then and pretended it never happened?

'What exactly did this witch they talk about do to get herself burned?' she asked Jack.

Sergeant Reid had done his homework.

'She was what they used to call a wise woman, back in the sixteenth century,' he said, trying to remember what the book he'd got from the library said. 'She brewed potions from plants to cure warts, that kind of thing. But then there was some kind of epidemic and the children were dying. The people were far too poor to call the doctor, so they turned to Hester Warren. She tried to help them with her plant medicines, and, when the children kept on dying anyway, the parson and the squire and the doctor all blamed Hester for their deaths and condemned her as a witch. The villagers burned her at the stake.'

Jack stopped and took a bar of chocolate out of the glove box. He broke it in half and handed Rachel the smaller share.

Then he said, 'More likely the children were dying of poverty and filthy living conditions and overcrowding. The toffs' children didn't die because their parents didn't have so many kids and lived in nice clean houses with good food. But the peasants were terrified and believed Hester was evil because the doctor said her potions poisoned their kids and the parson said she was unholy and an enemy of the church. Where they burned her was outside the village, just about where the housing estate is now. That's where she cursed them all.'

'But that was hundreds of years ago,' Rachel said. 'They can't still believe there could've been something in it.'

'1568 was the actual year,' Jack said. 'Hester cursed the village and its future inhabitants. And yes, a lot of them do believe there's something in it. They're very simple people, you know. They probably think we would've caught the murderer if the devil wasn't looking out for him. They think we're messing up a simple case; they're certain Kevin Miller did it. No one has any doubts about that.'

Reid was half laughing at the villagers' superstition, but he, too, felt that the murderer of Tim Baker was somehow protected by an outside power. Not witchcraft, of course, but something as powerful. Self-preservation, Jack called it.

We know who did this crime, he told himself, but the people who could bring Kevin Miller to justice are too afraid of what he might do to them. We've nothing to fight back with against that.

'Sometimes I wonder why we bloody bother,' he muttered.

Rachel Moody recognized the frustration in his voice.

'Hey,' she said, 'enough of that. As long as there's this conspiracy of silence about what people saw and what they know, we must just wait and hope. The rules of evidence aren't part of the black arts. We will get him in the end.'

'So what are we going to tell the public when he kills again and still no one admits to being a witness?' Jack Reid sounded angry, but his anger was at his own helplessness. 'Those people are so scared of the killer he can do what he likes,' he said.

'Don't go there, Jack,' Moody said. 'We can't give up on this.'

'I know, Boss,' Reid said. 'But what can we do? These people are giving that young thug a licence to kill, and there seems to be nothing we can do.'

'Take a grip, Sergeant,' Rachel said. 'It will be even worse if we take him to court without conclusive evidence and then he isn't convicted. Which he wouldn't be on what we've got. Or rather, haven't got. Then he really would have won.'

'Then what are we here for?' Reid asked.

'Because in the end we will get him,' Rachel said. 'Maybe he'll have to kill again before we do, more than once, even, but one day someone will talk or he'll make a mistake and then we'll get him.'

Jack knew she could say nothing else. They could do nothing else. But he was also disconcerted by the lack of human emotion in her attitude. She sounded as clinical as a computer. 'That doesn't sound like protecting the public to me,' he said.

DCI Moody's voice was harsh and uncompromising, devoid of emotion. Not very feminine, Jack thought, not very caring at all. But then she hadn't got to the rank she had simply because the police powers-that-be wanted to give the force a more girlie image. Perhaps they'd got more than they'd bargained for in Detective Chief Inspector Moody.

'The public made their choice,' she said. 'They must take responsibility if they're prepared to protect Kevin Miller rather than innocent people like that young vicar.'

Jack Reid was surprised at the contempt in her voice. 'You don't really like them, do you?' he said. 'The public, I mean?'

Rachel Moody turned to look at him.

'I don't like this case,' she said. 'I don't like what those people are doing, covering up for that bastard. But it's not a question of like or dislike. These people who won't help are getting in our way. We can't do our job because of them, and doing the job is the important thing. At least it is to me.'

Jack Reid hesitated. Then he decided that for the moment the way they were talking allowed a suspension of their professional relationship.

'About what happened in that shop . . .' he said.

Rachel Moody flushed. 'I needed some air,' she said. 'That's all.'

'Look,' Reid said, 'we're not all against you, you know, you're part of the team. I mean, if I was drunk on duty, my mates would cover for me, at least up to a point.' He was very embarrassed, but he couldn't stop now. 'Up to a point they would, anyway,' he said. 'What I'm trying to say, you should lighten up, let us help you. See yourself as part of the team. We're not enemies you have to defeat.'

'Is that how I come across?' Rachel asked.

'A bit,' he said. 'You seem defensive and it's not necessary. We're not chess pieces you're playing with.' He paused, then added, 'Ma'am.'

He waited in some trepidation for her to respond. He expected her either to explode, or retreat coldly into formality.

But she surprised him. She laughed.

'What do you want, mothering?' she asked.

'No,' he said, a little indignant, 'No. A bit more respect, that's all. You may be a graduate from university and have diplomas and all that before you joined the force, and, OK, you've been fast-tracked and that's fine; we don't doubt you're a good cop.'

'Hey,' Rachel said, 'don't patronize me.'

Jack ignored her and went on, 'You're not from around here, either, not one of us. But that doesn't matter. What we want is for you to know you need us too.'

Reid took a deep breath and finished in a rush, 'We've got a lot more experience than you and you could make use of that if you weren't so paranoid about not losing face in front of us.'

'You think I'm paranoid?'

Rachel knew he was right; she'd thought it didn't show. To establish her authority, she had kept her team at arm's length. She'd treated them like robots.

I'm afraid of them, she thought, I'm afraid they'll guess I'm flying by the seat of my pants most of the time.

'Do you hate working for me?' she asked.

Sergeant Reid shook his head. 'Of course not,' he said. 'I wouldn't be saying this if I did. I'd have applied for a transfer. But being a good policeman is more than just doing the job and you could do with getting yourself more of a life.'

She nodded. 'Point taken,' she said.

She didn't like to ask him for suggestions as to how she could do this.

Then he started the car. 'Well,' he said, 'what now? We won't catch a murderer sitting here chatting.'

'Don't be so sure,' she said, and smiled at him. 'I think we may just have made a real breakthrough in this case, Jack.'

FIFTEEN

Alice stood behind the curtain in her unlighted bedroom. She stared out at the bleak night.

The houses in Forester Close seemed to her to be skulking in the shadows, waiting for something to happen. Alice thought, it's almost as though the street has got used to being afraid, it's lost confidence in the people who live in it. She asked herself, isn't that the meaning of community, people knowing they can trust one another? That's what's happened in Forester Close, we've lost confidence in other people. And why wouldn't we, we live in fear?

There was no sign of Donna or Alan at Number Two, no lights on in the house. But outside Kevin and Nate Miller with a pack of their friends were gathered in the driveway, whooping and shouting.

Kevin, astride his motorbike, was directing his followers. He revved the bike engine like a war-cry.

Savages, Alice said to herself, they don't give a thought for anyone else.

If only that were all, she thought, but it was worse than that. They moved off; seeming to her like a pack of wolves hunting for a kill.

She heard the sound of breaking glass as the group gathered briefly round a vehicle parked at the far end of the Close. Then they turned and moved back up the street towards her. Alice moved away from the window out of the range of the headlamps of Kevin's motorbike so no one would see her outlined against the curtain and know that she was watching.

As she turned she caught sight of a slight movement in her garden, behind the front wall.

It came again, then stopped. In the faint light from a street lamp, Alice could make out a shape of more solid darkness against the corner of the wall. The baying of the teenagers seemed to be getting closer, and the dark shape shrank a little and shifted as though cowering closer to the ground.

Then Alice saw a white face raised and quickly turned away. It was only a glimpse, but in that flash she recognized terror. And she knew, too, who was hiding from that pack of thugs. It was Jess. They were hunting Jess.

Alice thought, is it a game? After all, they're just children. Are they playing hide and seek? It must be a game, she's family, she's one of them.

But Alice could not dismiss the terror she'd seen on that young face. If this was a game, it had gone too far. Everything those thugs did went too far. They were dangerous.

Without turning on the light on the landing she made her way downstairs and into her hallway. She crept to the front door and opened it.

'Jess,' she said in a whisper which in spite of her efforts quavered and betrayed her fear. 'Come in, quick, they'll find you if you stay out there.'

She didn't see anyone running towards the house, but almost before she had called out, she felt a rush of cold air, someone pushed her aside and then the door closed. In the light through the door from the kitchen, Alice saw Jess and a young man clinging together in the hall, leaning against the wall trying to catch their breath.

'They're after us,' Jess gasped. 'My God, they'll kill us if they find us. They're after Mark. They're crazy.'

'But why?' Alice said. She was bemused.

Jess was shuddering with shock. She managed to gasp, 'They've been on the piss all day. Mum's out and Kevin brought his pals home and they found Mark's pickup. God knows how they knew it was his. They've smashed the windscreen and the windows and kicked the bodywork. We heard them.'

She started to cry. 'They kept chanting "Kill, kill, kill". I couldn't stop them. They're crazed.'

She sobbed quietly and the young man took her hand and squeezed it. 'It's going to be OK,' he told her. 'It's a farm vehicle; no one's going to notice a few extra dents. That pickup's a lot tougher than your Kevin and his mates. No one will know the difference.'

'It's not the bloody truck,' Jess said. 'It's what they wanted to do to you. And me, *me*, can you credit that?'

Mark said to Alice, 'It was close. I can't believe what they were like.'

He'd had a bad scare, Alice could see that. He was babbling like a girl. 'We got out through the back garden of the house next door, but they came after us. If they'd found us . . .'

Jess kissed his face. 'It's OK now, they've gone,' she said.

The young man added, 'I couldn't risk tackling them, not on my own. There are too many of them, if they'd laid me out, God knows what they'd do to Jess. I really think they would've killed her.'

He put his arm protectively round Jess's shoulders, but he couldn't disguise how scared he was. Neither of them could.

'But, Jess, you're Kevin's sister,' Alice said, incredulous. 'You're one of them. Why were they after you?' Even as she said it, she could hear how silly she sounded. Like King Canute trying to turn back the tide.

'That makes it worse,' Jess wailed. 'They think they've got the right. I'm family, they think they're looking after me, they know what's right for me. Oh, Mark, what are we going to do? If they get their hands on you now, I honestly think they'll kill you.'

He gave her shoulders a squeeze to comfort her. 'It's all right,' he said softly, 'trust me, it'll be OK.'

Jess shook her head. She turned to Alice. 'It's all that crazy feud stuff between us and those villagers. Kev doesn't even have to know Mark, he hates him because he comes from the old village,' she said. 'It's like that old movie, *The Godfather*. They're born enemies. They don't know why, they just are. They're off their heads, they don't know what they're doing.'

Alice told her, 'You go in there, in the sitting-room. I'll come with you. We'll turn on the light. If they see us on our own together, without Mark, it may distract them. You,' she said to Mark, pushing him towards the kitchen, 'you go out the back and get out of here as fast as you can.'

They both obeyed automatically. Alice felt a sudden icy draught and heard the back door close as she and Jess went into the sitting-room and sat down as casually as they could in front of the television. Alice put her hand on the telephone.

'Should I call the police? In case he doesn't get away?'

Jess looked at her in horror. 'No, of course not. Are you mad? Kev would never let me get away with that.'

'Are you sure?'

Jess shook her head. Then she asked, slowly, 'You wouldn't really do anything like that, would you? You wouldn't ever tell the cops about something you saw that didn't have anything to do with you? You're asking for trouble.'

Jess was thinking, the first thing the old woman thought of was to call the cops. She could have been watching when that vicar man was killed. Could she be the one who told the police about Kevin?

'No,' Alice said. 'No, of course I wouldn't. But, the way they are tonight, if they see the telephone, it makes me feel better to know I could get help if they give trouble.'

Jess thought, she has no idea. It wouldn't stop them. Her life won't be worth living if they think she's shopping them to the police.

She said to Alice, 'They won't give trouble, not now. It's all over, at least for now. They wanted Mark. When they see he isn't here with us, they'll break it up. It started out they were having a laugh, but they were high and it went beyond that this time.' She shivered, then tried to smile at Alice. 'Brothers,' she said, 'who needs 'em?'

Jess sat staring impassively at her dirty fingernails. Tears squeezed like gel from under her smudged eyelashes.

The baying in the street seemed to get louder. Jess started to shake. Alice clenched her bony fists, trying not to tremble. She smiled at Jess as though they were talking about the weather, or a television programme. 'Just talk naturally,' she said.

Jess laughed and the sound surprised them both. 'What's natural?' she said. 'If I talked naturally the way that lot know me, you'd say I was starting a riot.'

Alice felt a sudden surge of affection for the girl. It took something special to make a joke against herself in this situation.

The baying outside was quieter. They heard feet splattering the gravel on the drive, then nothing.

'They've gone,' Jess said.

'Yes,' Alice said.

She got to her feet slowly. Now that it was all over she felt shaky. 'I'll make a cup of tea. It's as well to give them a little while to calm down, don't you think? Before you go out, I mean?'

With the immediate danger passed, Alice and Jess looked at each other as though they were creatures of different species. Jess stared at Alice's greyish skin, at her shapelessness under the screen of dingy clothing, and she shuddered at the bleakness of being such a creature. Alice saw Jess's curves tightly cased in cheap shiny cloth. She noticed the girl's white hands with their gruesome black-lacquered nails and the angry blackheads under the mask of make-up. She shuddered with distaste.

'Tea,' Alice said.

She went to the kitchen and filled the kettle. Jess followed her.

'You won't call the cops, will you?' Jess said. 'You won't tell anyone?'

Alice shook her head. 'No,' she said. 'What would be the use?'

'What can I do?' Jess asked suddenly. 'All I've got over Kev and them is getting angry and frightening the shit out of them. At least I can still do that. You can't talk to them.'

Alice shook her head again. She didn't know what to say. She was offended by Jess's language. Of course she heard worse on television but it was different hearing it from a real person in her own home. From a child, at that.

The kettle boiled. Alice took two mugs down from the shelf and put a teabag in each. 'Tea,' she said again. 'It'll help.'

'Oh,' Jess said with a sort of derisive snort. 'I know what you're thinking, but you're way off. You've no right to judge me. You're too old, you don't understand. You've got to get in first or you're dead.'

'Yes,' Alice said, 'I'm not judging you, I understand.'

Jess looked startled at that, then scornful. 'You think I'm wrong, right?'

Alice didn't dare answer. Jess stood there like a furious Rottweiler. She decided that Alice thought she had glimpsed vulnerability behind her show of aggression and Jess wanted to bully that moment out of the old woman's consciousness.

Of course, Alice had seen no such thing. To her, Jess was fearsome. Fear being part of Alice's life, she was afraid particularly of all young people, and most of all young people like Jess who defied everything about the world that might comfort someone like herself.

'That was Mark's pickup,' Jess said suddenly.

Alice had heard nothing, but then she made out the sound of a revved engine.

'I'd know it anywhere,' Jess said. She smiled.

'That's a relief,' Alice said. 'At least it still worked.'

'Yes,' Jess said.

Now that the crisis was over, they were both embarrassed.

'How's the baby?' Alice asked, thinking to placate the girl with a maternal reminder.

'What about it? Why does everyone think that my life begins and ends with that kid? What are you trying to say?' Jess sounded aggressive.

Alice didn't know what she was trying to say. Perhaps she'd hoped to soften Jess by mentioning the child; perhaps she was trying to sympathize with anyone bringing up her daughter in Jess's circumstances.

Jess suddenly turned on the old woman. 'It'll have a better life than you have,' she said. 'It won't be a weirdo. It's going to know how to get on in the real world. It won't hide away and suck the life out of people like you do.'

Alice smiled because she didn't understand what Jess was saying.

'You keep away from me,' Jess said. She banged the mug of tea down. Then she ran out of the house, slamming the back door behind her.

Alice walked slowly back into the sitting-room and closed the curtains. The pack of teenagers was still hanging around on the driveway of Number Two. Jess appeared and walked slowly towards them. Alice watched as one of them, she thought it was Kevin, broke away from the rest and approached Jess. It was a conciliatory move, it couldn't be anything else. Jess hit him, hard, on the ear, knocking him sideways so that he almost fell. Then they were both absorbed by the group, and they all moved away together down the street to the main road. They disappeared.

Gulls, Alice thought, they look like a group of dark and hungry seagulls moving off towards a new scavenging ground.

Alice turned on the television. She needed company.

He seems such a nice boy, Jess's friend, she thought. What on earth does he see in her? It's bound to end in tears.

SIXTEEN

The phone was ringing on Detective Chief Inspector Rachel Moody's desk when she came into her office first thing in the morning.

She took the call with her mind preoccupied by other things as she sorted the mail and wondered when someone would bring her a cup of coffee.

'Oh, my God, not again,' she said. 'Not that bloody Forester place again. Not another one.'

She found Sergeant Reid in the canteen. He had just sat down to a late breakfast, his plate heaped with fried sausages, eggs, and bacon, when the DCI caught up with him.

She saw the look on his face when she sat down opposite him at his table, and laughed. 'Don't look like that,' she said, 'I'll wait while you finish your cholesterol fix. It may be some time before you next eat.'

'What's the hurry?' he said.

'We're off to Forester Close,' she said, 'and if I never hear the name of that street again it'll be too soon.'

Jack Reid looked startled. 'What is it this time,' he said. 'Surely not another murder?'

Rachel Moody shrugged. 'Maybe, maybe not,' she said. 'Not technically, I suppose, but it could be another Kevin Miller victim.'

Jack Reid pushed his plate away. 'What's happened?' he asked.

Rachel told him what she knew.

'At ten thirty a.m. yesterday, Dr Peter Henson said goodbye to his wife on the doorstep of Number Four, Forester Close. He backed his blue Saab out of the garage, and drove off.'

The DCI spoke in a flat tone, as though she had learned the words off by heart.

Jack Reid nodded. 'And?' he asked.

Rachel Moody went on, 'At six thirty this morning a woman walking her dog in the woods a mile or so outside Old Catcombe saw the Saab parked in the gateway to a field. The dog got excited, jumping up at the driver's door and barking.'

'And then?' Reid prompted her.

'The woman approached the car. She saw the rubber pipe attached to the exhaust. She found Dr Henson dead behind the wheel.'

'How long had he been dead?' Jack asked.

'The car had run out of petrol. The ignition was still turned on. But the body and the engine were cold.'

'What's the wife got to say?'

'That's what we're on our way to find out,' Rachel said. 'I know it's not strictly our case, but the connection with Forester Close is more than a coincidence, so we're taking it on. This could well have something to do with Kevin Miller. Apparently he got the idea Dr Henson was a paedo and the family persecuted him.'

'I'd put money on it,' Jack Reid said.

He stood up. 'What are we waiting for?' he said. 'Let's go and see if we can't nail the bugger this time.'

Rachel Moody drove, while Jack gathered as much information about Dr Henson as he could on his mobile phone.

At last he snapped it shut and turned to look out of the car window at the depressing jungle of leafless winter undergrowth at the side of the road.

'Waste of time,' he said.

'Nothing to go on?' Rachel asked, prompting him.

'Model citizen, by all accounts,' Jack said. He sounded gloomy. 'Respectable doctor, specialist paediatrician. Wife a primary school teacher. Both retired. Not even a parking ticket between them, my friend said.'

Rachel turned into Forester Close and drove slowly up the street to park outside Number Four.

The house seemed deserted; indeed, the entire street appeared deserted. It was as though all human life had been evacuated because of an alarm about some sinister life-threatening danger lurking in the street. Rachel glanced over to Alice Bates's house, looking for the slightest twitch of a curtain, which might show that at least one person was part of the scene. But if Alice was watching, she was keeping well out of sight.

'I feel sorry for Dr Henson's widow,' Rachel Moody said to Jack Reid. 'This hateful place, she must think there's no one in the world who gives a damn for what she's going through. What price community here?'

'Selfish thing for the doctor to do, really,' Jack said. He sounded thoughtful. 'What made him leave her all alone to face whatever the Millers were dishing out?'

'Maybe they weren't,' Rachel said. 'We've no proof this has anything to do with the Millers.'

'What's that, then?' Jack said.

He pointed to slashes of red paint like knife wounds on the white garden wall outside the Henson house, and more on the front door. 'What's that say?' he said. The word paedo was painted on the wall. 'Look at that,' he said, 'and tell me that's got nothing to do with one of those Millers.'

'But why? What makes them think he's a paedophile? There's something we're missing here.'

'God knows,' Jack Reid said.

He got out of the car and Rachel followed him across the drive of Number Four to the front door.

Jean finally answered their knocking.

'I know what you've come to say,' she said, 'you don't have to tell me, Peter's dead. Two uniformed officers were here earlier. Thank you for coming, but I'd really rather be alone.'

She spoke in a bleak monotone, as though she had rehearsed the speech.

Rachel stepped forward. 'I'm so sorry about what's happened,' she said, 'but there are a few things we have to check.'

'What things? My husband killed himself. That's an end to it, there's no more to be said.'

Jean sounded surprisingly determined.

'Mrs Henson, was there any reason why your husband should be depressed? Was he under any unusual stress, for instance?'

'Nothing out of the ordinary,' Jean said.

'Perhaps we could come inside for a moment,' Jack said. 'It would be better than talking on the doorstep.'

Jean Henson looked hurriedly about. She seemed not to notice the ugly scrawled graffiti on the front door.

Perhaps she doesn't know it's there, Rachel thought. She

probably hasn't been out of the house since it appeared. But that was ridiculous, of course Jean Henson must know. She was just trying to ignore it because there was nothing she could say.

Rachel was trying to think of a way of bringing up the subject tactfully when she heard Jack say, 'Careful you don't get red paint on your clothes from that door. It looks as if it's still wet.'

Jean moved back, startled, and Jack moved forward into the door frame, as though he thought she had invited him in.

Reid said, 'Mrs Henson, what can you tell us about the word paedo splashed all over the outside of your front wall? What's that all about?'

Rachel was horrified at what she saw as the Sergeant's brutality. She, too, moved towards Jean Henson, but to try to comfort her.

'How long has it been there?' she asked.

'You'd better come in,' Jean Henson said. She sounded reluctant, and turned away to walk into the kitchen, leaving them to shut the front door.

Jack followed her to a stool at the breakfast bar in the kitchen and helped her up on to the seat. Then he pulled up another stool and perched close to her.

'We met your husband, you remember?' he said. 'He seemed to us then to be a happy man. No money worries, a good marriage, success in his career. What was happening in his life that made him do this?'

Jean Henson looked up at him, open-mouthed. She shook her head helplessly.

Rachel said, 'What about that stupid graffiti? Had someone got hold of the wrong end of the stick? Was someone threatening him? Or trying to blackmail him?'

'That was an idiotic mistake,' Jean Henson said. 'Jess Miller's baby fell out of her pram and Peter went and picked her up to see if she was all right.'

That was clearly as much as she wanted to say, but Jack would not leave it at that.

'Well, of course he did. What decent person wouldn't?'

He and Rachel both waited for Jean to say more. The silence grew oppressive.

At last Jean Henson said, 'Someone saw him touch the child and told Donna Miller he'd been abusing her.'

'So the Millers wrote that word all over your wall and the door?'

Jean's voice faltered. 'I don't know.'

'Do you know who told Donna Miller that your husband abused the kid?' Rachel said.

'He didn't abuse the child,' Jean Henson said, 'he picked her up and comforted her.'

'Of course he did,' Jack Reid said. 'But someone made a big mistake. Someone pretty stupid. Was it a mistake, or was it a malicious lie? Did your husband have any enemies that you know of?'

Jean hesitated. As his wife, she knew that a lot of people didn't like Peter. Even his own daughter had gone to Australia to get away from him. So she prevaricated. 'I don't know who'd make up a thing like that,' she said. She started to cry. 'But someone in this street must've seen him with the child and got the wrong end of the stick.'

'Who do you think that was?' Rachel said.

'Alice Bates,' Jean burst out, 'she's the one who watches what goes on here.'

Suddenly she turned on Rachel Moody. 'I can't help you,' she said. 'Go away and leave me alone, I've nothing to say. I know what you want me to say, you want me to tell you that Kevin Miller persecuted us and drove my husband to kill himself. But I don't know, I tell you, I don't know.'

She got off the stool and faced them.

Rachel noticed that in spite of everything she was going through, Jean Henson had put on her make-up and done her hair as though she were on her way out to a social occasion. It's the only way she knows to face the end of the world, Rachel thought, keeping up appearances whatever happens.

Jean started to recite at them. 'My husband has suffered from depression ever since he was forced to retire from the NHS. He didn't want to stop working, he'd lots more years work in him. He was bitter about that, and he felt there was no future to look forward to. That's why he did it.'

Suddenly, losing control, she shouted at them: 'And I feel just the same. I can't forgive him for not taking me with him. So get out of my house and leave me alone.'

Back in the car, Rachel and Jack avoided looking at each other. At last Jack said, 'Sorry Boss. I messed that up.'

Rachel shook her head. 'No,' she said, 'we both did. Poor woman, what's going to happen to her now?'

'We've got to get that bastard Kevin Miller for something,' Jack Reid said. 'His fingerprints are all over this, but we're absolutely hog-tied.'

They drove off and Forester Close itself seemed to take refuge in uneasy silence. The street lamps came on as the light began to fade in the late afternoon, but the Close was deserted.

Then a car driven at high speed turned off the main road with a squeal of brakes. It swerved, and came to a stop outside the Henson house.

Dave Byrne, Helen's deserted husband and a frequent and unwelcome visitor at Terri and Helen's, got out of the car and opened the boot. He made no effort to hide what he was doing; in fact, he looked about him as though defying an unseen audience of spies.

He took a bucket out of the boot, then scrubbing brushes and cans of spray paint. Carrying them, he went round the back of Terri and Helen's house, though there was no sign of either of them being there.

In a few minutes, he came out of the front door of Number Five with the bucket full of steaming hot water.

Alice Bates, watching from her front room, could see the steam rising. She thought, Helen must've given him a key. Terri won't like the idea of Dave coming and going as he pleases.

Alice felt a small thrill of excitement, anticipating ructions later between Terri and Helen.

Dave Byrne, having climbed over the wall dividing Number Five from the Henson house, started to clean off the daubed messages from the wall of Number Four. He scrubbed the front door, too. He seemed to be using a wire brush; the door paint was coming away. He got rid of the ugly words, but the bare unpainted patches were almost as unsightly. Dave had thought of that. He used the spray paint he'd brought with him to cover where the graffiti had been.

The paint didn't quite match the original colour, but almost.

Alice thought, Perhaps it will when it dries. Then Dave threw

the water away into the side of the road, packed his gear back
into the car boot, and drove off.

Alice watched the foam from the dirty water flowing away
down the hill. If only the harm that those words had done could
be washed away so easily, she thought.

SEVENTEEN

Bert Pearson was waiting for Mark when he came in from the milking. Bert had been waiting for some time, since he came back from his lonely wanderings in the fields at lunchtime, and he was impatient to get over with the confrontation he must have with his son.

Mark, taking off his boots at the back door before he came into the kitchen, was surprised to see his father there. 'What you doing still here, Dad?' he said.

'I wouldn't be here if there weren't something that's got to be said between us,' Bert said.

Two hours ago he hadn't expected to find what he had to say difficult. But now, faced with his son's plainly contemptuous hostility, and unsure about how he could explain what he had to say, Bert wished he could put it off until another day.

But he had to do something to break up Mark's relationship with that tart from the housing estate. His efforts to point the police towards Kevin Miller to show Mark the sort of family Jess came from, seemed to have come to nothing. There was only one thing for it, Bert told himself; he had to have it out with his son face to face.

Mark went to the sink and washed his hands.

'Well?' he said. 'If you've got something to say, you'd better spit it out.'

'You know what this farm means to me, don't you, son?' Bert said. He couldn't look at Mark, not talking like this about strong feelings.

'Not enough to make you pull yourself together and pull your weight running it,' Mark muttered. He couldn't look at his father's face, either, he was too embarrassed. It was worse than Bert trying to discuss his mother's withdrawal from him, what he'd call a man-to-man talk. Mark was always afraid his father was about to do that.

Bert pretended he hadn't heard what Mark said. He tried again.

'You know it's always been the best thing in my life that you came in with me? You know how much that means to me, don't you?'

Mark guessed what was coming. Bert was going to warn him off Jess. Someone who'd spoken to his father must have seen him with her and told the old man about it. Or maybe one of Mum's friends had seen them together and told her. He thought, whoever told Mum must've put the fear of God into her to make her speak to Dad about it.

Mark didn't want to talk to anyone about Jess. He wanted to tell his father that he had always felt the same way as he did about the farm and the land, but that he had his own way to make in the world and some day soon, if things didn't change, he was going to have to break away so that he could do that, Jess or no Jess. He knew that if his father said anything about Jess, he would have to defend his relationship with her. And once he did that, the thing would become something it wasn't. What he had with Jess was exactly the relationship he was looking for at the moment. The last thing he wanted was to be pushed into choosing between her and the farm, and that was what would happen if his father didn't back off. Mark knew only too well that if the thing was presented in those terms, he would have to choose Jess, not because his feelings for her necessarily justified his choice, but because he had to assert his right to make his own decisions.

'I don't want to talk about it, Dad,' he said. 'Leave it. It's not what you think, just drop the whole subject. You don't have to worry. It's time you were in bed, you know?'

'But I've got to make you understand . . .' Bert said. 'We've got to stand up for our . . .' He paused, trying to remember the big word people used. 'Our heritage,' he said at last and then paused again, embarrassed that in the heat of the moment he had used such a pretentious word. 'People like that Miller family are out to destroy us,' he said.

'You don't have to make me understand, Dad. I do understand. I know what I'm doing.'

Bert spread his hands in a helpless gesture, knowing that he had no way of communicating with Mark in this mood.

'I'm off out, Dad,' Mark said. 'Good night. Mum said she'd be back early tonight.'

Bert heard him laugh as he shut the back door behind him and went out into the yard.

Bert heaved a sigh of relief. At least he'd tried to talk to the boy.

A while later, in an old field shelter originally built for two pensioned-off cart horses to spend their declining years, Mark pulled away from Jess and started to drag on his clothes.

'Hey,' she said, 'what's the matter with you? I'm only just getting started.'

Playfully, she buffeted him with her impressive breasts, but he put his hands over them and pushed her gently away.

'Not yet, Jess,' he said. 'Let's talk.'

'Talk?' she said, looking puzzled as though talk were a sexual deviation she hadn't heard of yet.

Mark laughed. 'Yes,' he said, 'about you and me.'

Jess sat up, suddenly serious. She thought, this is it; he wants us to escape together.

'I've a bit of money saved,' she said.

She was thinking, Alice must have money stashed away in that house of hers. No one poor could live in a place like that. Alice certainly doesn't spend it, Jess told herself, she always wears the same clothes, she'll never miss it. Why should an old woman like that need a lot of money?

Mark didn't know what she was talking about, suddenly mentioning money as though that had something to do with what he had to say to her.

'What do your parents think of us going out?' he asked.

Jess looked at him in amazement. Had he forgotten how Kevin and Nate and their gang had hunted the two of them that night they'd gone to make love in the shed among the bushes at the back of Alice's house? She was still finding shards of glass down the back of the pickup's seat.

As though Mark read her thoughts, he said, 'I don't mean your moron brothers, I mean your mum and dad.'

'Same as Kevin does, I suppose,' Jess said. 'Best they don't know anything about it.'

'But if I met them?' Mark said. 'You know, if you took me to your house to meet them? Once we got talking to each other . . . ?'

'They'd hate you. They don't want to know you. They hate you because they think your lot are all snobs or hicks, that's enough for them,' Jess said.

She was thinking, Over my dead body you meet them. There's a limit to the number of times Kylie calls me Mum and I can make a joke about her being mixed up and not being able to say Jess. As if, she says Jess all the time, it's one of her noises.

Mark didn't say anything. He seemed unconvinced. Jess decided that the best form of defence was attack.

'Come to that, why don't you take me home to meet your mum and dad?' she said.

Not on your life, Mark thought, they'd turn her out of the house. He tried to tell himself, it's not that I'm ashamed of her, or of them, but I don't want to be part of the way they'd judge Jess if they met her. And then he thought, I am ashamed; I'm ashamed of what Jess would know about me, meeting them; and what they'd be able to tell about me if they met her.

'It's no good, you're from the new houses,' he said, 'they'd just hate you on principle.'

'But *why*? We don't do them any harm.'

Mark couldn't begin to explain. It wasn't something that could be explained, really. He remembered the day he'd met her, those two louts scaring the bullocks and leaving the gate open and her clinging to him, terrified, in her ridiculous red high-heeled boots. He knew from the start he couldn't explain to her. If he tried to tell her how he felt about the farm and the animals, she'd never understand.

'Oh,' he said, 'they feel threatened by all the people moving in, and what that means. They used to be free, in control of their own lives, and then there's all the stuff that comes with masses of strangers moving in you know; government interference, rules and regulations, restrictions, that sort of shit. Nothing stays the same.'

'That's crazy,' Jess said, 'we don't give a toss what those old villagers do.'

'That's part of the trouble,' Mark said, and he felt suddenly very sad. 'We know your lot have no idea what they're doing to us.'

'What's with this "us"?' she said, and moved closer to him. 'The only us that matters here is you and me. What does it matter what they think, they're well past it. It's what we want that counts.'

Mark gave up. There was no point in talking any more. All that mattered this minute was the way her hot wet mouth felt on him and the taste of her on his tongue.

She broke off to look up at him. 'D'you love me, Mark? Tell me you love me,' she said in a voice hoarse with lust.

'I love you, girl,' he cried, 'Oh, I love you.'

EIGHTEEN

Terri and Helen were having supper together. Nicky had gone up to her room to do her homework, and the house was quiet.

Terri said, 'Did you tell Dave I wrote that letter to the Millers?'

Helen looked flustered. 'What letter's that?' she said. Terri wasn't fooled; Helen was playing for time.

'Don't pretend you don't know,' Terri said. She was impatient with the little-girl way Helen always tried to deflect criticism. Terri resented being cast as the bully.

'God knows what made you write it anyway,' Helen said. 'He didn't do anything to that baby; he just picked her up when she fell down.'

'All men are the same,' Terri said. That was it, as far as she was concerned.

'Anyway, I didn't say anything,' Helen said. 'I didn't tell anyone you wrote it.'

Terri said, 'So why would an outsider like your ex-husband do a thing like that? Why should he care about a bit of graffiti, he doesn't live here.'

'Why are you making it into such a big deal?' Helen said, sounding irritated. 'After all, do you want to live in a street daubed with that kind of filth? Someone had to get rid of it. Think of Nicky.'

'That's not the point,' Terri said. 'What Dave did by cleaning up that graffiti was a deliberate act of criticism of me. He was making it obvious he thought it was my fault Dr Henson did what he did.'

'Oh, darling, that's rubbish. You know it is. Why should Dave even know about Dr Henson?'

Helen was still irritated. She didn't like talking about Dave to Terri. She let her irritation show as she said in a voice full of weary disinterest, 'Oh, Terri, what makes you think it had anything to do with you at all? It's far more likely Dave didn't want Nicky faced with those kinds of words at her age. He is still her father, after all.' Helen paused, then went on, 'If anything, it was more likely a way of getting at me if he goes for custody. He can say this isn't a proper place to bring up a child, when he has to protect her by cleaning up that muck.'

'What muck's that?' Nicky had slipped into the room without either of them noticing.

Terri was annoyed. It was frustrating that she and Helen could never even have an argument without Nicky butting in with her child's self-centred interpretation of everything they said. 'Nothing,' she said.

Then she saw Helen's face and knew that she'd said the wrong thing again. Helen seemed to have no qualms about Nicky being privy to anything that Terri considered confidential between them.

'No,' Helen said, 'there was nothing secret about it, darling. We were talking about the ugly graffiti those people painted on the walls of Number Four.'

'That wasn't people,' Nicky said, 'that was Kevin Miller and me and Jess. We did it. We all did.'

'We?' Terri said. 'We?'

She caught the child's shoulder and turned her to face her. She was shocked.

'What do you mean, "we"?' she demanded. 'Don't tell me you had anything to do with it?'

Nicky pulled away from her and went to her mother. She glared at Terri and put her hand in Helen's. 'I thought you'd be pleased,' she said. 'You told me Terri wrote that letter warning Jess's mother about that old child molester. I thought you'd be pleased I wanted to help make him suffer.'

Helen smiled at her. She said sweetly, 'But Dr Henson was innocent, darling. He didn't hurt Kylie, it was a mistake. You do understand that, don't you?' Helen sounded as though she wasn't convinced at all of Dr Henson's innocence.

'We were only supporting you,' Nicky said defiantly to Terri. 'It wasn't us who got it wrong, it was you.'

Helen was placatory. 'It was a misunderstanding,' she said, 'but what happened to Dr Henson was a tragedy for poor Mrs Henson, wasn't it?'

Nicky wanted to make peace with Terri. Life was much easier when she and Terri weren't at odds.

'I s'pose you only did what you thought was right,' Nicky said, sounding like a prim little old lady. 'It's sad he killed himself, but nobody forced him to. And surely it's better this way? An old man at the end of his life doesn't compare with one innocent child's life ruined by a paedophile. There must've been reasons why he didn't want to go on living. I'm surprised he didn't take that wife of his with him.'

Terri asked herself, why does she always sound like someone reading a political manifesto? She's thirteen, for God's sake. Where does she get the things she comes out with?'

But she smiled. She was glad that she and Nicky were friends again.

NINETEEN

Earlier in the day it had stopped raining and now the clouds had rolled back to reveal a mass of stars. Alice thought how stark everything suddenly looked outside. There was a full moon, and already the grass on the verges and in the Henson's front garden glittered with frost.

Before she went to bed, Alice took one last look out of her living room window. Now black ice covered the gardens and the street with a diamond sheen in the moonlight.

There was no wind and the scene was as still and dead as an old photograph. This was Forester Close as Alice wished it always was, quiet and peaceful and empty of people. There was an old-fashioned quality about the night here that comforted her. The daytime reeked of the twenty-first century and Alice felt discomfited and out of place; at night she was part of a formal order imposed by darkness.

But as she looked out at this wintry scene, Alice caught a movement in a parked car. She gripped the windowsill for support.

She recognized Dave's battered Ford. His was the only car she knew with a roof-rack piled with what looked like builders' equipment. When he first started to visit Helen, Alice had put him down as some kind of jobbing labourer. More recently, it had crossed her mind that he was sleeping rough in the car while he tried to get Helen to take him back. But she wasn't sure, she'd never seen him.

Now he was parked across the street from Terri and Helen's house. Against the glow of the street lamp, Alice could see him hunched in the driving seat.

He must be going to meet Helen, Alice thought. They must have planned a romantic assignation where Terri can't interrupt them.

As she watched, Dave got out of the car and took some kind of bag off the roof.

Then he jumped over the front wall of Number Five and disappeared round the side of the house.

Dave disappeared for so long that in the end Alice gave up and went upstairs to bed. I'm happy for them, she thought, it's for the best. If Helen goes back to Dave it's good for Nicky. They can be a proper family again.

Before Alice undressed, she took one last look out of her bedroom window. The moon had moved behind the house, and now black shadows made geometric patterns across the gardens and the street.

Alice was about to turn away and get ready for bed when she saw Dave come running round the side of Number Five. She could see him plainly as he crossed the front garden and vaulted over the wall into the street. He pulled open the door of his car, got in and at once drove off as though all the devils of hell were after him.

Alice sighed. He and Helen must have had a row. Or perhaps Terri caught them together. Really, she thought, Helen's hopeless. She might at least put him out of his misery one way or another.

Alice was wide awake now. She went downstairs in her night-dress to check she had put the cat out. She kept forgetting things like that these days. Then she remembered that she no longer had a cat. Fancy forgetting that, she told herself.

The thought of Phoebus made her want to cry. She must think of something else. She opened the back door to step into the garden to enjoy the beauty of the night for a moment before bed.

The air was crisp with a hint of woodsmoke, an old-fashioned, nostalgic smell. She sniffed again. Someone must have had a bonfire earlier, the scent of aromatic smoke was definitely in the air.

It was cold outside. Alice shivered and went back indoors. But that breath of fresh air had cleared her head of sad thoughts about poor Phoebus. And there was something consoling, too, about the smell of bonfire smoke, a nostalgic aspirin to ease the headache of tomorrow. Now she could go to bed and enjoy the simple pleasure of being warm and comfortable knowing it was cold outside, too cold for burglars. Or Kevin Miller.

She thought, I'll take a sleeping pill. Nothing will happen tonight.

Alice dreamed of a dark place full of confusion. She half woke and said aloud 'This isn't fair, this isn't part of this beautiful night,' but then she went back to sleep.

In the morning she felt as though she had spent a sleepless night. Even after she'd dressed and gone downstairs to put the kettle on, the dream still troubled her. She wasn't sure what had happened in it, or who had been there; she just couldn't shake off the atmosphere of ill-will that had permeated it and persisted now in spite of the blades of sunlight attacking her polished furniture through the window on this bright, clear morning.

What's the matter with me, she asked herself, looking down the street to make sure the Miller kids weren't hanging about before she opened the front door to bring in the milk. It had become automatic, that daily check that the coast was clear.

She couldn't see them, but when she opened the door she shut it again quickly against the smell. There was a horrible chemical smell out there, a sour stench of wet ash and burnt plastic.

From the window in her front room she had a better view. Something had happened to Number Five. There was a vast dark gash in the roof. The front of the house was stained black, and smoke crawled out of a broken window on the first floor. Part of the side wall of the building under the roof had collapsed and the remains of Nicky's bedroom were exposed. The bed was still smouldering, and a teddy bear, mutilated by the flames, hung by the threads of a knitted jacket from the end of a charred joist.

A police car drove up the street, did a screeching three-point turn outside Alice's house, and parked on the verge behind one of several red vans from the fire department. The actual fire-fighting appliances must have been and gone; what remained were Incident and Investigation vehicles.

Alice saw a curtain move in the front room of Number Two. Donna Miller must be watching, too. Has she seen me? Alice asked herself. Does she know I'm here? She wondered, does she think one of her teenagers was involved? And she thought, with satisfaction, whoever did it, they'll get the blame.

But of course Alice knew they hadn't done it. She could scarcely believe it, but there could be no doubt, she'd seen the way Dave had run away from that house in the moonlight.

Maybe Donna is looking at me, she thought, maybe all the Millers are in there together watching me and knowing that I know who did it. But I'm not going to tell. After what those Miller kids did to Phoebus, let them take the blame for this.

TWENTY

Because of their ongoing murder investigation in Forester Close, the Superintendent told DCI Moody and Sergeant Reid to treat the arson attack on Number Five as part of their inquiries.

'Here we go again,' Jack Reid said as he stopped the car.

'Ugh,' Rachel Moody said as she got out of the vehicle. 'What an awful smell.'

When they went into the house, the fire damage was not as bad as it had looked from outside in the street. Only the garage and the child's bedroom above it had suffered much more than cosmetic harm.

The fire investigators were on site.

Sergeant Reid knew their Chief. 'We might as well move in and save petrol,' Jack said. 'What's the story this time?'

'Hello again, Jack,' the Fire Chief said, 'how's the wife?'

'Not so bad,' Jack said. 'What's it this time, kids?'

'Could be. Deliberate, but it doesn't look as though it was much more than a prank. It could've been so much worse if it hadn't started in the garage.'

'Some kind of warning, d'you think?'

The Fire Chief shrugged. 'That's your problem. It was deliberate, but beyond that . . . The garage and the bedroom will have to be rebuilt, but there's no structural damage to the rest of the house. The insurance will be asking a few tough questions, I'd say. They won't be happy, that's all I can say at this stage, really.'

Rachel Moody was in the kitchen talking to Terri, Helen and Nicky. They sat round the table in the open plan dining area drinking coffee Terri had made.

'Are you all right?' Rachel asked her.

Terri seemed very calm, very efficient. She had already been talking to her insurance company, and to a firm of builders who were coming to secure the house and give her an estimate for repairing the damage.

Nicky was excited. Even, Rachel thought, thrilled.

'The spare room's my room now,' she told Rachel. 'Terri says I can do it as I want when the insurance money comes. I'll be able to get all new things.'

Helen alone looked devastated. Her hair, for some reason Rachel couldn't fathom, was dripping wet. She kept touching her face with her fingers, and there were black soot marks round her mouth and eyes.

'It was Dave,' she said. Her voice was shrill with hysteria. 'He always said he'd get me for leaving him, and this is what he's done. How could he do something like this to his own daughter?'

Rachel said, 'But surely . . .' She hesitated, then, sounding unconvinced, added, 'However bitter he was he wouldn't put his own daughter at risk. That's perverted.'

But Helen was certain. 'He knew Nicky wasn't in her room. He could see us all in the living room. I suppose he was desperate, he was afraid of losing me.'

Terri put her arm on Helen's shoulder. 'The man is mad,' she said. 'He's dangerous. Isn't that what I've said all along?'

'He's not really mad,' Helen said, 'he's desperate.'

She sounded as if this was something she could be proud of.

DCI Moody asked, 'Do you have any evidence that your ex-husband was involved?'

Helen quailed as though Rachel Moody had threatened her. 'Who else would it be?' she whispered. 'I've done everything I could to give him access to Nicky, but when he did see her, he was drunk and abusive and he terrified her with the scary things he said to me. She didn't want to see him ever again. She said so.'

'Yes, she did,' Terri said.

Helen started to cry. She looked abject, like someone made up to play the part of a waif.

'Then it all got messed up and suddenly he was saying I refused to give him access and it just got bitter.'

'But why should he say that if you didn't refuse?' Rachel said.

'The lawyer said it would be best if I refused to let him see her,' Helen said. 'And then after my lawyer said that, *his* lawyer went for full custody.'

'Why did his lawyer think he'd get that?'

'She – it was a she – said I wasn't a fit mother because I was living with Terri. Terri and I just wanted to settle down and make a home for Nicky, but then they started to say Terri was a corrupting influence and things like that. They said I was a man-hater and I would make it difficult for Nicky to form normal relationships with boys and other kids her own age.'

Helen broke off to blow her nose noisily. Then she went on, 'The lawyer also said Forester Close wasn't the right place to bring up a sensitive child. Dave would've done what he did to prove her right.'

Rachel found herself thinking that Dave had a point. The place gave her the willies. But of course ancient curses and silly super-stition had no part to play in a police investigation.

She asked, 'But why would setting fire to your house help your ex-husband's case?'

'Well, of course no one would know it was him, would they?' Helen said. 'He'd bank on that. He'd be able to say Nicky was in danger because Terri and I are being targeted because of our relationship. So this isn't a fit place for a child.'

Rachel nodded. Then she said gently, 'But surely he'd know that if he was caught, he'd lose all chance of getting custody.'

Helen started to weep again. She ignored Terri and Nicky, in fact she gave no sign of knowing they were listening to her.

'Dave was the one who wanted me to have a kid,' she said. 'I wasn't ready to be pregnant; he made me have a baby. And once I'd had her, she was weird, you must see that? I don't feel Nicky and I belong together at all, I never did. She always seemed like someone else's child. She still does. In fact, Terri's closer to her than I am.'

'She's very like you,' Terri said. She meant physically; the child's likeness to Terri's idea of how Helen must have been at that age was one of the reasons she wanted to protect Nicky.

'She's nothing like me.' Helen was angry. 'I was never like that. I was always a normal kid. She's not. She's on about some-thing she reads called *Crime and Punishment* all the time, she's obsessed with it. I think it must be some sort of report on prison statistics. It's not natural for a girl her age to study government reports about such things.'

'It's a book,' Terri said.

'Well, there you are, I told you so, she has unhealthy interests.'

It wasn't often that Rachel Moody was embarrassed by someone she was questioning, but now she was appalled by what Helen was saying in front of her own child.

'I think we'll leave it at that for now . . .' she said.

But Helen would not stop. 'I keep telling her she's got to get more normal,' she said. 'Like the other kids. What does she think's going to happen to her? She's got no interest in boys or the way she looks or anything normal. I've told her, she should watch out or she'll end up a lonely old freak like that Alice Bates up the road, but she takes no notice.'

Nicky suddenly shouted at her mother. 'I have got a boyfriend, I have,' she yelled. 'He loves me and I love him, but it's a secret.'

Terri said in a soft voice, 'Be quiet, Nicky.'

Nicky looked at her. There were tears in her eyes. 'I have,' she whispered.

Terri smiled at her. 'Of course you have,' she said, 'but that's your secret.'

Rachel got up to go. 'Where can I find Dave?' she asked. 'Whether or not he's involved in this attack, he should know it's happened. He is Nicky's father.'

Terri had already written Dave's telephone number on a scrap of paper. She handed it to Rachel.

'If it wasn't him, it could have been the kids,' she said. Then she remembered who she was talking about and quickly back-pedalled. 'Those Miller kids could've done it for a prank,' she said, and laughed as though trying to see the joke.

Nicky suddenly jumped to her feet. 'No,' she screamed at Rachel, 'no, it couldn't be them. You're a liar. Kevin wouldn't let them do this to me.'

Rachel looked at her with interest. Nicky was red-faced with passion or indignation, possibly both. Rachel was curious. She's not afraid of Kevin Miller, she thought, she's the only person I've met in this street who isn't. I wonder . . .

Jack was waiting by the car.

'Anything useful?' she asked. 'What does the Fire Chief think?'

'Deliberate, all right. Could be kids.'

'Or Helen's ex, according to the Odd Couple,' Rachel said. 'There's a custody battle over the child, apparently.'

'Even so, what kind of father would risk harming his own kid?' Jack said. He sounded doubtful.

'This is a kid who appears to be a friend of Kevin Miller's,' Rachel said. 'She seems to think he's protecting her.'

'What kind of friend?' Jack asked. 'Not the kind he picked up in a bar in Weston-super-Mare but he can't remember her name?'

Rachel laughed. 'Not yet, anyway,' she said. 'She reads *Crime and Punishment*. But let's see what Kevin has to say. He's at least nineteen, and she's about thirteen. You never know, we could get lucky.'

'*Crime and Punishment*?' Jack said. 'That's some kind of Russian story isn't it?'

'That's right,' Rachel said, 'I'm relieved to know someone in Somerset has heard of it at least. Most of the people in this street could be characters in it, as far as I'm concerned.'

TWENTY-ONE

Kevin was working on his motorbike on the concrete standing outside the Miller garage. He was concentrating on the intricacies of welding a split pipe on the exhaust system when Detective Chief Inspector Rachel Moody and Sergeant Reid parked across the driveway to Number Two.

'I don't care how you do it,' Rachel Moody told Reid as they got out of the car, 'but get him to resist arrest. That's the only way we're going to be able to hold him long enough to put the fear of God into him.'

Sergeant Reid nodded. He liked that about working with Rachel Moody, she wasn't afraid to take chances sometimes. This surprised him because she had come to them from the police force in Eastbourne and that wasn't a place he associated with the kind of crime and criminals you needed to take chances with.

He shut the car door and walked slowly to where Kevin was hunched over the red-hot blowlamp. Kevin didn't notice him coming, he was so intent on what he was doing.

'Kevin Miller?' Sergeant Reid said in the sort of tone an army sergeant might use to call the roll of raw recruits.

Kevin almost fell backwards in shock. Instinctively he raised his arm to steady himself, and instead brandished the lighted blowlamp as though it was a weapon.

'Back off, man,' Kevin yelled in protest.

Maybe it was a warning, but Reid needed no further excuse. 'Put down your weapon and kneel on the ground,' he said.

'I said back off,' Kevin said, waving the blowlamp to keep the policeman at bay. This time there was no room for doubt, it was a threat.

Rachel Moody had got behind Kevin and she grabbed his free arm and twisted it behind his back. Kevin dropped the blowlamp and once his hand was off the trigger, the flame went out.

Jack Reid handcuffed Kevin and dragged him to the car. Rachel got into the driving seat. 'Resisting arrest, threatening behaviour, assault with a deadly weapon,' she recited. 'That'll do for a start. We're taking you down to the station to question you about an arson attack on Number Five Forester Close.'

'*What?*' Kevin yelled. 'You can't pin that on me. I've got an alibi for that. I didn't have anything to do with it. You can't do this.'

'Yes I can,' Rachel said coldly. 'We're taking you in for questioning.'

'I was with a girl in Weston,' Kevin said. 'She'll tell you. I was with her all night.'

Rachel laughed. 'Oh, yes, you picked her up in a bar and went home with her but you don't know her name or where she lives. Don't tell me, I've heard it all before.'

At the station, the DCI and Sergeant Reid left Kevin Miller in the interview room before they talked to him.

'Give him time to cool his heels,' Rachel Moody said.

'What's our line?' Reid asked. 'Do we actually have anything against him?'

'We'll think of something,' Rachel Moody said.

'But we don't have anything concrete, do we?' the Sergeant insisted. 'We couldn't make anything stick then and we can't now on this arson charge.'

'Wrong attitude,' Rachel Moody said. 'This is what the Super wants. A fishing expedition.'

'It won't work,' Sergeant Reid said. 'I'll put money on it.'

'No dice,' Rachel said. 'We've got to go through the motions.'

The two of them went into the interview room and sat down opposite Kevin Miller.

'If you're going to fit me up I want a solicitor before I say anything,' Kevin said.

'Sure, when the time comes,' Rachel Moody said, smiling at him. 'This is just helping us with our enquiries.'

Kevin gave her a look which made Sergeant Reid start to get up from his chair to defend his boss.

'If that old witch at Number Three is the one who's trying to fit me up with this,' Kevin said, 'she's dead meat.'

Rachel Moody smiled again, very calm. 'Who do you mean, Kevin? Who do you think has told us about you?'

'That weirdo, Alice Bates,' Kevin shouted. 'She'd do anything to get me in trouble.'

'You mean because she sees what goes on in your street and you're afraid she saw you murder the vicar?' Rachel asked. She made it sound as if she were talking about the weather.

'She spies on everyone all the time,' Kevin said. 'But she didn't see me kill that vicar. She told you she didn't, isn't that right?'

Kevin realized he had made a mistake. He knew enough about the police to see that they would interpret what he'd said as some kind of admission of involvement in the vicar's death.

He laughed. 'Are you trying to make me think she's pretending she did see me murder him? Well, she didn't because she can't have seen me do something I didn't do, can she?'

Rachel said, 'This isn't about the vicar's death, Kevin. We're looking into the fire at Terri Kent's house. You say Alice Bates sees everything that goes on. Perhaps she saw you start the fire? What do you say to that?'

Rachel thought she detected a flicker of fear in Kevin's eyes.

He shouted 'No. She's lying.'

'Why should she lie, Kevin?' Rachel said.

'She's getting back at me because I killed her cat. I had nothing to do with that fire.' Kevin banged the table with his closed fist.

Jack Reid started to get to his feet again, but Kevin leaned back in his chair. Between gritted teeth he said, 'I swear, if she's fixed me up with this, I'll kill her.'

'Like you killed the vicar, Kevin?' Rachel Moody said.

'I want my brief,' Kevin Miller said.

Some time later, outside in the corridor, DCI Moody and Sergeant Reid watched Kevin Miller walk away with his solicitor.

'Well,' Reid said. 'At least we've got a confession to animal cruelty. He admits he killed Alice Bates's cat. I suppose it's a start. And he certainly threatened to kill the old woman. That was a definite death threat.'

'He's a nasty piece of work, with a limited vocabulary,' Rachel Moody said. 'That's just something he says. Even Kevin Miller isn't stupid enough to make a serious death threat against Alice Bates in front of us if he were serious about carrying it out.

Anyway, if we did make out a case for threatening behaviour, he'd get off with a caution. You know that as well as I do.'

Rachel was thinking of what the Superintendent was going to say.

Then she said, 'You don't think he'd really harm Alice Bates, do you?'

TWENTY-TWO

I t was early evening and Mark Pearson was hosing the yard after milking.

He heard a car drive up to the house and walked to the gate to see who it was. He wasn't expecting anyone.

The security light fixed to the front porch flooded the driveway. He recognized his mother's car. Joyce was opening the door to get out.

Bugger, Mark thought, I thought she'd gone out, what's *she* doing back so early? It's her bingo night.

He leaned on his broom, unwilling to break off his work. He didn't want Jess, when she came, to have to pick her way through the mess. Since the day he'd first met her, with the cattle chasing her down the lane, she didn't like the idea that he depended on animals for a living. She didn't like animals, any animals. And she'd be wearing those crazy shoes she always wore and they'd be ruined simply getting to the back door and that wouldn't be a good start to this first evening she'd ever spent at his house.

He thought, she'd expect me to carry her across. She'd like that.

But, rugby player though he was, he wasn't sure he was up to it.

He'd made sure Dad had gone up to bed. He'd seen the light in his bedroom go off half an hour before. His mother's bingo night was a regular fixture; she and her friends never missed it. And now here she was; she was going to spoil everything.

An hour ago he'd seen her off and waved goodbye. Mark hoped she had come home to pick up something she'd forgotten. It wouldn't be the first time.

He waved at her and turned back to his work.

Joyce Pearson waited in the car for a moment for him to come over to her, but when he didn't, she got out to go to him.

The sight of her came as a shock to him. It was the first time in a very long while that he had seen her not as his mother on the farm, but as the woman other people saw outside the home. Tonight she was dressed to go out, wearing a skirt and blouse instead of jeans and a T-shirt. He was startled that for a moment she was like a stranger and he saw her in an unfamiliar light. The woman he knew, with her unkempt hair and bags under her eyes, grumbling at the coldness of the kitchen floor through her slippers first thing in the morning, wasn't the same person as the smart and, yes, sexy figure who was making her way towards him across the gravel, wearing shoes almost as unsuitable as Jess's.

He began to walk to meet her.

'Is something wrong?' he asked. 'I didn't expect you back. Did the bingo get cancelled or something?'

What he wanted to say was 'You can't stay here, my girlfriend's coming and we'll be able to do it in a bed for the first time and please, please, don't spoil it for me,' but of course he couldn't. He knew he sounded surly because he wanted her to go but couldn't tell her.

He asked himself, is she trying to catch me out? Is that why she's here?

Joyce stopped smiling. She looked worried. He noticed how pale her face was.

Mark dropped the broom. 'What is it, Mum?' he said. 'Come into the kitchen. You look as if you need a drink.'

'I'd love a cup of tea,' she said, and suddenly she looked like the morning mum he was used to, with her old dressing gown wrapped round her.

In the kitchen she kicked off her shoes and sat at the table holding the mug of tea he'd given her in both hands to warm them.

'Dad's gone up,' he said.

She suddenly looked him in the eyes and blurted out: 'Mark, it's about that girl of yours from the new housing estate.'

At once he was on the defensive. She'd never mentioned before that she knew he had a girlfriend, let alone who the girl was.

'What's that to you?' he said, 'I'm not a kid any more.'

'Yes, but she is. Isn't she still at school?' his mother said. 'But it's not just that. My friends were full of it tonight. They're all worried about you. It's what they're saying about her family. I came to tell you as soon as I heard.'

'Heard what?' he said rudely. 'And what do those women know, saying things?'

'It's about that murder on the estate. When poor Tim Baker was beaten to death.'

'What about it?' he asked. 'What's that got to do with her? You don't think she did it, do you?'

It's just as Jess says, he thought, people like her get blamed for everything bad that happens.

His mother hesitated. She seemed frightened as well as concerned. 'A man in the post office told Rose Dacre it's true,' she said, as though trying to shift the blame for what she was about to tell him.

'What's true?' he almost shouted at her.

'The police have arrested the brother of that girl of yours for murder,' Joyce said, the words coming out with a rush.

Mark stared at her. It crossed his mind that she was making it up as part of some scheme to make him break off with Jess.

'He's only her half-brother,' he said. Then he added, 'That can't be true.'

He thought of Jess's brother, the thug who'd made the bullocks stampede, leader of the gang who'd hunted him and Jess like animals the night the old woman on Forester Close let them take refuge in her house. The brother was a moron, and definitely violent, Mark thought, but that didn't make him a cold-blooded murderer. The bullock business was brute ignorance, and the other thing probably started as a bit of drunken fun. Jess's brother was a bully; he wouldn't have the guts to do anything as bad as cold-blooded murder, not on his own.

'No,' Mark said, 'that can't be right.'

'People don't get arrested for nothing,' Joyce said.

'They've got to arrest somebody or people say they're not doing their job,' Mark said. 'They arrest a lot of people and it turns out to be for nothing and they let them go.'

Joyce looked at him and didn't know what to do. His face was stony, hostile in a way she'd never seen him. He's not my little boy any more, she told herself, he's got hard. I don't know who he is these days. And then she thought, is it my fault, what's happened to him? Between us, Bert and I must have driven him into taking up with that awful girl.

'It gets worse,' she said.

'It's nothing to do with Jess,' he said. 'Why do you keep blaming her?'

'Rose says she's got a kid. A little girl about a year old.'

Mark laughed. 'You shouldn't listen to gossip,' he said. 'That's her kid sister. I know about that.'

'Ask her, Mark, please make her tell you the truth. If it's not true, I'm sorry, but you've a right to know what people are saying. If it is true, she's taking you for a ride. Rose says the murdering brother is the child's father.'

'Half-brother,' he said again.

Mark wanted to hit her. Or, rather, he wanted to hit the man in the post office who'd filled his mother's silly friend's head with this poison.

'It's all a filthy lie,' he said. 'Tell that man in the post office who told your friend this rubbish that if he ever tells lies like that about Jess again, I'm coming to get him.'

His voice was very cold, and his eyes, meeting Joyce's, were hard as flint.

'Mark, be careful. Rose only passed the gossip on because that's what people are saying and she thought I should warn you. Are you so sure it isn't true?'

'Yes,' he shouted at her, 'yes, I am.'

'That's OK then,' she said. 'I thought I ought to tell you, that's all.'

Mark was thinking, Jess would have told me something like that. About the baby, not the brother. That can't be true. She wouldn't do it with Kevin. He probably raped her.

He realized that he was talking himself into believing his mother.

'No,' he said. 'It's not true.'

Joyce watched his face as he struggled not to doubt Jess.

He's beginning to think it could be true, she told herself, he doesn't trust her.

'Can I do anything for you?' she asked him. It struck her that she was treating him like someone bereaved, a bereaved acquaintance.

'No,' he said. 'You get back to your friends. Tell that Rose Dacre she shouldn't listen to gossip.'

'Pompous prat,' Joyce said, and laughed at him.

'Don't worry, Mum,' he said, and at last she detected a glimmer of affection in his voice, 'Jess isn't what you think she is. Once you get to know her . . .'

Was the affection for me or for her? Joyce asked herself.

But Mark, when his mother had gone, had no heart to go out and finish sweeping the yard.

Jess didn't come. He tried her mobile and it was switched off. He checked the telephone in the house to see if anyone had called. There was no new text from her on his mobile. He walked around the house in a daze, staying close to the telephone until he knew that it was too late, she wouldn't be coming.

At last he went out and started to walk up the lane. There was going to be a frost, he could feel how the cold air pinched his nose and fingers and toes. The night sky was very clear, the stars and the crescent moon shining bright and hard in the blue-black sky. Mark could smell the earthy scent of damp dead leaves and as he passed the field where he'd turned out the milking herd he could hear the cows breathing softly behind the hedge.

In spite of Jess and Kevin and his mother and all the mess of his life, Mark felt comforted by the enormity of the universe surrounding him. The stars went on forever. Nothing seemed to matter much in the face of that.

As he walked into the house, the telephone was ringing.

'Jess,' he said, 'where are you? Has something happened? I've been worried.'

'You're always worried,' Jess said. 'It's my fucking mum. She's gone out and left me to babysit my little sister. She said she wouldn't be long and she's been gone for hours. I'll come when she gets back, OK?'

'Jess, hang on, there's something . . .' Mark hesitated, unable to ask the question. He said instead, 'It's something they're saying about your brother; something about him being arrested for the murder of Tim Baker . . .'

There was a short silence, and then the quiet way she reacted surprised him.

'Well, he hasn't,' she said, 'he hasn't been arrested. They asked him questions about something else but they let him go. Even the cops don't think he's guilty of every bloody crime that happens. It's only those horrible old has-beens in your stupid village think like that and you should tell them to mind their own fucking business and not tell lies about innocent people or they'll end up in bloody *court*, OK?'

Mark tried to make light of it. He laughed. 'OK, OK,' he said, 'I just thought you ought to know what people are saying, that's all. Don't worry about it. When do you think you might get away?'

He was thinking, I ought to feel relieved, but I don't. It's not that I don't believe her when she says it's a lie, it's that I believe it could so easily be true.

Jess said, 'Not tonight. Not now, it's too late. I'll ring you tomorrow.' She sounded as non-committal as someone answering the phone in a call centre. There was something in her voice that made him feel relieved that she would not be coming after all.

It's this bloody feud between her lot and mine, he thought, it's even getting us involved. She didn't like me saying that about Kevin, she thinks I'm against him. And then he told himself, I am against him and she's on his side, she doesn't even think twice, she's defending him. Against me.

'Jess,' he said, taking a deep breath. He had to find out. 'There's something else,' he said.

He wanted to be cruel, to hurt her.

'What is it?' she said.

He could tell by a sudden eagerness in her voice that she was expecting him to tell her that he wanted her, that he loved her.

'It's about Kylie,' he said. 'Mum's friend told her she's your kid. He says she's not your sister. It isn't true, is it?'

He heard her gasp. Then she put the phone down.

TWENTY-THREE

Alice turned off the television. She was disappointed. Year after year the preparations on screen for the Christmas festivities – the cooking programmes, the jolly advertisements, and the decorations – made her feel part of something warm, friendly and fun.

But not this year. Now there was no help at all to get her into the Christmas spirit. She'd hoped to be transported in her imagination to somewhere thrilling, with ice and snow and a sky of sparkling stars outside, but it hadn't worked. It was hard to feel goodwill towards all men in a sodden, windswept, lonely, Forester Close.

In the street, only the Millers had made an effort. Donna and Alan had spent the afternoon outlining their home in bright coloured lights. A hugely obese inflatable figure of Father Christmas sat astride the roof of the porch over the front door, waiting for galloping reindeer etched in neon to pull a painted sleigh across the front wall of the house. From somewhere inside his vast belly came the tinny notes of a taped carol which could have been *Good King Wenceslas* or *The Holly and the Ivy*, Alice couldn't tell which.

The wind was strong enough to rock the Father Christmas figure and his decorated sleigh so that they actually seemed to be moving, setting the sleigh bells jangling. The red, green and blue lights on the house were reflected on the wet pavement, turning the street into a spangled 'fifties dance floor where dead leaves flickered like jiving feet.

It was like watching an old movie, Alice thought, one of those American films with music and singing and dancing and lots of chiffon dresses with sequins. Any minute now, Fred Astaire might whirl across the road from backstage in the ruins of Number Five to start his big number.

The ten o'clock news came on the television with its relentless catalogue of man's inhumanities to man. Alice turned it off.

In the sudden silence, she heard a muffled sound from the kitchen.

Alice felt the familiar prickling of sweat on her palms. Her hands and feet were suddenly very cold. The tightening fear in her chest left her breathless, painfully aware of the thumping of her heart.

She listened, holding her breath, but heard nothing.

Perhaps I imagined it, she thought. It was hard not to imagine things in this big echoing dark house all on her own. Perhaps, with Phoebus gone, a mouse had got into the kitchen. Then she tried to tell herself that the wind was catching the tarpaulin the builders had used to cover the open wall of the room above the garage at Number Five after the fire.

But Alice knew the noise she had heard did not come from outside. Something was wrong. It was in the room with her. A chill seemed to have crept through the house, filling it with menace.

Stop it, she told herself, you're imagining things. There's nothing there.

She got up slowly and tiptoed into the hall to go upstairs.

I'll go to bed, she thought, I'll check the kitchen tomorrow. I expect it was the wind.

There was a faint, unfamiliar smell in the hall, sweet and stale. Alice sniffed the air. What was it? Not scent, exactly, more like the way a crowded bus smells when the passengers have been out in the rain, attractive and repellent at the same time.

'Hallo, Miss Bates, come to join me?'

The voice stabbed Alice like the blade of a sharp knife.

She knew who it was, knew that cloying smell. She played for time.

'Who is it? Who's there?' she whispered.

Someone came towards her from the kitchen. She tried to retreat, but she could not move away from the wall, she was paralyzed with fear.

'It's me, of course. Surely you've been expecting me?'

The light was suddenly switched on.

Kevin Miller, wearing his motorcycling leathers and a helmet with the visor raised so that she could see his cold, pale blue eyes, came through the kitchen door and down the hall towards her.

'No,' Alice stammered. 'I was looking at the pretty lights on your house. I thought there must be a party.'

'You weren't invited,' Kevin said. 'You've been poking your nose in where you're not invited, haven't you?'

He lunged forward suddenly and gripped her thin arm, bending it back behind her.

Alice cried out in pain.

Kevin released her arm. He was disgusted at the feel of the dry loose skin covering the bones.

But Alice tried to take it as a sign of hope that he was not beyond human feeling.

'Thank you,' she said, 'I'm afraid even shaking hands can hurt when you're as old as me.'

The apparent confidence of her appeal to his sympathy enraged him.

'Shut up,' he said. 'You need to be taught a lesson. That's what I've come for.'

Her voice quivering because her teeth were chattering, Alice said, 'Did I leave the back door open? I keep doing that.'

'Shut up,' he said again, this time with more venom. 'I broke the lock.'

Alice was shaking with fright. She knew she must try to hide her fear, but she couldn't. She found she couldn't speak without stuttering.

'What do you want, Kevin? What are you looking for?'

He pushed her towards the kitchen. 'Stop asking me stupid fucking questions,' he hissed at her. 'You keep your mouth shut and we'll get on fine as long as you do what I tell you.'

'But why?' she said, 'why are you here?'

He snarled at her. 'As if you didn't know,' he said. 'Don't pretend you don't know the cops are watching my house. So I'm going to be staying with you for a bit. It's only fair. You set them on me, didn't you?'

'No,' she wailed, 'no, I didn't. I haven't said a word to anyone.'

'Don't tell me that,' he said. 'They said they had a tip-off. Who else would it have been?'

'It wasn't me,' she said. 'Please, Kevin, it wasn't me. I swear it wasn't.'

'D'you think I'm stupid?' he shouted at her. 'You were

watching, weren't you? When that vicar bought it? That's all you're good for, isn't it? Spying on people.'

'No, no,' Alice said, pleading. 'I never told anybody, I wouldn't dare.'

Kevin looked triumphant. 'So you did see?' He took off his helmet and smoothed his hair. That's the smell, Alice told herself, it's the gel he puts on his hair.

'You're going to be sorry,' he said. 'I'll make you sorry.'

He bared his teeth. He smiled like a dog, Alice thought, you couldn't be sure he wasn't going to bite.

She said in her quivering voice, 'I'd never tell, you know I wouldn't. What are you going to do to me?'.

He did not hide his disgust at her withered face and her knobbly body and her dry flaking lips.

'Shut up,' he said once more, 'shut up and get me something to eat. Don't you know how to treat a guest?'

Alice walked unsteadily to the fridge, but when she opened the door the shelves were empty. She'd been going to do her shopping tomorrow.

'There's cake,' she said. 'There's a cake in that tin in the cupboard. I made it in case Jean Henson wanted to come over and have a chat at teatime.'

Kevin reached up and pulled the cake tin from the cupboard shelf. He ripped open the lid and broke off a fistful of the sponge cake inside.

He spat it out. 'Yuck,' he said, 'it's like eating sawdust.'

'There's nothing else,' she said. 'I was going to do some shopping tomorrow.'

Kevin began to pull out the kitchen drawers, tossing cutlery and plates on to the floor.

At last he pulled out a new washing line Alice kept as a spare in case vandals cut the one in her garden. That happened several times over the year.

'This'll do,' he said. 'This'll keep you quiet until we get to understand each other better.'

'You can't stay here,' Alice said. 'You won't be safe. The police might come . . .'

She stopped, realizing what she had said, but it was too late.

'You see, I knew it was you. The coppers' nark.'

He sounded triumphant.

'No,' she said, 'it wasn't me. I'd never do that. I didn't see anything. I'd nothing to tell them.'

Kevin could hear how scared she sounded. He grinned at her. 'You're not my idea of a hot date for Christmas either,' he said. 'But you've only yourself to blame. You put the police on to me, and I can't stay at home till they lay off. This is the last place the cops will look for me, thanks to you.'

He suddenly started to laugh. 'As you sow, so shall you reap,' he said. 'Isn't that what that vicar would've said?'

Kevin shoved her back out into the hall, pushing her against the banister.

'Lift your arms up,' he said, 'stretch them out.'

As best she could, she did as she was told. He wrenched her hands upwards and outwards beyond their natural reach. She didn't know how she was going to be able to bear the pain. She moaned, but he took no notice. He used the new washing line to lash her wrists to the closest spindles, wrapping the cord round the handrail to prevent her sliding her arms lower.

'OK,' he said, 'you asked for this. You're going to pay.

He wound some of the line round her neck and the closest spindle.

'There,' he said, 'that's not too tight, is it? As long as you don't move there'll be no bruises to show.'

Then he stood back to survey his handiwork.

He laughed again, imitating her terrified expression and raising his arms in the shape of a vulture standing over its prey.

'There,' he said, 'you look like an old witch ready to be burned at the stake.'

Alice tried to speak but she could only make little whimpering sounds at the back of her throat.

'I'm going down the takeaway,' he said, 'I'll be back. Then I'll tell you what's going to happen. I'm going to be here for a while. No one is going to know where I am, got it? And you won't be telling anyone, will you, you ugly old bat? You won't be telling your police friends anything for a long time to come. Got it?'

He turned off the light. There was a faint click as he went out the back door, then silence. Alice, straining her ears for any sound, heard only the frantic thumping of her own blood in her ears.

In the alley that ran behind the back gardens of the houses on Forester Close, Kevin whistled and then whispered, 'Are you there, kid? You can come out now.'

There was a muffled yelp, then someone stepped out from behind a load of trash that had been dumped beside the fence.

Nicky Byrne's voice was muffled. 'How did you know I was here?' she asked.

'D'you think I don't know you've been following me around?' Kevin said.

'I can't help it,' Nicky said, 'I've got to tell you. I love you, Kevin, I really love you.' She was ready to cry. 'Please, don't send me away.'

'Piss off, you stupid kid. Does your mum know you're out?' he said.

Nicky came up close to him and pressed herself against him. She shook her head. 'No chance,' she said, 'she and Terri went to bed hours ago.'

Kevin grimaced at the thought of those two women in bed together.

Nicky's hot breath was in his ear. 'Let me stay with you, please, oh please, Kevin, don't make me go away. I'll do anything you want.'

'You'll have to make yourself useful,' he said.

'Anything you say, Kevin,' she said.

'OK, OK, get off me,' he said. 'You can run down the chippy for me. Get whatever you want too and bring it back here.'

'You mean me and you will be together?'

He pulled a twenty pound note out of the breast pocket of his leather jacket.

He said, 'This isn't kids' stuff. Don't let anyone see you come back here, right?'

'Oh, I won't, I promise I won't.'

'I'll be in Alice's place,' he said. 'She's asked me to stay there with her for a bit.'

'Oh, that's fantastic,' she said. 'I can come over every night and look after you, it'll be like we're really married.'

Kevin pushed her away from him. 'Don't be so fucking stupid,' he said.

'Why do you want to stay with her? She's gross.'

'I expect she's lonely,' Kevin said. 'It's Christmas, she'll be glad of the company.' He grinned at her.

Nicky said, 'Does Alice know? She won't like it.'

'Don't you worry about Alice,' he said. 'She won't mind. She doesn't have any say in it.'

'Oh,' Nicky said, trying to hug him, 'this is going to be the best Christmas ever.'

TWENTY-FOUR

Winter tightened its grip on Forester Close over Christmas. The temperature scarcely rose above freezing, even during the middle of the day, with a ruthless east wind and the dismal grey blight it carries with it across the landscape. The birds stopped singing in the leafless shrubs in the gardens, and daffodils which had ventured above the wet black soil to test the air retracted their green shoots to wait for more convincing signs of spring. Even at noon, it was as though daylight could not quite make up its mind to announce its arrival and started to tiptoe away before anyone noticed. People left the curtains in their upstairs windows closed all day, but there was no one looking up in the street to wonder if they were ill. Or even dead.

And then, as soon as New Year was over, the wind changed and great bluff grey clouds scudded across the bone-coloured sky. Suddenly Forester Close was jerked out of its deep sleep.

In Number Five, still shrouded in builders' tarpaulins waiting for the workmen to return from their holiday break, Nicky came into Helen's room early in the morning. She pulled the curtains open, shouting, 'Mummy, Mummy, something's happening.'

Helen and Terri both sat up in bed. The room was full of queer orange and bluish lights.

'What is it?' Helen said, yawning. 'Has something set off a burglar alarm?'

'If that bastard Dave's set fire to another house now, I'll kill him,' Terri said, but she did not sound convinced by her own bravado.

At Number Four, Jean Henson, an early riser since Peter's death, was downstairs looking out of the sitting-room window. 'What's happened?' she asked herself, speaking aloud as though Peter were still there, 'the street's full of police cars.'

Since the morning when the police had come to tell her of Peter's suicide, Jean was very disturbed by the sight and sound of any of the emergency services. And now here they were back in the road in front of her house.

For a moment she wondered if she were dreaming. Since Peter's death her dreams had been so real and so painful that she dreaded going to sleep. Perhaps this was one of them and in a moment she would wake up and find the scene in the street was just part of a nightmare.

Oh, Peter, she said to herself, if only you were here. How could you go and leave me alone like this?

Real or unreal, it didn't matter now. The sirens were screaming, and ghostly giants in weird masks and vast protective suits milled on the street outside her house.

Jean could not bear this alone. She pulled on her coat and slipped out of the house. If anyone knew what was happening, it would be Alice; she'd go and ask her.

But she could not reach Alice's house without running the gauntlet of a posse of police and fire officers. Taking care not to be seen, she fled past the demolished side wall of Number Five to hammer on the back door, calling Terri's name.

Terri, in striped pyjamas, opened the door and pulled her inside.

'What's Kevin Miller done now?' Jean said. 'What's happening, do you know?'

'No idea,' Terri said, 'but I don't think it's the Millers. Nicky says they're all over Alice's place.'

'It can't be. What on earth would Alice have been getting up to?' Jean said. She felt weak and dizzy.

Terri took Jean's hand. 'Don't worry,' she said, 'it's probably a false alarm. Or perhaps Alice thought she heard an intruder and dialled nine nine nine.'

But Jean could not be placated. 'Perhaps she did hear an intruder,' she said, and her voice sounded doomed.

'Those aren't ordinary cops,' Nicky said. 'It's terrorists at least; or a chemical leak. They've got breathing apparatus.'

She was excited, rushing round the house seeking the best view of what the emergency services were doing in the street.

All day people in white overalls, wearing masks and huge rubber gloves, moved in and out of Alice's house. Uniformed cops sealed off her driveway, and there was a police check point at the end of the Close where it met the main road.

And all day the other residents stayed hidden, watching behind closed curtains, conscious that they were silent witnesses to something stupendous, though they did not know what it was.

The drama was not diminished when they knew what had happened.

The milkman, barred from entering Forester Close, drove his float down the alley behind the houses to make his deliveries.

'All this is because of me,' he told Terri, Helen, Nicky and Jean, who were gathered in the kitchen of Number Five. 'I'm the one discovered it.'

'Discovered what?' Terri asked.

The milkman, called Fred, looked shocked at the enormity of what he had started.

'Here,' Helen said, 'sit down and have a cup of tea. You don't look well.'

'Tell us what happened,' Nicky said. 'Why are all those men wearing all that special gear?'

'It was all the milk bottles she never took in,' Fred said. 'I thought she must've gone away for Christmas and forgotten to leave me a note.'

'Alice never went away anywhere,' Jean said. She sounded full of foreboding.

'I took the bottles away when she didn't take them in,' Fred said. 'It doesn't do to leave milk bottles on the doorstep; it's a signal to thieves. Then after ten days I tried looking through the letter box and saw the post she hadn't collected. But that didn't mean anything, not if she'd gone away, did it?'

'No,' Terri said, 'not if she'd gone away.'

Fred began to look green and had to take a swig of tea before he could go on.

'It was the smell,' he said. 'I couldn't help noticing the smell.'

'What smell?' Nicky said.

'Perhaps she'd put a turkey out to defreeze and forgotten it before she went away?' Terri prompted him.

'But if she was going away, she wouldn't have had a turkey, would she?' Jean said.

'No,' Fred said, 'that's the conclusion I came to myself. I knocked at Mrs Miller's and asked if she knew if her neighbour at Number Three was taking a holiday?'

'What did she say?' Helen asked.

'She said she's not the friendly type, I haven't seen her since before Christmas,' Fred said. 'Some people, eh? No sense of community.'

'Quite,' Terri said.

There was a pause. Then Fred said, 'I called the cops. I thought I'd better.'

'But what's happened?' Terri almost shouted at him. 'What did they find?'

'They found her,' Fred said. 'She'd been dead all that time. She was lying dead at the bottom of the stairs.'

Terri gasped.

'Alice is dead?' Jean Henson whispered. 'My God, Alice is dead.'

'What are the police saying?' Terri asked Fred. She looked as though she was about to shake the information out of him.

'Her face was frozen in an expression of abject horror, one of the young cops told me,' Fred said.

'Do they think she was murdered?' Nicky asked.

Her clear childish voice in that context shocked them all.

Fred got up to go. 'I don't know what's happening now,' he said. 'That's what they're doing now, I suppose, finding out if someone killed her.'

'It was probably an accident,' Nicky said. 'Old people fall down stairs.'

'More likely Kevin Miller's got his own back,' Jean said. Her hands were shaking and she was very white. 'He said he would,' she said. Then she started to cry.

In Alice's house, DCI Moody and Sergeant Reid watched as the body was removed from the house.

Rachel Moody sighed. 'Well,' she said, 'what do you make of it?'

Jack Reid closed his notebook. 'Not suicide, anyway,' he said.

Rachel gave him a quick look. 'Are you saying that because you really believe it, or because this is Forester Close and you think the odds favour a violent death?' she asked.

Jack said, 'There's just no reason to think she killed herself. No note, nothing. And she hadn't made her bed. She was the sort of woman who wouldn't want a stranger finding an unmade bed. It looks like an accident to me. A frail old woman caught short in the middle of the night trips on her way to the bathroom and falls down stairs. It's easily done.'

'What about that gash on the back of her head?'

'She could easily have hit her head on the newel post on her way down. There was a lot of bruising and that would explain it.'

'And the facial injuries?'

'If she did a somersault after bashing the back of her head in she'd land face down on those tiles in the hall,' Jack Reid said.

'But the body wasn't face down when we found it, was it?' Rachel said. 'She was staring up at us with that terrified look on her face.'

'Are you saying you think she was murdered?' Sergeant Reid asked. He looked doubtful. 'What would anyone gain from killing someone like that?'

'Quite,' Rachel said. 'But then you'd think no one would want to murder a poor harmless little vicar, but someone killed Tim Baker, didn't they?'

'Don't tell me you think you can pin this on Kevin Miller?' Jack Reid said. He was startled at her attitude. She seemed to be complicating a simple issue, which wasn't like her. 'What makes you think you could?' he said.

She didn't say anything. She knew that he was thinking she'd taken leave of her senses. Part of her agreed with him.

She shrugged. 'Hope springs eternal,' she said, 'but you're probably right. At the moment, accident looks the most likely cause of death. But we'll keep an open mind, right?'

'Forensics are nearly finished here,' Reid said. 'We'll have to wait for the autopsy, anyway.'

'Find out what's known about her, will you?' Rachel said. 'Alice Bates, I mean. Who was she? Where did she come from? Who did she know? Perhaps the neighbours can tell us something.'

Jack Reid laughed. 'This is Forester Close,' he said, 'I wouldn't put money on it.'

'Maybe,' Rachel Moody said, 'but we've got to go through the motions. You go back to the station and do what you can there.'

'If you think it's worth the effort,' Jack said. 'What are you going to do?'

'I'll stay on here and look through her personal stuff,' Rachel said. 'There may be papers, letters, photos, anything to give us some idea why anyone would think it worth killing her.'

'I thought we'd agreed no one did kill her,' Jack said. 'She fell down the stairs.'

Rachel shrugged and didn't answer.

He said, 'You really don't think it was an accident then?'

'Oh, probably,' she said. 'But bear with me. I can't help thinking there's something not quite right about this. That look on her face.'

'Falling down stairs would be enough to make her look like that, surely?' Jack said.

'We'll do this my way all the same,' the DCI said.

Jack was shaking his head as he walked to his car.

When the last of the Scene of Crime people gathered up their equipment and left, Rachel Moody was alone in the house. The flashing blue lights in the street had gone, and all the unmarked cars except her own. It was once again as though nothing had happened in Forester Close.

Rachel tried to search Alice Bates's desk and cupboards. She had a feeling like a series of faint electric shocks every time she touched something that had belonged to Alice, as though she were feeling Alice's distress at the invasion of her privacy. There was an atmosphere of disapproval throughout the house. Rachel felt she was violating something secret and personal in Alice's life; something that when she grasped it would be full of menace.

Why menace, she asked herself. Where does that come from? What could intimidate her in her own home?

God, Rachel thought, all I know is how scared and unhappy she was.

But why, she asked herself, why do I think that?

Rachel was getting nowhere. She rang Jack Reid to see how he was doing. Nothing.

Jack had even rung a contact on the local paper to see if the press was doing any better.

The paper had set out to try to discover details about Alice's past. There weren't any. The journalists' best efforts were embarrassed finally by the pathetic facts; a scraped pass at Grade One in piano at the age of twelve; a few undistinguished 'O' Levels; lapsed membership of a library in a suburb of the Midlands city where she'd lived most of her life in a tower block with her mother before moving to Forester Close. The reporters could find no evidence that she'd ever been abroad on holiday, or worked in an office; she'd never learned to drive, she'd had three teeth filled as a child, and she was registered with a local doctor in the Community Centre at Catcombe Mead. He had never met her.

No ex-lovers, no friends, no life at all, as far as the police were concerned. What possible motive could there be for killing Alice Bates?

'Until you tell us different we've put this one down as accidental death,' the reporter told Sergeant Reid.

But when Rachel ended the call to Jack, she could not leave it at that. For several minutes she stood at the living-room window staring down the empty street. She was trying to imagine how it would have felt to be Alice Bates.

Somewhere in one of the houses on the main road a dog was barking. A small dog, Rachel thought, probably a terrier. Did Alice like dogs? No one would ever know now.

Then a cat leapt down from the garden wall of Number Five and streaked across the road.

Alice had a cat, Rachel told herself. Hadn't Kevin Miller admitted to killing it?

He must have had something against her to do that, Rachel thought. He was punishing her for something she'd done. Or, of course, something he thought she'd done. Perhaps that was just the beginning of Kevin's retribution.

Rachel opened the drawers in a desk by the radiator. Surely there must be some evidence somewhere of Alice's life before Forester Close; photographs, perhaps, old letters, or bills addressed to Alice at an old address.

After more than an hour, Rachel admitted defeat. She had to hold on to the image of that broken old body at the foot of the stairs to convince herself that Alice Bates had existed at all.

There were no letters, no family photographs, no old bank statements. Rachel had to accept that the woman really had no life. Poor old thing, she thought, she'd died at Christmas. And yet there was no festive food in the fridge; no celebratory bottle of wine; no greetings cards or wrapped presents. There was an old TV listings magazine for the Christmas week. Alice appeared to have planned to spend the festival watching television. That seemed to be the extent of her contact with the world outside Forester Close.

Half-heartedly, Rachel started asking the residents of Forester Close what they knew about Alice Bates. She had a bad feeling about this inquiry. People weren't being obstructive; they simply had nothing to offer. It soon became clear that the old woman's neighbours were aware of her only as an almost unseen presence, watching them from behind the curtains at the window of her front room. They rarely saw her, but they were conscious that she was there, part of the background scenery.

As for knowing something about her, no one had anything to tell.

Alice Bates had arrived in Forester Close leaving no trace of how she got there. Her neighbours moved in, and she was already there. And now that she was dead, it soon seemed to Rachel Moody that she was not so much looking for a killer, she was trying to find out who it was who had been killed. Alice seemed to have arrived and stayed where she was put as dumbly as a house plant moved to a larger pot.

Rachel finished her interviews with neighbours. She returned to Alice's house and stood in the sitting-room listening to the heavy silence that so often, in her experience, froze the atmosphere in a house after something momentous had taken place there. Jack Reid called it her doom mood to mock her, but it wasn't so different from the policeman's hunches he was prone to himself.

She was about to leave the house when she heard the front door open.

'It's me, Boss,' Sergeant Reid shouted.

'Anything to report?' she said, going out into the hall to meet him.

He shook his head. 'Any chance of a cup of tea?' he said. 'I need cheering up.'

They went into Alice's kitchen and Jack filled the kettle while Rachel found teabags in the cupboard and milk in the fridge. She sniffed the bottle.

'It's off,' she said. 'It must've been sitting there since the day she died.'

'Black tea, then.' He grimaced. 'I've tried all the neighbours,' he said, 'but not one can remember when they last saw her alive. They're not trying to be awkward; at least I don't think they are. She seems to have been someone people didn't register.'

'I know,' Rachel Moody said. 'I've found the same thing.'

'Surely you don't still think it wasn't an accident?'

She frowned, biting her lip. 'I wouldn't put money on it,' she said, teasing him. 'But don't ask me why I'm so sure, Jack. I mean, who'd want to murder someone like that. What the hell was the point?'

TWENTY-FIVE

Mark Pearson, on his way late in the afternoon to meet Jess on the road outside the supermarket in Catcombe Mead, called in at the Co-op in the village to buy cigarettes. Not for himself, but for Jess. She was always out of them because, she said, Kevin and Nate stole them if she bought them for herself.

Mark hadn't seen Jess since the night before Christmas when she'd put the phone down on him. He had tried to ring her over the holiday, and left messages, but she hadn't returned any of his calls.

Then this morning he'd sent her a text asking her to meet him that evening. He'd told her when and where he'd pick her up. He'd ended the message 'I miss you'. Then he turned his mobile phone off. No point in giving her the chance to refuse.

He didn't know what he was going to say to her, but it would help to put her in a good mood if he bought her cigarettes and maybe chocolates as a peace offering. It crossed his mind that he should not give her chocolates, she should lose weight. She'd never speak to me again if she knew I thought that, Mark told himself.

The Co-op was unusually crowded. Mark joined the queue for the checkout. He was used to the leisurely pace of the service, but today was different. Nobody seemed to want to move forward. They were all involved in what seemed to be a single whispered conversation, all part of a sort of suppressed glee as though they were licking their lips after eating forbidden chocolates.

'What is it?' Mark asked a young woman holding a child's hand in front of him in the queue. 'What's happened?'

'Another death on the new housing estate,' the woman said. 'A poor old woman battered to death in her own home. On Christmas Day, too.'

'He must be some sort of Satanist fiend,' said another woman with her.

An old lady looked puzzled. 'Who, dear?'

'The murderer of course,' said the mother's friend. 'Wasn't his previous victim the vicar? And now this one at Christmas. Was this new poor victim a churchgoer?'

The old lady ignored this. 'Homicide Close, my Herbie calls it,' she said. 'Can you believe it, all that death in one place?'

A middle-aged man in front of them in the queue picked up his shopping and turned away from the counter. He tipped his tweed cap to the women. 'They should declare that Forester Close an open prison and have done with it,' he said. 'There's nothing but criminals and perverts living there.'

'The poor woman who was murdered wasn't a criminal,' the old lady said.

'That's why they killed her then,' the man said, pleased that he had proved his point. 'You mark my words.'

'Bullies and criminals and perverts every one of them,' the old lady said. She hesitated and then lowered her voice as though she had a secret to tell. 'They'll all be up in arms because of the effect on the value of their houses, won't they? That's all they really care about, you know.'

'I wouldn't live in a place like that if you paid me,' the young mother said.

'Didn't we always say that no good would come of building those houses and bringing all those townies here?' said the man in the cap.

It's not fair, Mark thought, not everyone on the estate is like that; Jess isn't. Should I say something, he asked himself, should I stick up for her?

He knew there was no point. He didn't really believe his own argument. Jess *was* like that, he couldn't deny it; she'd never pretended she wasn't, hadn't she defended Kevin against him.

'I've got to go,' Mark said.

He pushed his way past the people crowded round the checkout and out of the shop. Jess would have to go without cigarettes for once, he had to get away from those people and what struck him as their vicarious enjoyment of a local murder. He couldn't bear their air of expectation of disaster vindicated.

As he walked towards the pickup he thought, that's because I feel the same way, I'm like those gossips; I can't defend Jess against them.

He wondered, as he drove off towards Catcombe Mead, who had been murdered this time.

He thought, it has made a difference to me and Jess, the things that have happened. I know she didn't have anything to do with it. But then he told himself, I don't know that. I'm not sure. I don't know which side she's on. If it's that brother of hers who's killed the old woman, she'd cover up for him, I know she would.

I don't trust her, he thought, that's the trouble. I can't trust her now. But I can't tell her that, can I?

He tried to think of how it was with him and Jess when they were together. When he was with her everything else in the world was suspended and all that mattered was to make her his own.

But when he wasn't with her, it was different. We don't have anything to say to each other, he thought. I don't want to talk to her, I don't want to listen to her, there's only one thing I want and that's to fuck her.

He felt lust stirring as he thought of Jess and how hot her mouth was as she kissed him, and the damp feel of her skin and the thrust of her . . . well, he mustn't think of that, although he knew that when he saw her that was all he could think of.

He pulled off the road into a lay-by and sat with the truck window open to cool himself down. He had to think before the folds of Jess's body wrapped him round and squeezed all thought from his head.

He didn't understand how, but the news of the second murder in Forester Close had changed the way he thought of Jess. He wished now that he hadn't sent her that text, or that he was the sort of person who could stand her up. He tried to ask himself why the new murder had changed his mind. Why should it, it wasn't her fault? But he couldn't rid himself of the feeling that in some way it was.

He'd tried to believe that the differences between the two of them didn't matter, that they were created by other people who were protecting their own prejudices. What was between the two of them had nothing to do with that.

It did, though, he knew that now. Those new estate people were different, they lived worthless, depraved lives and she was

part of that. Killing and crime and violence meant different things
to Jess than they did to him; she was used to them, not afraid
of them. And he was afraid. He was afraid of what was inside
her head. He didn't like to think it, but it was true, he was afraid
of Jess.

No, he told himself, no, this is Jess. Laughing, loving, lustful
Jess who smothered him with her affection, who wanted him,
who made his head explode with the secret things that were
between them. She would never hurt him.

For the first time, Mark tried to understand how Jess
experienced their love. He told himself, she can't get enough of
me; she's *hungry* for me all the time. But when she's feasted,
what then?

He thought, Why me? She's not interested in anything about
me except sex. I make love to her, I don't just bang her and get
up and go away. I try to make her happy. That's what she likes.
All the rest treat her like a tart.

Mark leaned his head out of the window to feel the cold wind
in his face. He wished he hadn't started this business of thinking
about what was between him and Jess because now he knew too
much about how he felt. I treat her like a tart, too, he told himself;
those things she likes, that's just because I don't do it like those
yobs like Kevin. I can't get enough of her.

He thought, it's harder having a girl in a place like this, a
village, you know you can't avoid seeing her again and again,
she won't let you forget it ever happened. In a big town, you
don't have to bump into her all over the place. What's so great
about Jess, she's not always on about getting married like one
of the local girls.

That wasn't true, though, was it? Jess talked about nothing
else but the two of them going away together somewhere new.

It's worse with her, Mark told himself, she thinks of me as a
way for her to escape. God knows what'd happen after that.

And then he thought, I don't want to escape. Not to the kind
of life Jess wants.

Mark started the truck and moved out into the flow of traffic.
One more time, he thought, and then I've got to talk to Jess
about us.

He saw her standing under a lamp post on the kerb. He could

tell from the way she was moving on the spot that she was impatient waiting for him. The street light turned her purple hair and clownish make-up to eerie colours unknown to the palette of Windsor & Newton; colours mixed in mud by a child.

He drew up beside her and she opened the door of the pickup.

'About time too,' she said. She slammed the passenger door as she got into the vehicle.

'Don't you know there's a murderer on the loose?' she snapped. 'What do you think it's like for me, waiting alone like that?'

He laughed. He wouldn't have said to her face that she'd no cause to be afraid, the murderer was probably one of her family. But she knew at once that's what he was thinking, it was why he had laughed.

'The woman who was killed,' she said, 'she's the one who let us hide in her house when Kevin was after you.'

'Oh, God,' he said, 'I didn't know. I'm sorry.'

Jess shrugged. 'She was a weirdo,' she said, 'she's better off dead. What did she have to live for, after all?'

They drove to a quiet track through a wood close off the road to Old Catcombe.

She turned to him, panting. 'Put your hand here,' she whispered, taking him by the wrist.

He leaned towards her across the gear lever. He felt he was slipping into a vat of honey. He closed his eyes.

She started to moan, clutching at him.

Then suddenly he pulled his hand away and leaned back against the door away from her.

'I can't,' he said. 'I'm sorry, Jess, I can't. That poor old woman . . .'

'You think it was Kevin, don't you?' she said. She sounded very sad.

'I don't know,' he said. 'Tell me it wasn't.'

'Well, I know it wasn't me,' she said. 'But you're not sure, are you?'

'Oh, Jess . . .'

'You'd better take me home,' she said.

'I'm sorry, Jess,' he said. 'I can't help it.'

They neither of them spoke. Jess stared fixedly out of the passenger window as he drove, staring ahead at the road.

He dropped her under the same lamp post near the supermarket. When he stopped under the street light, he could see oddly iridescent tears quivering in her eyes, like tiny bubbles blown by a child.

'I'll ring you,' he said. 'We've got to talk.'

She shrugged and turned away. He put the pickup in gear and moved off.

When he was out of her view, he reversed into a side street and then drove slowly back to make sure that she was safe. He felt ashamed, sorry for her, but also relieved. He thought, I made a stand, I made her take me seriously.

Under the street light, she was talking on her mobile phone. Shouting, really, Mark could hear her.

Within minutes, he saw a dark figure on a motorbike draw up beside her. Mark knew it was Kevin. Jess got on to the pillion seat and put her arms around Kevin's body.

Long after the bike had disappeared, Mark could hear the snarl of its engine and the squeal of brakes grow gradually faint as it raced into the darkness.

TWENTY-SIX

Rachel Moody was working late in the office. Really, she was putting on a show of having to work late because she didn't want to go home. Alone there, she knew that thinking about this case would force her to face disturbing truths about herself and the state of her own life. She could just about hold these at bay at her desk in the police station. At home, though, these questions were harder to set aside.

She wasn't usually so involved in an investigation – not on this disconcertingly personal level.

Tonight, though, two days after the discovery of Alice Bates's body, even going through the motions of working was getting her nowhere. Anyone who was still on duty in the detectives' room was either out on enquiries or in the canteen, and Rachel, looking out of her office across the empty desks, found herself remembering what she had told the Superintendent earlier in the day.

'Our questions may be forcing everyone in Forester Close to concentrate on what they knew about Alice Bates,' she'd said, 'but what's becoming more and more obvious is that none of the woman's neighbours really knew anything about her at all.'

The Super had grunted and told her to keep at it.

I don't need telling that, Rachel thought, I'm going to put Kevin Miller behind bars if it kills me.

Rachel hated this case. She found her eyes brimming with tears for no reason every time she thought of how lonely Alice must have been. Alice's death hadn't been tragic, not like the young vicar's was; it was just pathetic.

She remembered how, when the Reverend Tim Baker died, great heaps of flowers in cellophane had been piled against the wall outside the Millers' house. The Millers of all people! There'd been messages, too, saying how much the Reverend would be missed, and what a good, kind, Christian man he was. Comforting for the family, Rachel told herself.

There was not a single bunch of flowers left outside Alice's house. Sergeant Reid, even, had noticed this. He'd pulled a stem of winter-flowering honeysuckle out of a bush in Jean Henson's garden and laid it on the wall of Number Three. He'd glared at Rachel as though daring her to say anything.

Apart from Jack and Rachel, no one seemed to notice that Alice left a gap in their lives. Of course, she didn't have a family; she didn't have friends, either. She was an outcast from the human race.

Rachel asked herself, does this death depress me so much because I identify with her. A few years on and I could be Alice Bates – alone, unloved, unimportant. She thought, I wonder when she had the Change? I wonder if she felt the future was as empty as it seems to me? Premenstrual tension is taken seriously; why does everyone ignore what happens to a woman after that?

While she was talking to the Super, Rachel had thought – but did not say aloud to her boss – that, in a sense, Alice's actual death seemed to mean very little to anyone because her life had passed almost unnoticed. As a result, all the residents of Forester Close seemed to see what had happened to her simply in terms of its implications for them and theirs.

Rachel hadn't tried to explain that to the Super. He wouldn't know what she was talking about, or why it mattered. He'd probably have put it down as another reason why women weren't really suited to police work. Too bloody fanciful, he'd tell himself. Rachel thought, it's probably not relevant to our enquiries anyway.

Even so, to support her theory that Alice's death was murder, not an accident, DCI Moody felt that she had to discover something about the woman which, if she were ever going to find her killer, might reveal a motive for murdering her. If there was a killer . . .

Moody asked herself for the umpteenth time, who was Alice Bates? Where did she come from?

But, alone in her office surrounded by the darkness of the deserted CID section, the question Rachel was really asking herself was not about Alice Bates. If Alice hadn't been killed, she might not find herself driven now to ask herself, who am I? What kind of person am I? What am I doing with my life?

My God, she thought, looking out across the empty desks in

the open-plan detectives' room, am I making such a meal of this because I'm afraid I'm turning into Alice Bates? A lonely old crone with nothing to look forward to and very little to remember?

No wonder I don't want her death to be an accident, she thought, at least I want her to have made enough impact for someone to have wanted to kill her.

If that someone was a vicious no-mark like Kevin Miller, so be it. It was better than nothing.

Rachel tried to remember what the neighbours had said about Alice.

At Number Five, Terri said, 'She never mentioned anyone. No family at all.' Terri was plainly gratified that there was no one to suffer from Alice's loss. For her, it was the living who counted, not the dead.

'She had a cat and it was killed,' Helen said.

'She used to watch people,' Nicky said. 'She spied on us at night.' She added in her prim little child's voice, 'I think she was a masochist, if you know what that means.'

DCI Moody said nothing.

At Number Two, Jess Miller said, 'She was a witch.'

'A *bitch*?' Rachel was astonished.

'I said witch,' Jess said, sulking. 'She looked like a witch.'

Rachel wondered now if Jess had perhaps opened the door to new lines of inquiry. So far, the DCI hadn't thought that sex could have had any part to play in this case, but now she wondered if she might have been mistaken. Just because she'd taken it for granted that Alice was post menopausal, that didn't mean she had no interest in sex. Look at me, Moody told herself, I'm not all that much younger than Alice Bates and I certainly don't feel I'm past it.

And then she thought, it's other people who think that.

Rachel kept asking herself whether any of her own neighbours would pay any more attention than Alice's if she were murdered. Quite likely they wouldn't notice. At least, she told herself, I've got work and the people here, they know who I am. Alice lived a totally invisible life, and that includes her death.

Funny, Rachel told herself, how she thought of the victim as Alice now, as though she'd known her as a personal friend. There were very few people in her own private life she called by their first names. Oh God, she thought, don't say my life's in such a mess that dead people are the only ones I can feel close to.

She knew she shouldn't be wallowing in self pity like this, but she felt helpless to stop herself.

Then the phone on her desk suddenly started to ring. Saved by the bell, she thought.

She recognized Jack Reid's voice at once. He sounded excited.

'What's up?' she asked. 'I hope you don't expect to be paid overtime for this.'

'This one's on me,' he said. 'You're not going to believe this. I've been given a steer on the forensics results. They'll be official first thing in the morning. Guess what?'

This must be good, Rachel thought, Jack doesn't play games.

'What?' she said.

'Kevin Miller's fingerprints are all over Alice Bates' house. Including the body.'

Rachel jumped to her feet. 'Bingo,' she shouted. 'We've got him now!'

She was exultant. It was a professional crow of achievement. The personal angst was gone; now she knew who and what she was.

There was a short silence while they both took in the implications.

'Where are you?' Rachel asked.

'I'll be there in five minutes,' Jack Reid said.

'I'll wait for you downstairs,' Rachel said. 'I'll alert the custody sergeant. We'll be bringing Kevin Miller in for questioning about the murder of Alice Bates. As soon as we get the forensics report in the morning, we'll charge him with murder.'

'Sounds good to me,' Jack said, 'Forester Close, here we come.'

In the car, Rachel said, 'It would be just our luck if he's not there.'

'What, you think he's in Weston with one of his anonymous pick-ups?' Jack said. 'He's not afraid of us. He got away with the vicar, he thinks he's in the clear.'

'Let's hope so,' Rachel said.

'He'll be there, I'd put money on it. I've got a good feeling about this.'

'Me too,' Rachel said.

'We're here.'

Jack turned into Forester Close and stopped at the bottom of the road. They waited for the squad car with two uniformed officers to pull up behind them.

The houses in Forester Close looked like a huddle of hibernating animals, Rachel Moody thought. It was a cold, damp night and there was no sign of life behind the closed, curtained windows. She looked to the top of the street to Number Three and thought of Alice. I hope you're somewhere you can see what's going on, Rachel thought, you wouldn't want to miss watching this. For once in your life, you're getting your own back.

She got out of the car and walked back to the waiting uniformed officers. The driver opened his window and she told the men, 'Follow us up to the house and park the squad car across the drive,' she said. 'We don't want him sneaking past on his motorcycle. Then, one of you, get round the back. He may make a run for it.' She added to the driver, 'You've got the Enforcer? We'll probably need to break the door down.'

The two cars moved slowly up the road and stopped outside the Millers' house. A uniformed man disappeared round the side of the building to cover the back door.

Rachel followed Jack Reid and the squad car driver with his battering ram across the driveway to the front door.

The tattered remains of a giant drunken-looking Father Christmas trailed electric flex across the porch as though holding the reins of a lost team of reindeer.

Jack Reid pounded on the door. 'Open up. Police,' he shouted.

'OK,' Rachel said to the uniformed man.

He swung the ram and the door splintered and fell open.

Rachel ran into the house and up the stairs, Jack close behind her. The uniformed man went through to the kitchen and unlocked the back door to let his colleague into the house.

On the landing at the top of the stairs Donna Miller staggered out of one of the bedrooms. She was wearing an inadequate T-shirt and nothing else.

'What the fuck d'you think you're doing?' she yelled. 'There's a child asleep here.'

'We need to speak to Kevin, Mrs Miller,' Rachel Moody said. 'Which is his room?'

'How dare you burst in here like this?' Donna shouted. 'What time do you think it is?'

Jack moved forward to open the bedroom doors. Donna stepped forward to stop him. The fight had gone out of her.

'No, don't wake the baby,' she said, 'that's Kevin's room next door.' She turned away, afraid to watch. 'You'd better have a good reason for this.'

'Oh, we have, Donna, believe me, we have,' Rachel said.

Jack Reid went into Kevin's room. There was a crash, then the sound of a struggle.

'I didn't do nothing,' Kevin said. 'Get your fucking hands off me. You've no right.'

Jack pushed him out on to the landing. Kevin was wearing jeans and a denim jacket.

'He was making a break for it through the window,' Jack Reid said. 'He resisted arrest.'

He smiled at Kevin. Kevin glared at him but it was bravado. He looked cowed.

God, he doesn't look much now, not without the other thugs to back him up, Rachel told herself. What is it about him that made so many people scared of him? And then she thought, I'd never realized there's something quite frightening about Jack when he's on the job. I'm glad he's on my side.

'I'm arresting you on suspicion of the murder of Alice Bates,' Rachel said. 'We're taking you in for questioning. Take him down to the car, Jack, and read him his rights.'

Kevin tried to twist away from Jack Reid's hold.

'I didn't,' he said, 'I didn't kill her.'

He sounded as though he couldn't believe what was happening.

Donna stepped forward. 'This is harassment,' she said, 'You've nothing on him. Kevin didn't kill her.'

'You've got it wrong,' Kevin said, whimpering. They could hear real panic in his voice.

'Then why are your fingerprints all over her house?' Rachel asked.

'Our Kevin's never been in her house,' Donna said, 'why would he go in there?'

'OK, I did go to her house,' Kevin said. 'I went to warn her about her spying on everyone. People didn't like it, I told her that.'

'Save it,' DCI Moody said. 'Take him away, Sergeant. Sorry you've been disturbed, Mrs Miller.'

'You will be,' Donna said in an attempt at venom. But her lack of conviction made her sound pathetic.

'She thinks he's guilty,' Rachel said quietly to Jack as they got into the car.

'Well, she would, wouldn't she?' Jack said.

Kevin was slumped beside Rachel in the back seat.

'You've got it wrong,' he said. They could hear the fear in his voice. 'I didn't do it.'

TWENTY-SEVEN

Next day the news that Kevin Miller had been charged with the murder of Alice Bates was the lead story on the local television lunchtime news.

By teatime, reporters were crawling all over Forester Close. They were there the next day and the one after that. But they discovered no new information to shed light on the murky details of Alice Bates's death.

Curiously, though, the reporters succeeded in opening lines of communication between the residents of the Close. Where people had instinctively always been wary of each other, or actually afraid, they began to recognize a common humanity even in those they distrusted most. They could not remain in fear of people whose faces they were seeing in their own homes in the news-papers or on the television screen.

If this was the first labour pain in the birth of a community, Jess Miller became its unlikely midwife.

A reporter from a Sunday tabloid asked Jess how having a second murder in the street had affected her life, especially as her brother was accused of the killing.

Jess was in a bad mood. She had recognized that something important had happened in her relationship with Mark on that horrible night when he rejected her advances, and then dumped her on the street to find her way home as best she could.

She'd tried to shrug it off, it hadn't meant anything much. He was all mixed up, that was all.

But she was desolate. She'd spent all the next morning trying to text him. He didn't reply. But then, she told herself, Mark wasn't at all mobile-literate. He treated the cell phone as a tool of his farming trade, and his messages to her might as well have been to DEFRA or the Milk Marketing Board for all the intimacy they had in them.

So when the reporter asked his question, she snapped, 'How much?'

'What's it worth?' he asked. 'Depends what you've got to tell.'

'Give me a grand and I'll tell you plenty,' Jess said.

'OK,' he said. He told himself that if the editor objected to the payment, by then he'd have got his story and he could run out on her and there wasn't anything she could do about it. If she had nothing to tell, he wouldn't pay anyway.

Jess let rip. She told him about the warring families from Catcombe and Catcombe Mead who would not let her and Mark be together; she told about their secret trysts behind Alice's house, and that was why Alice Bates had to die.

Jess was carried away by the drama she was creating. 'Why not?' she said. 'Alice helped us before. She once rescued Mark and me from my brothers. This feud, it's like *The Godfather*. She didn't obey the rules; she had to die.'

'You're having me on?' the reporter said. 'Aren't you?'

Jess shrugged. 'Ask around,' she said. 'We all knew that if Kevin found out Alice helped Mark, he'd kill her, no sweat. She knew it, too, she was terrified of Kev.'

'It's incredible,' the reporter said.

But incredible or not, it would make a terrific story for the paper.

'It's like we belong to rival gangs,' Jess said. 'God knows what started it. It's to do with history. It's the way things are. It's not just Mark and me; it's the whole village against everyone on the estate. It's primordial.'

Primordial was a word Nicky used all the time, to express contempt. Jess had taken it up because she liked the way it sounded.

The reporter didn't know this. He liked the idea of a primitive local feud as a background to murder. The alleged murderer, after all, was this girl's half-brother.

'Wonderful,' he said. 'It's like Shakespeare.'

So Mark and Jess briefly became Romeo and Juliet. The reporter set their romance against a background of barbarian warlords and undercover violence set in a despotic no-man's-land in rural England where the forces of law and order were helpless to act.

Jess was right, the reporter told himself, it was primordial. And it all happened quite close to where, only a few hundred years before, the Monmouth Rebellion and the Bloody Assizes had ravaged backward farming families in Somerset.

The publication of his story was devastating to the residents of Forester Close.

As long as they had kept themselves to themselves, they had been able to see where lay the unspecified but nonetheless present danger which haunted all of them. As long as each family saw its neighbours as the source of that danger, they had felt that they could contain the perceived threat.

But once the residents of Forester Close were revealed publicly as all equally vulnerable, the fear that pervaded their lives seemed to have been set free. Kevin Miller might be gone, on remand in prison awaiting trial, but still they were all afraid. So there must be something to fear. And what made it harder to deal with was that no one now knew where the threat came from. They had to acknowledge that they were not imagining the violence and the viciousness and lack of care of the world outside. The newspaper published it, it must be true.

Curiously, too, the residents of Forester Close began to see Kevin Miller as the victim of the historic feud between Old Catcombe and Catcombe Mead. They saw him as a martyr to the vendetta. They began to feel ashamed that they had misunderstood a young man whom they now cast as someone brave enough to keep their enemies from the old village at bay. First the vicar who had come as some sort of spy, then the traitor Alice, who had betrayed them all.

It was the people of Old Catcombe, they thought, who were to blame for pushing Kevin over the edge into real violence. They agreed that they had always known that he killed the vicar from the old village. He must have thought that in murdering Alice, he was dealing out just punishment to a traitor.

Jean Henson was the first to wonder if, after all, Alice hadn't contributed to her own death. Meeting Helen Byrne with Nicky in the supermarket one morning she said in the course of conversation, 'Don't you think perhaps there was something about Alice that was a bit provocative to people? She was so helpless she laid herself open to abuse. It's a recognized psychiatric argument, you know, that the victim of crime is equally responsible with the perpetrator for what happens. She must've contributed in some way to what the Miller boy did to her.'

Later that day, Nicky met Jess in the alley behind the Miller house.

'Heard from Kevin?' she asked.

Jess was still missing Mark. She'd hoped that the story in the newspaper would make him get in touch with her, but it hadn't. She was not inclined to be sympathetic to Nicky's schoolgirl crush on her brother.

'Yes,' she said. 'Mum went to visit him.'

'Did he mention me?' Nicky said, oddly breathless.

'You? Why should he? He said he didn't kill the old witch, that's all. He told her to ask you, you'd know who did it. Mum wasn't sure he was guilty till then, but after that she knew he was, making up something as desperate as that.'

'Perhaps he didn't kill the old woman,' Nicky said.

'Of course he did,' Jess said.

Nicky was twisting her hands together in a helpless way that irritated Jess.

'If someone else came forward and said they did it,' Nicky said, 'would you believe Kevin didn't?'

'No,' Jess said.

TWENTY-EIGHT

It was a January of drizzling winter days and damp fog, smelling sour like wet ashes from a dead fire. Fallen leaves which had not been swept up during December gales lay rotting in the gutters. They blocked the drains, and a small torrent of water flowed past the houses, leaving convoluted patterns of grit and debris strewn across the road like a dark design embroidered on grey canvas.

Dave Byrne had given Nicky a new bike for Christmas. He dropped it round to Number Five on Christmas Eve. It was his attempt to propitiate Helen's bitterness over the fire.

Terri answered the door. She didn't ask him in. Helen was out with Nicky and at first Terri wanted to tell Dave Byrne to take the bicycle away, neither Helen nor Nicky wanted his presents.

But she couldn't do that. It was a beautiful bike, red and shiny chrome; Nicky would love it.

'Please, Terri, let her have it,' Dave said. 'Tell her it's a present from me and Helen together. It's not good for the kid for us always to be fighting over her.'

'I don't know what Helen will say to that,' Terri said.

'Look,' he said, 'I was wrong to do what I did, I know that. I went too far. Helen didn't shop me to the police, she must know I didn't mean that to happen. It's all got out of hand since the lawyers got involved, it was all fine till then, but it had gone too far to go back. What Nicky needs is for me and Helen not to be fighting.'

'I can't speak for Helen,' Terri said. 'I'll tell her what you say.'

'Tell her I mean it,' he said. He leaned the bicycle against the wall of the house.

'Yes,' she said. 'I will.'

Terri watched him walk away. Will I, she asked herself. Will I tell Helen about his visit?

She felt threatened by Dave's coming to the house, and by

what he said. She was scared. She'd never allowed herself to realize that her relationship with Helen had come to depend on Dave Byrne being cast as a villain. And if that was so, what was it worth, what was between her and Helen? If Helen and Nicky would be happier with Dave than she could make them, she had no right to hold them back. She had to face that. Oh, God, she thought, what will happen to me if I lose them?

She wheeled the bike round the back so Nicky wouldn't see it before she'd had a chance to talk to Helen. I've got to have it out with her, Terri thought, I can't go on like this, not now.

That night, as they were getting ready for bed, she told Helen about Dave's visit.

'I didn't know what you'd want me to say,' she said. 'Should I have told him to take the bike away?'

'Of course not,' Helen said. 'Nicky needs a bike, she'll be thrilled.'

'Dave wanted you to tell her it's from the two of you,' Terri said. She gave Helen an agonized look, expecting her to see the implications of what Dave had said.

But Helen simply laughed. 'That's great,' she said, 'I could never've afforded to give Nicky a present like that, but now she'll think I've made a special effort for her.'

She went into the bathroom. Terri got into bed and turned out the light. She heard Helen singing as she ran her bath.

Terri lay on her back staring into the dark.

She doesn't want to understand, she doesn't care, Terri told herself. Why do I love her so much? Sometimes I think I don't really like her at all.

It was Terri who told Nicky that the bike was a present from her father.

'Wicked,' Nicky said, 'it's the best present I ever had.' Then she laughed and grinned at Terri. 'One of the advantages of a guilty conscience, don't you think? Worth pursuing, I'd say.'

Terri couldn't help laughing at Nicky's contrived cynicism.

'Don't bank on that,' she said. 'But it's nice work if you can get it. It's a beautiful bike.'

Since Christmas, Nicky had been trying to teach herself to ride it in the street outside the house, but Nate and Jess jeered at her and she'd stopped taking it out on the road any more.

Instead she went out early in the morning by the back alley that ran behind Forester Close to practise on a patch of waste land adjoining the supermarket.

On the Wednesday after Jess's photo had been splashed all over the Sunday paper, Terri went upstairs to call Nicky before she left the house to go to work. During the school holidays, she did this every day so that Nicky could make Helen's breakfast and take it up to her in bed. Terri thought Helen should have the time alone with her daughter.

But today Nicky was not in her room.

Terri woke Helen, but she didn't know where Nicky was.

'What are you worried about?' Helen asked Terri. 'She's probably taken the bike and gone somewhere those other kids can't tease her.'

But Terri was worried. It wasn't like Nicky to disappear without telling her mother where she was going; and Terri worried too that no one seemed to be concerned that the other kids could be bullying Nicky. Terri herself had been bullied at school, in spite of being a big girl well able to stand up for herself and flatten most of the boys in her class. It had been the girls who had been able to hurt her, because she had never been soft and feminine, and they made sure she knew she did not belong amongst them.

So her heart bled for Nicky, who was too studious, and not pretty enough, ever to belong amongst what Terri called 'the dolly brigade'.

Of course it was the holidays; no one expected Nicky to stay around the house. Terri went to work as usual, but she rang Helen at lunchtime. Nicky hadn't come home. Terri began to panic.

'Oh, for goodness sake,' Helen said. 'She's thirteen years old, she's off somewhere with her friends.'

'She hasn't got any friends,' Terri said.

'Not that we know of,' Helen said, 'that doesn't mean they don't exist.'

But the January days were short, and when it got dark around four o'clock and there was still no sign of the child, even Helen began to look concerned.

Terri came home from work early in the car and drove straight off out again to search for the child.

After about an hour, she came home. 'It's too dark,' she said, 'it's pointless. I've checked all the places with street lighting. She could be anywhere.'

'Should I tell Dave?' Helen said, 'he's her father, he should be dealing with this.' She was angry with Nicky; she thought the child was doing this to get attention. She added, 'Of course, she could be with him. Perhaps he's abducted her.'

'Tell the police first,' Terri said.

She had to go upstairs away from Helen because she was afraid she would not be able to stop herself grabbing her and shaking her until her teeth came loose.

Why am I taking this out on Helen, she thought, she's Nicky's mother, she must be in hell.

She heard Helen's voice on the telephone. She was calling the police, at least that was something.

Terri went into Nicky's bedroom. It was like a nun's cell, completely unadorned. The narrow bed had a white duvet, and the walls were white, too. The only colour in the room was the dark red of the curtains Nicky had chosen herself after the fire for her new room.

Terri sat on the edge of the hard little bed and picked up the single pillow. 'Where are you, Nicky?' she said, pressing the cool white cotton against her cheek. She could smell Nicky's shampoo.

She was surprised at the strength of her anxiety about the child. She'd always thought she'd tried to love Nicky for Helen's sake, but now she was overwhelmed by her feelings. Oh God, she thought, clenching her arms around the pillow, let her be safe, let her come home.

She saw the note as she went to replace the pillow. The envelope was addressed to her – Terri Kent printed in capitals in black ink, underlined twice.

Terri opened it.

'By the time you read this letter, I will have escaped this Vale of Tears,' she read.

This isn't real, Terri thought, it's like something out of an old novel. She wanted to weep for the child who felt so unloved she had to hide her misery behind such unreal words in order to express her deepest feelings.

Perhaps Nicky had felt the same when she wrote it. Anyway,

she'd abandoned that approach and the rest of the note was scrawled out as though written in a great hurry.

She wrote, 'It wasn't Kevin who killed Alice Bates, it was me. I can't keep it to myself any more. Kevin forced her to have him live in her house to hide from the police, and I helped him guard her because I love him. I really love him and I wanted to show him how much. You may not understand this because you have probably never read a book called *Crime and Punishment* which is the greatest book ever written. I love Kevin because he is the hero of the book, Raskolnikov, even if he doesn't know it yet. He is a special person who has the right to commit murder and Alice Bates was a parasite like the pawnbroker in the book.

'But Kevin didn't kill Alice. He wanted to, but he didn't, so I did it for him. It was late at night and he was in bed. He told me to watch Alice didn't try to escape. Alice didn't understand what was happening by then. She told me to get out of there while I had the chance. She said Kevin was wicked.

'I hit her over the head with a lamp on the landing and pushed her so she fell down the stairs. I wanted to show Kevin that I'm not a silly little schoolgirl but worthy of him.

'The noise she made falling woke Kev up, and he came to see and he said she was dead. I was scared and I told him she'd fallen by accident.

'I'm sorry, Terri, but you and Mum will be better off without me. I know this will disappoint you because you wanted the best for me and I've let you down. Please ask Jess to say I'm sorry to Kevin, I never meant for him to get the blame. Please try to make Mum understand and not hate me.'

The note was signed Nicky Anne Kent.

Terri sat on the edge of the narrow bed staring at Nicky's childish rounded handwriting for some time. Then she put the note back in the envelope and put it in her pocket.

How am I going to tell Helen? Terri asked herself.

Helen looked at Terri's face and screamed at her.

'My God,' she said, 'what's the little idiot done now?'

'Poor, poor child,' Terri said. She started to cry.

'Stop it,' Helen shouted at her, 'for God's sake stop that noise. She's my daughter, why are *you* crying?'

Terri's tears were awful, as though heavy metal started spontaneously to melt.

Then Terri clenched her fists and ground them into the sockets of her eyes to stop herself weeping.

'Where would she go?' she said to Helen, 'where would your daughter go to kill herself?'

Helen gave her a terrified look and curled up on the sofa in what looked like the foetal position. She sucked her thumb and whimpered like a child.

Terri glanced at her, then turned away and ran out of the house. She scrambled over the dividing wall between her house and Jean Henson's.

Jean opened her front door to the frantic knocking. Terri tried to explain that Nicky was missing.

Jean pulled her into the hall. 'Tell me?' she said. 'What's happened?'

Terri scarcely knew what she was doing. She thrust Nicky's note into Jean's hands. Then, as Jean read it, she spilled out the whole story as though the words were lava erupting from her. She was helpless to stop the flow in spite of her fear of the consequences for Helen and for Nicky of what she had to tell.

Jean was very calm. She asked, 'Are the police looking for her?'

Terri nodded.

Jean said, 'If she took her bike, she can't have gone far. She couldn't ride it very well.'

'But she's been gone all day.'

'Yes.'

They looked at each other and then Terri said, 'What are we going to do about the other thing? About Kevin Miller? And Alice? Do you think anyone would believe it? Do you think it's *true*? Was she trying to protect Kevin?'

Jean took her by the shoulders and shook her. 'Is, Terri. Is, not was. We don't know she's dead.'

'Poor little thing,' Terri said, 'she doesn't think she's got anything to live for. That note's so sad.'

'Burn the note,' Jean said. She handed it back to Terri. She sounded as though she had no doubts that they must do this.

'But the police must see it,' Terri said. 'They've charged Kevin Miller.'

'Has Helen seen the note?'

Terri shook her head. 'No,' she said, 'Nicky wrote it to me. That means she didn't want her mother to see it. She trusted me.'

'Helen mustn't see it,' Jean said. 'The police mustn't see it, either. If they do, they'll put her in care, and the psychiatrists will get hold of her. You've got to destroy it.'

Terri hesitated.

'Come on,' Jean said, taking Terri's arm and marching her out of the house and back next door.

Helen was still curled on the sofa, her eyes closed. She was still sucking her thumb like an infant.

'She's out of it,' Jean said. 'That's something to be thankful for.'

There was a loud knocking at the front door. Helen started to whimper, retreating further into the sofa cushions.

'Quick,' Jean said. She snatched the note. 'You answer the door.'

She was tearing the note into shreds as she ran upstairs to the bathroom.

She could hear Terri talking to the police in the hall. From the top of the stairs Jean recognized the voice of the female Detective Chief Inspector who had come to question her after Alice's death.

Damn, Jean thought, how did they get here so quickly?

She flushed the pieces down the lavatory.

Terri, white-faced and her forehead beaded with sweat, stood in the hallway like a fat bull terrier barking at the postman.

'We'd like to speak to Mrs Byrne,' the Chief Inspector said. 'We need to talk to her. We've found her daughter.'

TWENTY-NINE

The light was already fading as Mark Pearson set off to check the electric fence in the fields by the river where the cows were grazing with the stud bull. While he was at it, too, he could make sure the water troughs were in working order.

Bloody public rights of way, Mark was thinking. If the government didn't force him to protect intruders on his own land, he could let the animals get down to the river bank to drink.

'Bloody vandals,' he muttered, 'letting their dogs off the lead with the in-calf heifers, and their children running all over the crops. Ignorant yobs, the lot of them. And I get prosecuted if that old bull so much as looks at them.'

Mark had been grumpy like this for days. The endless cold grey days, the gloom everywhere, the boredom of being unable to get on with work that needed to be done because of the weather, all got him down. He knew he was being absurd and unreasonable. But thinking of yobs invading his land had reminded him of meeting Jess. Mark missed her. He felt very lonely without her.

Close to the river, where the bank curved and left a small muddy inlet in the field, he found the wire fence had come loose from one of the plastic posts. It was trailing on the grass. He could hear the crackling sound where it was shorting out.

He moved the electric fencing post to a point where it could hold the wire off the ground. He got a shock as he raised the wire and broke the point of contact with the earth. It was too much. He almost succumbed to a childish urge to stamp his foot and swear. At least there was no one to see him, and it might make him feel better.

The crackling ceased. In the sudden silence, he heard a sound.

At first he thought it was a wounded wild animal too damaged to flee. A small animal, not one of his heifers, anyway. It might even be a frightened bird with an injured wing,

He walked slowly towards the sound, as quietly as he could. He did not want to scare whatever it was making the noise. It was coming from beyond one of the old pollarded willow trees which stood like the ruins of ancient forts guarding the river bank.

Mark approached the tree. He stopped, listening to see if the noise had changed or stopped.

It came again, but more faintly now.

Long ago, a bough had split from the old tree and now lay like part of the skeleton of a prehistoric beast in a hollow where the river bank sloped down to a quiet pool. It was a favourite place where families often came on picnics in the summer because it was safe for the children to paddle in the water.

Mark saw the child's red bicycle leaning against this broken bough. The chain-guard and the wheels were clogged with mud, but the handlebars and the mudguards looked too bright and shiny to have been left there since the summer visitors. He told himself, anyway, I'd have seen it when I came down to check the fence if it was here yesterday.

He felt his heart pounding and sweat prickled under his collar in spite of the cold. He didn't know what he was afraid of, but he was afraid.

The whimpering seemed to be coming from somewhere beyond the bike, behind the rotting bough of the old tree; a sound of moaning mixed with some kind of feeble threshing movement. Mark thought some animal was trapped. Some stupid child playing games, he thought. Cruel little beast.

'Who's there?' he called softly.

There was a sudden silence, then a renewed moan as though whoever was making the noise had tried to keep quiet and couldn't hold back the sound.

Mark ran the last few strides to the rotting bough and looked over.

A child was writhing feebly on the muddy grass. A thin, gawky girl with strands of almost colourless damp hair stuck to her pale skin. She was clutching her stomach and moaning in pain. Her face was contorted and the skin around her mouth looked to him to be bluish.

He jumped down beside her.

'What is it?' he asked, 'what's happened?'

But she did not seem to know that he was there. She couldn't speak.

He lifted her to wipe her hair away from her damp face. She felt cold as stone. He took off his anorak and wrapped it round her. She was staring at him through half-closed eyes. He didn't think she saw him; she seemed to him half-dead.

He had to root in the pocket of his anorak, now wrapped round the child, for his mobile phone. He was shocked at how quickly the garment that a moment before had been warm with his body heat had become chilled by the coldness of her body.

He dialled 999.

Mark knew the ambulance could not make its way across the water meadows from the road, so he told the paramedics where to meet him in the lane. 'I'll carry her up there,' he said.

'Do you know who the child is?' the switchboard operator asked him.

He looked down at the girl. She had stopped the writhing now, and her eyes were closed. He thought she had lost consciousness.

He did not know her. At the back of his mind, he thought he might have seen her before, somewhere he had been because of Jess. But beyond that, he couldn't place her.

'No,' he said, 'but she may come from the Catcombe Mead housing estate.'

He was frightened to see how pale the child was. Not white like ivory, more the colour of Lalique glass.

'Hurry,' he said, 'please, hurry, or you'll be too late.'

'Is there anything around to show what she might have taken?' the calm, matter-of-fact voice on the telephone asked him.

At first he could see nothing. Then, close to the bicycle, he noticed a plastic freezer bag.

'Wait,' he said, putting the child down and fetching the bag. 'There seem to be a few berries in it,' he said. 'It looks as though they came off Christmas decorations. There's holly and mistletoe, anyway, I recognize those. There's something here looks like laurel, too. She could have taken them accidentally.'

Why did I say that, he thought. It makes it sound as though I really think she did this deliberately.

'Take them with you,' the voice said, 'it may be vital to know what she's ingested.'

He nodded, as though the calm speaker were there beside him.

'The ambulance is on its way,' she said. 'It should be with you in about five minutes.'

Mark lifted the unconscious child and started back the way he had come, towards the lane.

He heard the siren well before the ambulance reached him.

'Hold on,' he urged the unconscious child, 'it won't be long now.'

When he reached the lane, he saw the flashing blue light on top of the ambulance above the hedge, racing towards him. And then the paramedics were there and he felt an overwhelming relief that the child was in safe hands.

A police car arrived and Mark went to open a gate into the field so that it could reverse into it out of the way of the ambulance. The driver, a cheery young woman with cropped blonde hair, went to check what was happening in the ambulance. The girl in the passenger seat got out and put on her helmet before approaching Mark.

'Are you all right?' she asked.

Mark found that he was shaking. He felt very cold. 'I found her,' he said.

'You look pretty shaken,' she said. 'Don't you have a coat?'

'I wrapped it round her,' he said, 'she was freezing cold.'

'Come and sit in the car for a bit,' she said. 'You can tell me what happened. Jo will go in the ambulance, I expect, so I'll drive you home when they take her to hospital. I'm at the end of my shift anyway.'

She opened the passenger door for him and then went round to the driver's seat. The car smelled faintly of spearmint.

'Here,' she said, 'have some chewing gum.'

Mark shook his head. 'Do you know, for the first time in my life I'd give anything for a cigarette,' he said.

She smiled; a nice smile with perfect teeth, he thought.

'Can't help you there,' she said. 'My name's Penny, by the way. Penny Harrison.'

'I'm Mark,' he said, 'Mark Pearson. I live on the farm here; I was checking the fences when I found the child.'

'I've always wanted to live on a farm,' Penny said. 'I'm a country girl, born and bred.'

Mark was about to ask her where she came from, but then her blonde colleague, Jo, knocked at the window.

Penny opened it. 'Are they ready?' she asked.

'I'll go in the ambulance,' Jo said. 'Can you go and check out where she was found?'

'Sure,' Penny said. 'Mark here found her, he'll show me.'

Jo nodded and hurried back to the ambulance. Mark and Penny watched it move off. They listened to the sound of the siren until it died away in the distance.

Penny smiled at Mark.

She said, 'I'll drive you home first. You could do with a hot drink after what you've been through. There's no crime involved – I think we can skip the formalities for now. I know where to find you if I need anything more.'

'I don't know about you,' Mark said, 'but I'm starving. Funny that, wanting to eat now.'

Penny laughed. 'It's probably a nervous reaction to being a public hero,' she said. 'Ever since I joined the police, I'm always ravenous.'

She started the car and drove slowly into the lane. 'Down here?' she asked.

Mark nodded. 'It's about half a mile further on,' he said.

As they reached the farm and Penny parked in the yard, Mark suddenly felt nervous. It seemed all at once very important that she wasn't put off by the dilapidated buildings and the farm smells that had so horrified Jess Miller.

'Oh, this is wonderful,' Penny said, looking about her with an expression of excitement Mark associated with Hollywood movies when the humble heroine finds herself in the bridal suite at the Ritz Hotel. 'It's a real farm, a real live farm. Like farms used to be.'

Yes, Mark thought, and Dad's still up, so now you're going to meet a real live farmer.

He was surprised to find he didn't care. It was extraordinary that he trusted her. Whatever his Dad did or said, Mark knew it would not change what she thought of him.

So he did not try to offer explanations.

He stood back to let her go first into the kitchen.

Mark heard the panic in his father's voice as he saw Penny's uniform.

'What's happened?' he said, 'has something happened to Joyce?'

Before Mark could say anything, Penny had got to Bert and grasped his hand. 'It's all right, Mr Pearson,' she said, 'your wife and Mark are fine. Mark saved a young girl's life this afternoon and I've brought him home.'

'It's all right, Dad,' Mark said. He was shaken by the intensity of his Dad's reaction. 'A young girl from the estate tried to kill herself down by the river and I found her and called the ambulance. Everything's fine now. This is Penny Harrison. We got cold; we need something hot to drink.'

Bert took the kettle and filled it at the sink. 'Of course you do,' he said. 'Sounds as though you both deserve it.'

'Where's Mum?' Mark asked, and then wondered what on earth had made him say that.

There was an awkward silence. Then Penny said, 'How old is this house, Mr Pearson? I didn't know places like this existed any more. It's a real traditional farm, isn't it? How many acres do you have?'

She turned to Mark, 'You're so lucky,' she said, 'it's beautiful here. And so *real*.'

The kettle began to boil. Bert made the tea. 'Here,' he said, 'get this down you.'

He handed mugs of tea to Mark and Penny. 'Now,' he said, 'what about this girl you found? Is she all right?'

'She will be,' Penny said. 'But if Mark hadn't found her . . .'

She had to go, but still she seemed to linger.

'I'd better start the milking,' Mark said.

'Of course,' she said, 'I've got to hand in my report.'

She smiled at Mark. 'I'll pick up your anorak when I can and bring it back here,' she said. 'Perhaps on my day off.'

'Great,' Mark said, 'Thanks.'

He felt like an idiot. He wanted to offer to take her for a drink or a meal, but it was impossible in front of his father.

But then Bert said, 'You come back on your day off, Penny, and I'll show you what a real old-fashioned farm looks like.'

Mark felt furious with his Dad, who was stealing his thunder; and with his mother, because if she'd been a proper farmer's wife, she'd have been at home cooking a meal he could have invited Penny to share.

He muttered and growled at the cows, who stared at him

with detached curiosity. Watching their soft puzzled eyes, he saw he was being ridiculous, childish, even. But nonetheless he felt it was unfair that his parents, even unconsciously, still dominated him.

We're all wasting so much time, he thought, and there's no time to waste.

He told himself that it was the attempted suicide of the young girl from Catcombe Mead that was making him feel like this. It had left him painfully aware that time for everyone was fragile and finite.

He went to bed to think, falling asleep immediately.

In the morning he slept through the alarm clock. When he finally came downstairs, his mother was cooking eggs and bacon.

'I've no time for breakfast,' he said, 'I'm late for milking. We'll miss the tanker if I don't hurry.'

'Dad did the milking,' his mother said.

'He did?' Mark didn't try to hide his surprise. 'Why?'

'Something's happened to your Dad,' Joyce said. 'Last night we talked.'

'God,' Mark said, 'what the hell about?'

'Us,' Joyce said.

'There is no us,' Mark said, 'not any more.'

He had not meant to sound so bleak.

Joyce started to say something, but then they heard Bert at the door, taking off his boots in the porch.

I'm not going to apologize, Mark told himself. He doesn't on all the days I cover for him.

'Thanks, Dad,' he said. 'You should've called me.' Where did that come from, Mark asked himself, why did I say that?

Bert sat down at the table. 'I've had an idea,' he blurted out. 'A terrific idea.'

Joyce put plates of bacon and eggs on the table in front of Bert and Mark. Then she sat down facing them.

'It was that girl from Catcombe Mead coming all the way out here to find herself a quiet place to . . .' Joyce started and trailed off. She seemed excited, but doubtful, too, as though she couldn't trust what was happening. 'It seemed so sad, a child that age wanting somewhere private and having to look for it in the country like that.'

Bert interrupted her. 'That Penny you brought here,' he said to Mark, 'a girl like that with a good job and everything, she couldn't believe the farm, it fascinated her. It did, didn't it? She couldn't get enough of it.'

'Yes,' Mark agreed, 'it did, didn't it? I'll bet she does turn up and get you to show her round.'

Bert thumped the table. 'You've got it,' he said.

'Got what?' Mark asked. He looked to his mother to explain, but Joyce was laughing.

'I've been thinking,' Bert said, sounding more sober. 'If those incomers got the chance to understand what we're on about—'

'What are you trying to say, Dad?' Mark sounded anxious now. Had his Dad lost his reason?

'We'll open the farm and invite them to come in and see what we're on about. All about the traditions of farming, what we do and how we do it. They can join in and learn some of the old crafts, like stone walling and thatching a rick. Parties of school children, that sort of thing. We'd do that together, you and me.'

'You're crazy,' Mark said. 'You know what they're like.'

Joyce got up and came round the table to put her hands on Bert's shoulders.

'I'd run a farm shop,' she said. Her eyes were shining. 'I could do cream teas in the summer.'

'We'll get the farm cleared up and on its feet again,' Bert said. 'It'll be hard work, but worth it. And then we'll invite them in.' He took a deep breath and said with an obvious effort, 'That girl of yours, Jess, she could start by bringing her little girl.'

'Jess is history,' Mark said abruptly.

'Well, she might have been a hard nut to crack anyway,' Bert said. 'That Penny will help. There's no harm visitors like those people from the housing estate knowing there's a police presence.'

Mark laughed. He couldn't help it. He and his Dad needed something like this, something to work on together.

Mark was silent for a moment. Then he said, 'If that's what it takes to bring this farm of ours – and us as a family – back to life, then yes, let's try it.'

THIRTY

Nicky had eaten a cocktail of Christmas berries – holly, mistletoe and ivy. There were traces of all three in the freezer bag Mark Pearson had picked up from the grass near her red bicycle.

By the time Terri and Jean reached the hospital, though, the doctors had pumped the child's stomach and she was out of danger.

She looked like a waxwork, lying in the stiff hospital sheets with a drip attached to her arm, her thin pale hair damp and flat against her skull.

Terri stood awkwardly by the bed and touched the child's hand.

Nicky opened her eyes and said, 'Mum?'

Terri and Jean exchanged glances.

'She'll be here later,' Terri said.

Helen had become hysterical when the Detective Chief Inspector told her what had happened to Nicky. She refused to listen to what Rachel Moody was saying, or to speak at all. She simply lay curled on the sofa with her thumb in her mouth, crying out if anyone tried to touch her. In the end Jean fetched the sleeping pills that had been prescribed for Peter before he died.

'She'll sleep for hours,' Jean said when Helen had finally been persuaded to take two of them.

Terri grasped Nicky's hand. 'Your Mum was so upset thinking she'd lost you, we had to give her some medicine. She's asleep now. You'll see her very soon. You've given us all a terrible fright . . .'

'She should be here,' Nicky said. 'I want her here.'

Terri leaned over Nicky and whispered, 'It's all right, Nicky. Don't get upset. About your note . . .'

A look of terror crossed the child's face. 'You've read it?' she said. In spite of the tubes, she put up her arms and clung to Terri. 'You know what I did? What's going to happen now? Will I go to prison?' She began to cry. 'I don't want to go to prison,' she wailed.

Terri used a box of hospital tissues to wipe away the tears.

'Shhh,' she said, 'listen to me. It's all right. We've destroyed the note. Me and Mrs Henson. It's gone. No one saw it except us. We're all going to forget it existed. It was an accident. What happened to Alice was an accident. You must forget it ever happened.'

Nicky looked from Terri to Jean as though she couldn't believe what Terri was saying.

'What about Mum?' she said. 'Does Mum know what I did?'

'No, I didn't show it to her. Leave her to me,' Terri said. 'We all want what's best for you.'

A nurse came into the room. 'You should leave now,' she said. 'She needs rest.'

DCI Moody was waiting in the corridor outside Nicky's room.

'Can you give me some idea what happened?' she asked. 'Why did she run off like that?'

Terri shrugged. 'She wanted to practise riding her bicycle,' she said. 'Round Forester Close the other kids laugh at her because she doesn't know how. You know what it's like, they're all like stunt riders these days. Nicky felt left out.'

Jean smiled at Rachel. 'That's Nicky all over,' she said, 'she's such a perfectionist, she couldn't bear to make a fool of herself in front of the others.'

'Oh?' Rachel Moody sounded doubtful. 'Well, I'll talk to her in the morning. Perhaps she'll be able to fill me in.'

'She's a child,' Terri said. 'She's confused . . . I don't think she knows what she did.'

'No.'

The expression on Rachel's face seemed to accept this, but both Terri and Jean imagined there was a question mark after Rachel's 'No'.

'We'll all know more when we've had a chance to talk to Nicky in the morning,' Terri said. 'Thank you for finding her, Chief Inspector. If the police hadn't been so quick off the mark she could've died.'

'You've a lad from the old village to thank for that,' Rachel Moody said. 'He found her when he was checking a fence on his farm. His name's Mark Pearson. He's the one who called the paramedics.'

Her mobile phone rang. 'It's the station,' she said. 'I'll have to take this.'

She turned her back and moved away from them.

Terri and Jean looked at each other like naughty schoolgirls; they fled.

They drove home in silence. Then, when Terri stopped the car outside the Henson house, Jean said, 'How are we going to play this with Helen? She mustn't know about the note.'

Terri hesitated. Then she said, 'Jean, it's possible Nicky's lying to protect Kevin Miller. She may be making it up. I mean, all that stuff about that book. I thought what she was reading was part of her research for her social studies class at school.'

Jean got out of the car. 'I'll be over first thing in the morning. You go to Helen now and see how she is. We can't do anything now.'

Helen had not woken. She slept through until the next morning and came into the kitchen where Jean was sitting with Terri at the table over cups of coffee.

She still looked distraught.

'Where's the paracetamol?' she asked Terri. Jean she ignored. 'I feel terrible, I've got the most awful hangover,' she said. 'What happened last night?' She sounded irritable.

'You were upset,' Terri said, taking her hand. 'Nicky went off for the day and we reported her missing. The police found her.'

'Where is Nicky?' Helen asked. 'Why didn't she bring my breakfast?'

'They kept her in hospital last night, just in case.' Terri poured coffee for Helen. 'Toast?' she asked.

Jean made an attempt to explain. 'She got hungry and ate a few berries to keep herself going, but unfortunately they were poisonous,' she said. 'They had to pump out her stomach but she'll be fine now.'

'So that's why I'm angry with her, is it?' Helen said. 'I knew she'd done something stupid.'

She frowned as if there was something she was trying to remember. Then she gave up and appealed to Terri. 'So she put me through hell running off for the day, did she? What am I going to do with that child, she's such a drama queen? You wait till she gets home, I'll make her sorry.'

Jean smiled at Terri and Terri shrugged. Neither of them could quite believe what they were hearing. Helen seemed to have no memory of yesterday. It seemed incredible to them that a mother could have blotted Nicky going missing right out of her mind.

'As soon as you're dressed, I'll take you to see her,' Terri said.

'I can't do anything without a decent cup of coffee,' Helen said. 'This stuff's cold. There's no hurry about Nicky now, she might as well stay there. Serve her right, it'll teach her not to be so selfish in future.'

THIRTY-ONE

J ess asked Donna, 'Can you take care of Kylie today?'

'No, I bloody can't,' Donna said. 'You can't leave her with me whenever you feel like it.'

Jess tried cajoling. 'Oh, Mum, please,' she said. 'I'll fix your hair for you tonight.'

'No,' Donna shouted. 'She's your child, you look after her. If you don't like it, you should've thought of that before.'

'Why won't you?' Jess said. 'You won't lift a finger to help me, all you think about is what's happening to frigging Kevin. It's not my fault he's in jail.'

'Meaning you think it's mine?' Donna said.

'Meaning I don't give a fuck, I'm going out,' Jess said.

It was as good a time as any, Jess thought.

She had laid her plans very carefully.

Her palms were sweating and she could tell her voice sounded funny because she couldn't get her breath properly.

It's now or never, she thought.

She said, so quietly that Donna turned and stared at her in astonishment, 'I can't stand this place any more, I'm moving out.'

'Yeah, yeah.' Donna didn't argue, she'd heard it all before.

Jess waited a moment for her mother to react, to beg her to stay. But Donna said nothing.

Jess said, 'I went to the council and said I had to move and because of me being homeless and having Kylie, they've found me a flat. It's in the Midlands, in a place somewhere near Birmingham. It's on the seventh floor of a tower block on a big housing estate, that's what they said.'

Donna didn't believe her. Jess would say anything, threaten all sorts of things, to get her own way.

'You and Kylie?' Donna said. 'What about Kylie?'

She's expecting me to say I'll look after her, Donna thought.

'What about Kylie?' Jess said. 'We'll be fine. There's bound to be lots of other kids.'

Jess sounded irritated. She didn't like it that Donna assumed Kylie would go with Jess. She's not even going to offer to take on the kid until I've got a life going for myself, the selfish cow, Jess told herself.

'Do you think you'll be able to get a job in Birmingham?' Donna said. She was deliberately taking Jess's plans at face value, pretending she believed what the girl was saying.

'Job?' Jess said, 'Why should I get a job, I'll be on benefits. I'll even get new furniture and a washing machine.'

'Won't you be scared?' Donna said. 'I can't imagine living in one of those places.'

'It's better than this dump, miles from anywhere,' Jess said. 'I'd put up with almost anything to get away from bloody Kevin,' she added.

'But Kevin's not here,' Donna said.

'Don't bet on it,' Jess said. 'His slimy lawyer will get him off.'

She was thinking, There she goes again, bringing everything round to Kevin. Why doesn't she listen to me? She thinks I'm kidding. Well, she'll be sorry . . .

Jess slammed the door as she left the house.

On the bus going into Haverton, she watched a young mother struggling to cope with two young boys.

They ignored her efforts to amuse them. They fought noisily among themselves, refusing to sit still, charging up and down the aisle of the bus.

The other passengers sat with pained expressions, occasionally giving the harassed mother looks of hatred.

One of the boys knocked against Jess. She caught his fat little arm to stop him in his tracks.

Between clenched teeth, she snarled at him, 'Shut up or I'll thump you.'

The child skulked back to his mother, snivelling.

The other passengers, instead of being grateful, glared at Jess. But with her purple hair, her tattoos, and the safety pins apparently holding parts of her body together, they didn't dare confront her. Jess heard the mother mutter to her kid, 'She can't hit you, it's illegal.'

Jess didn't care. She was sorry for the mother in a way, except she wasn't worth being sorry for, she didn't matter. Jess despised her. She knew how it felt, being tied down like that, except she wasn't going to let it happen to her.

And, briefly, she thought of Donna, and suddenly saw how her mother must see her own life. Of course she didn't want to look after Kylie, she wasn't interested in her. She wasn't interested in me, Jess thought, why should she care about Kylie? I think she's a pain in the arse, and I'm supposed to be her mother.

Then she asked herself, why's it always the mother who gets lumbered, not the dad? If I was Kevin I wouldn't mind having Kylie, I could still do what I wanted.

Jess glared at the young mother as the bus stopped at the coach terminus near the town centre. Her two boys rushed off, shouting.

'Careful of the traffic,' the young woman cried.

I'm not going to let that happen to me, Jess told herself, I'm going to have a life.

She followed the instructions the reporter on the Sunday tabloid had given her. He was the paper's regional correspondent and worked from an office in the same building as the local daily. He'd told her to go there and ask for him at the desk. He would come down to meet her.

Jess had told him she wanted to be paid for her Romeo and Juliet story in cash because she didn't have a bank account and wasn't likely to be allowed to open one. The reporter had agreed to that. It suited him. He could make up the money on expenses and it saved having to produce an invoice to justify the payment to Jess.

A blonde middle-aged woman at the reception desk looked at Jess over her glasses.

'Yes?' she said. 'Can I help you?'

The way she said it, Jess knew she meant 'What's the likes of you doing here?'

Jess showed her the letter the reporter had sent telling her what to do. 'I've come to see him,' she said. 'He has something for me.'

The blonde woman raised her eyebrows and pursed her sticky red mouth.

'Wait, please,' she said.

She lifted the receiver in a way that reminded Jess of a brightly coloured parrot taking a peanut. She said something that Jess couldn't hear, then put the phone down and opened a drawer. She took out a sealed envelope and pushed it across the desk.

'Here,' she said. 'He hasn't time to see you.'

Jess grinned as she picked up the envelope, opened it and looked inside. 'Fine by me,' she told the woman, 'I'm not here for the pleasure of his company.'

Afterwards Jess walked aimlessly round the centre of Haverton. The money, in its envelope, was hidden in the inside pocket of her jacket – an old black leather vest Kevin had discarded. She didn't even look at the shop windows.

The money actually felt hot against her breast, radiating warmth that spread through her body making her feel like Popeye with a bellyful of spinach.

She caught the bus back to Catcombe Mead and got off at the bottom of Forester Close. It was already getting dark and the street lamps cast spotlights on to the wet pavement. She moved from one patch of light to another imagining herself a ballet dancer who had conquered gravity. The money in her inside pocket seemed to give her wings.

As she walked up the road towards Number Two, she was singing '. . . *you are the wind beneath my wings* . . .'

She saw Forester Close as she had never seen it before, as a place that would not exist if she no longer lived there. She could be the rocket projected towards the star, Forester Close the useless casing left behind in her meteoric wake. That's how much this money means, she thought.

As she came into the kitchen, Donna looked up from peeling potatoes to scowl at her.

'Where've you been?' she demanded. 'I told you I wouldn't look after Kylie and you just went ahead. Where do you get off being so bloody selfish?'

Jess laughed. 'Here,' she said, 'I won on a scratch card.'

She tossed a twenty pound note on the table in front of Donna.

Donna picked it up and tossed it back at Jess. 'Keep your dirty money,' she said. 'Spend it on someone to take care of that poor child.'

'OK,' Jess said, picking up the note and forcing it into the back pocket of her jeans.

Somewhere in the house Kylie was crying. Donna picked up another potato to peel.

'Your baby's crying,' she said.

'I'll go,' Jess said. 'I might as well.'

'She's the one with blonde hair and blue eyes, in case you've forgotten what she looks like,' Donna said.

Jess laughed.

'What's got into you?' Donna said. 'Are you on something?'

'You wouldn't understand,' Jess said.

'You'll have to feed her, Jess,' Donna said. 'I'm doing a night shift on the till at the garage.'

'OK, OK, I know,' Jess said.

Kylie continued to cry.

Donna threw down the potato she was peeling. 'To hell with it,' she said, 'I'm not going to cook. Tell Alan to get down the takeaway and get something for supper, I'm off.'

'OK,' Jess said.

Donna collected her purse. At the door she turned back. 'See you in the morning,' she said. The front door slammed behind her.

'Goodbye, Mum,' Jess said.

She told herself, It's too late to have second thoughts.

Very early the next morning, Jess opened her bedroom door and listened to the rhythmic sound of Alan's snoring.

How does Mum put up with him? Jess asked herself. I'd rather die than be her.

She crept across the landing to Kylie's room. The child was awake, lying on her back making soft gurgling noises.

Jess picked her up and carried her downstairs, moving as quietly as she could.

In the kitchen, she called a cab to take her and Kylie to the mainline station about twenty miles away from Catcombe Mead.

'I'll be at the bottom of the Close,' she said. 'I don't want to wake the whole street.'

'Ten minutes,' the taxi firm controller told her.

Jess didn't take much luggage, only what was in the washing

machine. She stuffed the clothes into one of those canvas bags that people with babies always carry around on their backs.

Then she picked Kylie up and walked out of the house. She did not look back as she hurried down the street towards the main road.

'You're going to have a new life now and everything should start off new,' she said to Kylie.

There was no one about. A dog barked twice, then someone shouted at it to keep quiet. Two cats were squaring up to fight in one of the gardens, but they fled as she passed by.

The taxi was waiting for her. The driver was listening to the car radio.

Jess opened the back door and got in. She put Kylie on the seat beside her.

'Station, right?' the driver said. He didn't want to talk.

He set off without waiting for confirmation.

At the station, she gave the driver a tip because if she hadn't he might have taken more notice of her. She didn't want to arouse suspicion. But she didn't argue about taking the money back when he told her to spend it on the kiddie. Good, she told herself, he didn't even look at me; he only noticed the baby and all babies look the same.

Then she bought a ticket for the early morning stopping train to Liverpool via Crewe.

The train was crowded. Commuters from outlying areas were on their way to work in the city. Most of them were slumped in their seats half asleep, or reading the morning newspaper.

No one took any notice of Jess with her baby. A young man grudgingly moved his laptop from the seat beside him so that she could sit down.

Best sit next to a man, she told herself, a woman would start talking about the baby.

The train rumbled through suburbs and into a busy station. Jess's carriage emptied as though someone had shouted 'Fire'. She watched the passengers move along the platform to the exit and the crowd seemed to her a live thing in its own right, all the expressionless faces the scales on some giant lizard.

Jess listened to the list of towns the train would stop at. To her, the names sounded romantic and strange, a new world full of promise.

Then a whistle; the train lurched and moved slowly forward. Jess watched out of the window as the tracks merged and disappeared. The railway sidings slid away behind her as they picked up speed between rows of terrace houses, then new housing estates which reminded her of Catcombe Mead.

And then they were in the country, flashing through villages, speeding past farm buildings and cottages. Jess thought of Mark. He'd be out in the fields by now. She asked herself, is he thinking of me? She could see men just like him at work as the train flashed past, moving across fields of churned mud under a low leaden sky.

Goodbye, Mark, she said to herself.

She picked up the baby and looked down at her sleeping face. Funny how they screw up their eyes when they're asleep, she thought, as though they're afraid of the light.

'It's all new to us from now on,' she murmured to Kylie. 'We've escaped, you and me. We live our own lives from now on, you and me.'

Poor Mum, Jess thought, she'll miss Kylie. She wanted me to leave her there, in that no-hope dump. But how could I? What kind of life would that be for the kid? She'd end up exactly like me, trapped and dragged down like me.

She said to Kylie, 'You wouldn't want to end up like me and Kev, would you, kid? Your Gran will just have to make do with visiting your Dad in prison, won't she?'

In Crewe Jess left the train. She stood on the platform and watched it disappear down the line, taking her old life with it.

Then she boarded a train for London. It was important to cover her tracks. So far, so good. She'd warned Donna of her intention to leave; her absence should be covered by that, for a while at least. But if her plans didn't work out, and Donna got the police looking for her, they would waste a lot of time searching in the North before they ever thought she might be in London. That's if the man in the ticket office remembered a young woman with a baby buying a ticket to Liverpool. He would, Jess thought; with the kid and the way she looked, she wasn't one of the run of the mill commuters he was used to.

In the train from Crewe, Kylie lay on the seat beside Jess, lulled by the rhythm of the wheels on the track.

Jess watched her sleeping. 'Don't think I never loved you,' she said softly, 'this isn't going to be easy. It's the only way to give you a better life. That's the best I can do for you.'

An elderly woman walking up the carriage towards the buffet car leaned over to look at the baby. 'What a lovely child,' she said, 'what a beautiful baby.'

Jess smiled. 'Yes,' she said, 'I wish she was mine. I'm just minding her. Her mother had to go to the toilet.'

It had started. It was easier than she'd expected it would be.

THIRTY-TWO

Detective Chief Inspector Moody sat at her desk facing Sergeant Reid.

'Where are we on the Kevin Miller case?' she asked.

'Are you worried we haven't got enough?' Jack Reid said.

Rachel got up and stretched. Then she sat down again.

'I don't know, Jack,' she said. 'We've got the DNA, but it is circumstantial. There could be all sorts of explanations why he was in her house. Including burglary.'

'His DNA's all over the bedclothes in the spare room,' Jack said. 'And in the bathroom. Everywhere, in fact.'

'Perhaps she asked him to stay,' Rachel said.

'Why would she do that?' Jack asked.

'Because she was too scared to refuse,' Rachel said.

'But why would he want to?'

'Hiding out,' Rachel suggested.

There was a pause, then she said, 'All I'm saying, we've plenty of evidence he was there, but that doesn't mean he murdered her. You and I may be certain he did, but a jury may not be so sure. They might even think that if he'd murdered her on the spur of the moment, there wouldn't be nearly as much DNA as there was.'

'You're saying it could've been an accident. She fell down stairs and he moved the body checking to see if she was dead? Is that what you think?'

It was plain Jack Reid didn't disagree with this. He had always thought that Alice Bates's death could have been an accident.

'That would explain the look on her face,' Rachel said, 'suppose she wasn't quite dead and the last thing she saw was Kevin Miller bending over her? She'd think he was going to throttle her. She'd look like that then.'

Jack Reid walked over to the window. There was never any doubt when the Sergeant was thinking seriously about something, he always stood hunched forward supporting his prominent chin on his clenched fist, a bit like a moving version of the Rodin statue.

'You want to have another go at the neighbours?' he asked. 'Kevin's been out of the way for some time now, they may feel able to tell a different story now.'

Rachel Moody looked relieved that he had made the suggestion. She hadn't wanted to say anything herself, because she was convinced Jack thought she was flogging a dead horse.

'If Kevin was hiding out in Alice Bates's house, you'd think someone would see him going in or out,' she said. 'Perhaps someone saw him.'

'He'd make damn sure they didn't,' Jack Reid said. 'He must've had that poor woman terrorized. If anyone asked, she'd say he wasn't there. She'd be too scared to say anything else.'

'Well, let's see what we can dig up,' Rachel said. 'We'll start with those two gay women with the kid who took the accidental overdose. That girl wasn't the type who'd get hungry and pick berries to eat. She wouldn't have gone into the countryside at all, by the look of her; she'd have stayed in the pavement zone and bought vegetarian takeaway. And there weren't any holly trees or mistletoe or whatever it was she took where she was found. She must have taken those poison berries with her.'

'Go easy on her, though,' Jack said. 'That mother of hers looked fit for the funny farm. The kid's probably vulnerable.'

'Don't mention the word farm round Forester Close,' Rachel said. 'It's like a red rag to a bull.'

'Well, I don't really know what we're looking for, Boss, but we've got to start somewhere, I suppose,' Sergeant Reid said, picking up Rachel's car keys from her desk. 'I'll drive.'

Building work to repair the fire damage had started on Number Five. There was scaffolding on the gable end, and a breeze-block wall to what had been Nicky's bedroom. There was a mechanical digger parked in front of the garage, and the front garden had been churned into a morass. But at the moment there was no one working on the site.

Rachel Moody looked at the mud and shuddered.

'We could start next door,' Jack Reid said. He was a man with daughters and he knew what she was thinking.

'No,' she said, 'we start here. I've got a hunch about this.'

Jack muttered, 'I won't be putting money on it, whatever it is.'

Terri opened the front door to them before they reached the house.

'I'm glad you've come,' she said. 'I've been thinking things over. About Kevin Miller.'

Rachel and Jack looked at each other, puzzled. 'How's Nicky?' Rachel said.

'She and Helen are out shopping in Haverton,' Terri said. 'That's why it's good you've come now. I need to talk to you when she's not here.'

She looked like a bulldog trying to learn to read, Rachel thought. Fierce and uncertain, but determined.

'About Kevin Miller?' she said. 'What's this got to do with him?'

'Come into the kitchen,' Terri said. 'I don't want anyone to see us talking.'

There's a lot of hidden talking goes on in the kitchens of Forester Close, Jack Reid thought, but then, there were a lot of secrets. He followed Rachel down the hall.

Terri did not offer them tea or coffee. She turned to confront them as soon as Jack closed the kitchen door behind him.

'I want to be frank with you,' Terri said. 'That business with Nicky . . . well, she's a teenage girl with all that brings with it, and it seems she had a bit of a crush on Kevin Miller. You know what girls her age are like? Of course, to him she was just some silly kid. These girls always seem to go for the wild ones, don't they?'

She was appealing to Rachel, but Rachel had no idea what she was talking about. It was Jack who nodded in understanding.

'My girl was just the same,' he said. 'Those weirdo pop stars!'

'Well, we've put all that behind us,' Terri said. 'But I want to be sure you've got enough to put Kevin away?'

Rachel looked startled. 'He's been charged,' she said. 'He'll be tried.'

'I know, but it sounds to me that it's not an open and shut case,' Terri said. She was very red in the face. 'I know I must sound a bit mad, but if there's any chance that he could get off in court, I've got to tell you something that'll make sure Kevin

Miller is put away for years. I don't want Nicky to have it all dragged up again . . .'

'What exactly are you saying?' Rachel Moody asked.

'If he's going to get away with Alice Bates's murder,' Terri said, speaking unnaturally loudly as though she were reading from a script, 'I want him convicted of the murder of the vicar from Old Catcombe. I know you haven't found any proof but I'm here to tell you Kevin Miller did it and I was a witness to it. So was Alice. I saw her watching. If he found that out, it could be why he killed her.'

DCI Moody licked her lips. Jack Reid, watching her, thought, she's a predator, a killer. She looks as though she's purring; she thinks she's finally got her man.

Terri sat down suddenly on a chair at the kitchen table. There were tears in her eyes.

'Please,' she said, 'take me to the police station and I'll give you everything you want. But Nicky and Helen might come home any time. I don't want them to know about any of this.

'Did anyone else see what happened?' Jack Reid said. 'I'm not suggesting you're not a reliable witness, but corroboration would clinch it, I should think.'

Terri took a deep breath. 'Try Jean Henson next door,' she said. 'I think she may have seen something.'

The DCI and the Sergeant left Terri alone while they went to ask Jean Henson if she had seen the murder of the young vicar from the village.

Terri put the kettle on to boil. They'll want tea when they come back, she thought, the police drink a lot of tea.

Her hands trembled as she set out four cups and saucers, in case they brought Jean with them.

He deserves it, Terri told herself, he did murder the vicar, even if he didn't kill Alice.

It was all planned. She had already talked to Jean about what she intended to do. Nicky had to be protected at all costs. That's why I sent her off with Helen to spend her Christmas money, Terri thought. If Jean and I can provide proof that Kevin Miller killed Tim Baker, any doubts a jury might have about his guilt for Alice's death will be set aside. They won't look for anyone else, anyway.

Terri was surprised that she didn't feel more guilty about what she was doing. She had seen Kevin Miller among the group who attacked the young vicar, but she hadn't seen him kill him. Unlike Alice, she had not been able to watch what was happening. She had run out of the house and through the garden into the back alley behind the Close, looking for Nicky. She had been terrified that the child might be one of the gang involved.

But, Terri told herself, I know who was responsible for Tim Baker's death. Kevin Miller was the leader of that gang.

She'd said to Jean, 'I'm going to tell them I was a witness. I'm going to give them the evidence they need to put that brute away for life.'

Jean's eyes were unexpectedly shrewd as they met hers. She said, 'It's your word against his. It would be better if there were two witnesses.'

Terri could not believe what she understood Jean was trying to say. Was she really volunteering to be the second witness? Why would she be willing to commit perjury to protect Nicky?

'Did you see anything?' Terri asked.

'I think so,' Jean said.

Terri thought, she must hate Kevin Miller because she blames him for driving her husband to commit suicide, but does she hate him that much?

'But I saw you in the garden,' Terri said. 'You can't have seen what happened.'

'No, that's not right. You saw Peter in the garden, not me, not then,' Jean said. 'I came out later when I'd seen what Kevin Miller had done. I came out because I had to warn Peter to keep out of the way or he might get hurt. Kevin had threatened him, you know?'

'So . . . ?' Terri said.

'Yes,' Jean said.

They smiled at one another. Like conspirators, Terri told herself, but almost like friends, too.

THIRTY-THREE

Donna Miller parked her car outside Number Two. She was tired and her eyes felt raw from lack of sleep. Someone on the day shift had failed to turn up and she'd had to stay on the till for another six hours at the twenty-four hour petrol station on the Haverton Road.

She couldn't bear to open the garage and drive in because she knew Kevin's motorbike was inside. It was covered with a waterproof sheet but knowing it was there reminded her painfully of his absence every time she looked at it, so she tried not to.

She was still thinking of Kevin as she got out of the car. She thought she'd seen that woman DCI who'd put Kevin away drive out on to the main road as she turned into Forester Close, and that, too, had helped to bring it all back.

I hope you get what's coming to you, you sour old bitch, Donna thought. Suing you for false imprisonment's just the start of what I've got in store for you.

Donna told herself she was probably whistling in the dark, but maybe not. Kevin's solicitor had said the case against him might be dismissed because all the police evidence proved was that he'd been in the house. Kevin could plead guilty to attempted burglary to explain the DNA all over the place; the police hadn't anything else to make the murder charge stick. Kevin's DNA on the corpse only showed he'd touched the body when he found her dead at the bottom of the stairs. It could easily have been an accidental death and Kev had checked to see if she was still breathing. That's what anyone would do naturally, without thinking.

The house seemed unnaturally quiet as Donna went through to the kitchen.

She shouted, 'Jess?'

There was no reply.

The bloody girl's gone out and left Kylie in her play pen, Donna thought. She told herself, something's got to be done about Jess and Kylie. Perhaps it would be best if they did move out, away from here. Jess would soon be running home, but even a short time on her own would give the girl a reality check to find out what being a mother really involved.

But why was Kylie so quiet? She wasn't making any noise at all.

Donna started up the stairs, calling to the baby, 'I'm coming, love, I'm coming to get you.'

On the landing Donna was suddenly afraid. It was too quiet. My God, she thought, the baby's dead. Something's happened to her. Oh, no, Jess . . .

She was really afraid that Jess had somehow caused the baby's death. Filled with dread, she opened Kylie's bedroom door and looked in. The playpen was empty. There were toys left scattered on the floor. The bed was unmade, but Kylie was not there.

Donna turned and ran to Jess's room. She burst in without knocking. There was no sign of Jess.

She heard someone come in through the front door and, thinking it was Jess, raced down the stairs.

'Hi, babe,' Alan said. 'Is the kettle on? I've got the paper.'

'Where are they?' Donna screeched at him.

'Where's who?' Alan said.

'Jess and Kylie, of course. They've gone,' she said.

'What d'you mean, gone?' Alan said.

She followed him through to the kitchen.

'Didn't you hear anything?' she asked. 'She's taken Kylie.'

'Don't tell me you want me to go out looking for her? She'll be back. She can't get far, she's no money, for one thing.'

Donna sat down at the table and took a cigarette from Alan's pack.

'She said she was going to move out,' she said, taking Alan's half-smoked cigarette from his mouth to light hers. 'I thought it was just talk. Social services gave her a flat in Birmingham, she said. She said she'd be glad to get away from here.'

Donna's face crumbled. 'I thought she was having me on,' she said. 'She must've lied about her age.'

'Probably forged your signature,' Alan said. 'D'you want to get the police?'

Donna thought about Rachel Moody with her perfect hair and

make-up and her way of staring at you as though she saw you as something different from what you were.

'Not yet,' she told Alan. 'She wouldn't thank us. She'll let us know when she gets there. I'll ring her.'

She rang Jess's mobile. From upstairs, they heard the ring-tone.

'She's left her phone,' Donna said. She started to cry. 'She doesn't want us to find her.'

'Fine by me,' Alan said. 'I'll save a packet not having to provide for her and that kid of hers. Ungrateful cow.'

Donna was too tired to argue.

'I'm going to bed,' she said. 'Call me later. We'll get a takeaway.'

But, tired as she was, she couldn't sleep. She didn't know what she was going to do without Jess. The boys were all right but they'd always been off doing their own thing. And Kevin . . . Jess was different; she needed her mother. They might fight all the time but they understood each other. Jess hadn't even said goodbye, not properly. She hadn't been able to say goodbye to Kylie. It was a total rejection, and Donna felt bereft. And there was the child; Kylie needed her. Jess would never cope.

Perhaps she'll find that out and bring her back in a day or two, Donna told herself.

That thought cheered her. She slept for a while, then got up and went downstairs where Alan was in the lounge watching television.

'It's the news,' he said. 'D'you want me to turn over?'

'No, leave it on,' Donna said. She thought, if something has happened to Jess . . .

On the television screen, a very young policewoman was holding a baby wrapped in a hospital blanket.

The baby on the television had been found abandoned in a station waiting-room somewhere in the commuter belt north of London, some town Donna had never heard of beginning with H on the main line to the North. The child had apparently been well looked after. Police were appealing to the mother to come forward. They wanted to help her. Nurses at the hospital which had examined the baby were calling the kid Kylie after Kylie Minogue, because she was a little waif with a powerful set of lungs.

'That looks like our Kylie's coat,' Donna said. 'I bought one just like it for her at Asda.'

'You and a million others, I expect,' Alan said. He lit a cigarette and switched channels on the television.

Donna sat in silence for a while, then she said suddenly, 'You know, I can't help thinking about Jess and Kylie. That kid on the television – the one they found abandoned at the train station, the one they called Kylie . . .'

Alan grunted. 'What of it?' he said. It was the nearest he could get to showing sympathy towards Donna.

'Oh, I was just thinking . . . if that kid's mother was anything like Jess, the poor little thing's bloody lucky her mother abandoned her.'

'How do you make that out?' Alan said.

'Well, the mother can't have been any good,' Donna said. 'Now the kid will be adopted by some nice family who'll love her and give her the chance of a good life.'

Alan pressed the remote to turn off the television. He stared at Donna, not sure that she was serious.

'Are you trying to say you wish your Jess had left her Kylie like that other mother did?'

Donna's voice trembled. She said, 'Rather than take her away to some dump in Birmingham to live on benefits and grow up like Jess to get pregnant by men who don't even know her name?' She sounded close to tears. 'Yes, that's what I'm saying; I suppose it is.'

'Jess'll be fine,' Alan said. 'She's got her head screwed on, that one. Selfish cow.'

He leaned across to give Donna a friendly cuff. 'What's brought this on?'

Donna sighed. 'I can't help worrying what's going to happen to them – the kids?' She couldn't explain. Alan wasn't even their father.

'You did everything you possibly could for them,' Alan said. 'We both did. They never wanted for anything. They'll be all right.'

THIRTY-FOUR

Rachel Moody thought that the bleak room in the remand centre where she and Jack Reid had come to charge Kevin Miller with the additional murder of the Reverend Tim Baker was the most soulless place she'd ever seen.

Rachel would not have admitted to anyone else, even to Jack Reid, that she felt an unprofessional degree of personal satisfaction when Terri Kent and Jean Henson provided the new witness evidence which made the additional charge possible. She had always recognized the potential weakness in the police case against Kevin as the murderer of Alice Bates. Now, as the Super would say, they'd got him bang to rights.

She had never stopped hoping to nail Miller for Tim Baker's murder. It seemed to her much more important to do that than put him away for killing an old and – dare she think it? – insignificant victim like poor Alice Bates. That could have been an accident, a burglary gone wrong; it was an isolated small tragedy compared with the killing of the young vicar.

That murder, Rachel thought, was a deliberate blow against the whole concept of social order. It affected numerous lives and groups, making a mockery of the law and the very purpose of the police. If the murderer of Tim Baker could get away with what he did, society itself was undermined. Rachel was relieved that at long last Terri Kent and Dr Henson's widow had realized where their civic duty lay.

Jack Reid, sitting beside Rachel at the formica-topped table, shifted in the uncomfortable chair.

'It's just another case,' he said out of the blue.

Rachel thought, how does he know what I'm thinking?

'Of course it is,' she said. 'But this is one I began to think we wouldn't be able to solve.'

'What do you think you have to do to get a cup of coffee round here?' Jack Reid said. He fidgeted on the hard chair, which was nowhere near broad enough for a man of his bulk.

The door opened then and Kevin Miller was brought in to sit opposite them at the table. His solicitor, an eager young woman in a black suit, sat down beside him.

Rachel Moody watched Kevin. He looked thinner than when she had last seen him, and whiter. Without the motorcycle gear and the swagger, he was reduced to a nondescript young man with greasy hair, acne, and an air of rat-like defiance.

How could that Byrne child have a crush on someone so ordinary, Rachel asked herself. And, she thought, how could a weasel like that ever seem to embody evil incarnate? That's what Alice Bates thought.

She couldn't believe that she was trying to stop herself from seeing Kevin as pathetic.

Kevin Miller showed no interest in what anyone said until Jack Reid told him the police now had a witness to prove his guilt.

Kevin shook his head. He gave Rachel Moody a pitying smile. 'I didn't do it,' Kevin said. 'I didn't kill that Alice Bates. That four-eyed kid Nicky from next door did it. You found my prints in the house, sure, but hers were there too if you'd bothered to look.'

'It's not going to look good for you in court if you accuse a young girl of something like that to save your own skin,' Rachel said.

'Maybe not,' Kevin said, 'but that's what happened. You can't prove it didn't.'

'It's not Alice Bates's murder we've come to ask you about,' Jack Reid said.

Rachel leaned forward across the table towards Kevin. 'We've got a witness who's prepared to give evidence in court that she saw you murder the vicar of Old Catcombe outside Number Two, Forester Terrace on the seventeenth of December last.'

Kevin jumped to his feet and tried to leap across the table to grab Rachel.

A burly warder held him back, then dropped him on to the chair.

'You'd listen to that dirty bull-dyke and her lies?' Kevin screamed. 'Don't you see, she knows that moron kid killed the old witch and she's doing this to cover for her. She's lying, don't you see that?'

'She's not our only witness to the vicar's murder, Kevin,' Jack Reid said. 'Someone else saw you do it.'

Kevin curled his thin lip in contempt. 'That bloodless lesbian partner of hers . . .' he said, and laughed.

'No,' Jack Reid said, 'this evidence has no connection with that family. She's an independent witness.'

There was a silence. They all, including the solicitor, knew then for certain that Kevin Miller had killed the vicar. It was written all over his face that he had done the murder, that he knew he could have been seen doing it, that he had made the mistake of being too sure that no one would dare admit to witnessing what he did.

'She's lying too,' he said. 'Mum'll tell you I wasn't there.'

'Well, she would, wouldn't she?' Rachel said. She nodded to the Sergeant.

Jack Reid stood up. 'Kevin Miller, I am charging you that on the seventeenth of December 2009 you murdered Reverend Timothy Baker at Number Two, Forester Close, Catcombe Mead . . .'

Kevin sat hunched over the table. His face was expressionless.

Suddenly he looked up and interrupted the Sergeant as he began to read him his rights.

'Wait,' he said. He said to his solicitor, 'Give me five minutes alone with them.'

The solicitor protested. 'Don't say anything now,' she said. 'Shut up, that's my advice.'

Kevin said, 'Get out. You and the screw.'

'This is irregular,' the solicitor said.

'It's what I want,' Kevin said.

His solicitor was unhappy about leaving, but Kevin insisted. He was left alone facing Rachel and Jack Reid.

'I want to talk straight,' Kevin said. He looked surly but his voice betrayed something else.

He's scared, Rachel thought. But it wasn't just that, she told herself, there's something else, it's like he's afraid . . .

'I want to make a deal,' Kevin said. 'I'll plead guilty to the vicar if you drop the murder rap for Alice Bates. That was an accident, right? And you know you won't make it stick.'

'But you told us Nicky Byrne killed Alice,' Jack said. 'You're the one called it murder. You might be able to help your case by giving evidence against her.'

Kevin ignored him and said to Rachel, 'It was an accident. I found the old girl lying dead at the bottom of the stairs. That's the truth.'

'What were you doing in the house?' Rachel asked.

Kevin shrugged. 'What do you think?' he asked. 'It was Christmas, I was short of cash.'

'Weren't you staying there to hide out from the police?' Rachel said sweetly. 'I must say we would never've thought of looking for you there, not after the things you said about Alice.'

'OK,' Kevin said, 'I moved in on her. She didn't get the choice. I didn't even have to rough her up. The kid ran errands for me.'

'So let's get this straight,' Rachel said, 'you want to plead guilty to killing the vicar if we record Alice Bates as an accidental death and do you instead for attempted burglary? Is that right?'

'Yup,' Kevin said.

'And we forget about incidentals like demanding money with menaces and false imprisonment and kidnap and—'

'Yup,' Kevin said.

'But why?' Rachel asked. 'Why would you give up without a fight? If you plead not guilty there's a chance you'll get off. The jury might not believe the evidence against you in Alice's murder. Your brief could cast doubt on our witnesses, you know. The jury might not be convinced. They might think your neighbours in Forester Close held a grudge against you.'

'Whose side are you on?' Kevin said. 'I've told you what I want to do. Can't we get this over with?'

Rachel nodded; Jack got up and went to bring the solicitor back into the interview room.

Rachel sat facing Kevin across the table.

'Why?' she said.

Kevin met her eyes. 'What's the point?' he said. 'I'm going down one way or another. That kid had a thing for me; she thinks I'm something special. She's the only person who's ever thought that.'

He smiled, but not at Rachel; it was the thought of Nicky Byrne did that.

'Those witnesses of yours,' he said, 'they've come forward because they think they're protecting her, isn't that right? They think I'll blame the kid to get off killing the old woman, right?'

'Well you just did that,' Rachel said.

'That's before you mentioned the vicar,' Kevin said. 'OK, if I've got to go down for that, I don't want to take the kid with me on the other thing – the old lady. That kid thinks a lot of me, you know? She told me once I may do bad things but only for good reasons. What the fuck does that mean?'

Rachel said nothing.

Kevin Miller ran his hands through his dark hair and went on, 'I'm a father myself. OK, my kid's not going to have much of a chance, not with the mother she's got, but that Byrne kid might be all right. I don't want her forced to be in court to listen to that lesbian freak who's the best hope she's got giving evidence against me. I don't want a trial.'

Rachel said, 'Why?'

Kevin grinned at her. 'Like she said some old fart said, I want to do one good thing before I die, OK?' he said. 'It's that kid, she thinks I'm some sort of hero and I don't want to disappoint her.'

Suddenly Rachel understood why Nicky Byrne and all those nameless girls in Weston-super-Mare might find something to attract them in Kevin Miller.

'What old fart said that?' she said.

'Who cares, I'm saying it, me, Kevin Alan Miller, murderer in the first degree. OK?'

He hesitated, then asked her, 'Did you ever read a book called *Crime and Punishment*?'

Rachel was startled. 'Dostoevsky? Where did you hear about that?' she said.

'The kid read it. It meant a lot to her.'

Rachel remembered one day in Forester Close when Helen Byrne, almost in tears, was wailing on about Nicky not being a normal kid. One of the reasons she gave, as far as Rachel could recall, was because the child read *Crime and Punishment*.

'It's a great classic, but I'd have thought Nicky's much too young to understand it,' she said.

'She got it into her head I was like the hero in it,' he said. 'She said I was the future, whatever that means. Maybe I'll get it out of the library,' he said. 'It sounds like my kind of book.'

Rachel was going to laugh, but then she didn't.

Jack came back into the room.

'Your brief will be back in a minute,' he said. 'She went to get a coffee.'

He produced a pack of cigarettes from his jacket pocket and lit one. He inhaled slowly and deeply. Then he handed it to Kevin.

'Here,' he said, 'and take the pack. I've given up. I don't want to start again.'

'We're charging Kevin with Tim Baker's murder,' Rachel said. 'He'll plead guilty. I'm satisfied now that Alice Bates's death was accidental.'

'I'd have put money on it,' Jack said. 'But what changed your mind?'

'Cheers,' Kevin said, picking up the pack of cigarettes and putting them in his pocket.

THIRTY-FIVE

Detective Chief Inspector Rachel Moody was in her office sorting through a bundle of house particulars from estate agents when Jack Reid brought her a second cup of coffee.

Sergeant Reid did not usually take on the responsibility for keeping the DCI topped up with the caffeine which as a rule helped to put her in a good mood first thing in the morning.

But today he wanted to ask her a favour.

His wife, Sandy, had been particularly grumpy as he'd got ready to go to work that morning. She didn't say goodbye, but stomped off upstairs and turned on the vacuum cleaner. When he'd asked his teenage daughter, Kate, what he'd done to offend her mother, Kate told him that today was his wedding anniversary and he'd forgotten it and that was why.

From upstairs, Sandy had shouted to Kate, 'Tell your father to leave a cheque for the oil bill before he goes out.'

'Oh, my God, how am I going to get out of this?' he asked his daughter.

Kate laughed. 'I'll tell her you haven't forgotten but you're picking up something to bring home as a special surprise tonight,' she said. 'But it's going to have to be something special if you're going to get away with it.'

'But what can I get her that I wouldn't have got yesterday?' Reid said. 'She'll know I didn't remember.'

'Take next week off and get tickets to Paris or somewhere romantic,' Kate said. 'That would be special.'

'I can't afford to go gallivanting off to Paris for a week at a moment's notice,' Reid protested.

'Dad, you can't afford not to,' Kate told him.

But Sergeant Reid wasn't a detective for nothing. He suspected conspiracy.

'Did your mother put you up to this?' he asked.

Kate laughed again. 'Of course not,' she said, 'she only said that if you forgot your anniversary this year, that's what it would take for her to ever speak to you again.'

So Jack, who well knew the value of a wife who for years had been prepared to put up, without protest, with the demands of the job he loved, wanted to put his boss in a particularly good mood before suddenly asking to take a week off with almost no notice at all.

When he brought Rachel the second coffee, she gave him a funny look and said, 'What are you after, Sergeant Reid?'

'I was wondering if we've got much on today, that's all,' he said.

She was making him nervous, and as he put the coffee down on her desk, he accidentally tipped the cup and spilled the steaming liquid across some of the house particulars.

'Damn,' he said, trying to mop up the coffee with his handkerchief.

Rachel produced a box of tissues from a drawer of the desk and cleared up the mess in a moment.

'No harm done,' she said.

Reid did not know what to do with his now soaked and stained handkerchief. Surreptitiously he dropped it into her wastepaper basket, which was already half full of more rejected house particulars.

'Are you thinking of moving?' he said, trying to make conversation. It didn't seem quite the right moment to ask for a week off, but he didn't want to turn tail and have to come back to try again later.

Rachel Moody shuffled the estate agents' lists so that they made a fan shape on the desktop.

'It's my particular way of dealing with a mid-life crisis,' she said. 'I've decided it's high time I began to plan for a singleton future, and get myself some sort of private life outside work. Buying my own home in a nice friendly suburb where I can put down roots seems a good place to start.'

Reid was disconcerted by this. The DCI had never talked to him in such personal terms before and he was flattered as well as embarrassed.

'Trouble is,' Rachel Moody said, 'I can't find anything I like the sound of. They keep sending me details of cottages with roses round the porch, but that's not what I want. I'm not retiring, for God's sake, I'm investing for my future, that's all.'

Reid picked up a typed page at random. 'What about this?' he asked, and read aloud: '"Three-bedroomed modern property in quiet tree-lined cul-de-sac on architect-designed housing estate on outskirts of picturesque traditional country village. Close to all amenities, ideal for commuting".'

He handed Rachel Moody the first page of the particulars. At the top of the page was a coloured photograph of a modern executive home with a small front garden where magnolia was in full bloom and clematis montana rampaged over the front wall.

DCI Moody glanced at the picture, then looked more closely. 'It looks familiar,' she said.

'Well, it's stock housing estate design, I suppose,' Reid said. 'That doesn't mean those houses aren't a good investment.' He turned over the page and checked the price at the end of the particulars.

'Wow,' he said, 'if this is right, it's bloody good value for the money.'

He tipped the paper so that Rachel could see the figure printed at the bottom of the page.

'There must be something wrong with it,' she said. 'The local authority must be going to build a waste disposal site over the road, or put a dual carriageway in the next street. It can't be right.'

Reid put the particulars back on his boss's desk. 'I can check that on the Internet if you're interested,' he said.

'Where is it, anyway?' Rachel Moody said.

Reid picked up the paper again.

'Well?' Rachel prompted him when he said nothing.

'I don't think you're going to like this,' he said. 'You do know it. We both do. It's in Catcombe Mead.'

Rachel Moody stared at him. 'Don't tell me,' she said. 'It's Three Forester Close, isn't it? The house where Alice Bates died?'

Reid put the paper back on the desk. 'They call it *Mon Repos* now,' he said. 'But yes, it is. It's Three Homicide Close.'

Rachel picked up the cup of coffee and drank it in silence. Then she said, 'Well, thank you, Sergeant, but I don't think I'll be asking for a viewing. There's not much an estate agent could tell me about that house that I don't know already. I wonder if the younger Miller boy – wasn't his name Nate? – has turned into another Kevin?'

'Of course, I knew there was something I meant to tell you, Boss. Kevin's up on a charge of GBH for stabbing his cell-mate in prison. Nearly killed him, apparently. Life's going to mean life now, I'd say.'

'I suppose an estate agent could use that as part of the sales pitch,' Rachel said, 'but I think I'll pass.' She added, 'Poor Kevin, he wasn't all bad, you know. He never had a chance, though.'

Reid remembered the first of the many visits he and Rachel Moody had made to Forester Close, way back last winter when they were investigating the death of the vicar from Old Catcombe. He'd said something about it being a nice place to live and she'd sounded almost frightened when she said it was spooky. She'd actually said it was spooky, as though it was going to be haunted some day. And he remembered now that at the time he hadn't dismissed what she said as the whimsicality of a woman of a certain age, he'd known what she meant. And then later, when he'd learned that a witch had been burned there four or five hundred years before, he'd told himself he'd better be careful in future how he mocked talk of women's intuition, because maybe there was something in it after all.

So he didn't even try to tell Rachel Moody that Three Forester Close was the investment opportunity of a lifetime. He understood how she felt. 'Well,' he said, 'it's not the only house for sale, is it?'

'You know,' she said, 'I'm not sure I am cut out for suburban life. I'd forgotten what it was like, how all those people we talked to seemed to be frightened of their own shadows. I mean, can you see me living in a place like that?'

'Well, in the circumstances . . .' Reid said.

'No,' Rachel Moody said, 'it was more than that; it was part of the way of life. All those awful things happened and it was as though those people weren't surprised, they'd been expecting the worst but at the same time they couldn't believe any of it was real, as though it was just something they'd seen on television, so they didn't think there was anything they could do to change it.'

'That's part of the normal way of life for most of us now,' Reid said, and thought of his teenaged daughter Kate. One of the reasons he was glad his work made it hard to spend much time at home was because he was frightened enough himself of the future Kate was going to face without having to confront his wife being worried about her too, and neither of them with a word of real comfort for the other about it.

'Boss?' he started to say.

'Yes, Sergeant,' DCI Moody said. 'And yes, you can have next week off to take your wife to Paris. As long as you don't bring me any more coffee.'

Jack Reid laughed. 'Thanks Boss,' he said, 'but how did you know?'

'Your wife rang up and asked me yesterday,' Rachel Moody said. 'But she made me promise I wouldn't tell you.'

Rachel Moody picked up the prospectus for the house in Forester Close and tore it up before she threw the pieces of paper into the waste bin.

'Well, that's the end of that,' she said, and they grinned at one another.